To Lois
with pleasure

Theophanes' Virgin

By
Peter Georgas

Also by Peter Georgas:

Dark Blues
The Fifth Slug
The Empty Canoe
Curse of the Big Water

Copyright © 2017 Peter Georgas, Minneapolis, MN

All rights reserved.

ISBN: 1544804725
ISBN-13: 9781544804729
LCCN: pending

In Memory of my Family
Theodore Georgas (1890-1975)
Chrysoula Villas Georgas (1900-1975)
Angeline Georgas Underwood (1925-2001)

The screams.

The constant pounding on the metal door, the shiny walls painted brilliant white, the 300-watt bulb hanging over his head that was never turned off, the cold concrete floor, the cot that served as chair and bed, the urinal which was nothing more than a drain in the floor—none of these could match, for sheer terror, the awful screams.

Not far off, certainly within earshot, was an interrogation room where prisoners were taken for a kouvenda, a conversation, as the guards liked to call it with snide laughter. Questions were asked, and if the person did not know or refused to answer, the screaming started. He shuddered. There was nothing else to do because soon it would be his turn, and his own screaming would begin.

1

The letter was stamped Urgent, Special Delivery, and it still took ten days to reach 3941 Xenwood Avenue, St. Louis Park, Minnesota 55416 USA. It was addressed to Stamatina Giannou who, after reading it with growing anxiety, immediately called her son, Marcus, interrupting a staff meeting with Senator Jeff Tolson, Room 231, Senate Office Building, Washington DC 20610 USA.

There was a delicate tap on the Senator's office door. His secretary, Edith Miller, leaned in a bit flustered. "Mr. Giannou, it's your mother."

Marcus looked down to avoid his boss's disapproving glare.

"Didn't I tell you to hold calls?"

"Yessir, but…"

"I know," the Senator replied resignedly, "your mother."

Marcus said to the secretary, "Tell her I'll call her back."

"She said it was a matter of life and death."

The Senator rolled his eyes behind half-rimmed spectacles implying that everything with Marcus's mother was a matter of life and death.

"In that case, you better take it, Mrs. Giannou's only son." There was more than a hint of sarcasm in his voice. "We'll try to carry on without you."

"Sorry, Senator." Marcus got up and went to his desk in the adjacent office he shared with two other staffers. Fortunately they were with the Senator, drumming their pencils on their notepads waiting for him to return, and so he was able to talk to his mother privately.

"Mom," he said into the phone, "didn't I tell you not to call me at work?"

"How else can I call you? You're hardly ever in your apartment."

She was right about that. The trouble with his mother, he came to realize, was that even though she was in Minneapolis and he was in Washington, she was still omnipresent. Part of it was his own doing when he showed her how to direct-dial. No more long distance operators to place her calls, giving her the illusion that her son was just down the block. With this newfound method of communication her monthly phone bills sometimes exceeded her social security check. But the telephone was her chief link to Marcus ever since he moved to Washington after Jeff Tolson got elected—from the Attorney General's office in the Minnesota State Capitol to the Senate Office Building in Washington DC. Mother cried when it came time to say goodbye. St Paul was bad enough on the other side of the Mississippi River but now her son would be "five thousand miles from home."

"Eleven hundred, Mom."

"What difference does it make? You are out of my sight."

"You have the neighbors, the Ladies Philoptohos, the Church."

"But only one son."

"And you are speaking to him when he should be in a staff meeting with the Senator."

"I don't call you at work unless it is important, you know that," she said defensively. "I got a special delivery letter from Caliope in Kremasti."

Caliope was his mother's sister and Kremasti was a village on the southeastern corner of the Greek Peloponnese.

"You haven't heard from her in a long time. Is everything all right?"

"Eleni is engaged."

"That's great," Marcus replied, wondering what the emergency was all about. Eleni was a World War II orphan adopted by Caliope and her husband Dimitri. They were too poor to have a dowry and getting Eleni engaged was reason to celebrate.

"Not great, terrible."

"How can this be terrible?"

"*Siopee*," she admonished. Hush. "Let me explain."

"I'm in a hurry."

"Everything from you is in a hurry. You say that to your Senator?"

Marcus sighed with guilt. His job had grown exponentially since he got to Washington two years ago. He had flown home only once and got in the habit of cutting her off whenever she called.

"Sorry, I'm listening. Go ahead."

She must have unfolded the letter with the receiver in one hand because he heard paper crackling. Then more noises as, apparently, she put on her reading glasses.

"Caliope does not write very often, so when she does…"

"I know, Mom. What does the letter say?"

"She is afraid for Eleni."

"Why? What's the matter?"

"This man, Kostas—Kostas Kanellos."

"Who is he?"

"Elleni's betrothed. Let me read the letter."

Caliope wrote in simple unadorned Greek, which is why Marcus could understand, but his mother kept translating every sentence, concerned that he might miss something.

My Dearest Sister Stamatina:
I think of you often, you and your wonderful son, Marcus. I pray to God that you are both in good health and that His blessings shine upon you.
Ever since you left Kremasti to go to America, we have grown old. I must confess that Dimitri is no longer in good health. He has bad knees and must use a cane. His lungs fill up in the winter when the snow is in the mountains and it takes longer for him to recover in the good months. That is why we have not written you in such a long time.
But something serious has forced me to bring pen to paper—words that are written with a heavy heart. Our dear Eleni has just passed her 27th birthday. She is a beautiful girl and even though she did not grow in my body I think of her as my own daughter. I hesitate to burden you with our troubles but Dimitri persuaded me to write you.
Eleni is engaged to be married, a blessing if it weren't for the fact that the man she is betrothed to is fifty-five years old. But even worse, he is an agent for ESA.

Marcus's mother stopped reading to let this sink in. "You know ESA don't you?"

This was an obvious question because ESA was an agenda item of the Committee on Foreign Relations chaired by Senator Tolson and whenever Marcus talked to his mother, the painful subject of the dark side of Greek politics inevitably came up. ESA was the acronym for the Military Police.

In the Good Old Days—pre-junta, that is—working for the Military Police would make a future father-in-law proud because it not only brought prestige to the family, it also provided good income and guaranteed retirement. But since the coup d'etat by the despotic Colonels in 1967, ESA had become a fearful tool of right wing extremists and anyone working for it was instantly suspect. Known for the torture of prisoners in the infamous Special Interrogation Section (SIS) in a building not far from the American Embassy, its motto was *Friend or Cripple He Who Exits Here*.

Marcus involuntarily shuddered being reminded of this. "But what has this to do with Eleni?" he asked his mother.

"Listen to the rest of the letter, *paithi mou*, my son, and you will find out…"

I have reason to believe Kanellos wants to spy on our village. We have anti-government loyalists in Kremasti, including Dimitri. There is fear any of us could be arrested.

In addition he has a special interest in Eleni that I dare not explain in this letter. Dimitri cannot deal with this emergency alone. If anything happens to him, Eleni will be at the mercy of Kanellos. I fear for her safety. That is why I make this urgent request that you return to Kremasti, the village of your birth. May God rush you to our side and embrace us in his arms.

Mrs. Giannou began crying. "I am going to write Caliope right away," she said between sniffles, "and tell her we are coming."

"We?"

"Of course. Who else can go with me to Kremasti, the President of the United States?"

Marcus looked at the active files on his desk, the memos waiting to be answered, the call-back messages, the draft of a speech to the Washington Press Club—everything ASAP. Besides it was election year and he was planning to spend the recess mapping out the Senator's fall campaign.

"Mom, it's hopeless. I could not possibly leave until after the November election."

"Didn't you hear what I said?"

"Of course I did, but Greeks are emotional, they tend to overreact. It is probably nothing that can't wait. Besides, Caliope didn't say when the wedding is taking place. I need to know a lot more if you want me to fly all the way to Greece with you."

"She was afraid to write more in case someone would open the letter and read it. You know what Greece is like now."

Marcus had to admit his mother made a point. This very morning he read a classified telex that an American tourist in Greece was detained for singing the theme song from Never on Sunday in a taverna. The regime that toppled Greece's uneven yet democratic government was not known for treating dissent with an even hand. More like an iron fist. And from what Caliope wrote, Kostas Kanellos could be an informant for that repressive regime. Marcus also wondered why this man had a special interest in a woman living in a remote village whose name, Kremasti, literally meant hanging from a mountain.

"How about going alone?"

"I am too old to travel alone, even to Greece. Besides you are a man of influence."

"Me?"

"You are Press Secretary for a powerful Senator," she replied, upset that her son took his profession so casually.

"It would be unethical to involve an elected representative of the US government in a private family matter. Caliope doesn't need a senator, she needs a marriage counselor."

Marcus could see his mother crossing herself.

"And even if I could get the Senator to intervene," he continued, "it would be the kiss of death for Caliope, if I may speak bluntly—if what she says is true about that Kanellos guy, that he is associated with ESA."

"What do you mean?" she asked warily.

"Tolson did more than any other Senator to get Andreas Pappandreau out of jail."

Pappandreau, who had once taught at the University of Minnesota, was a political thorn in the side of the Colonels when he moved back to Greece in the late 1950s, and was arrested when they took power eight years later.

"The Senator was on Meet the Press as well as the McNeil-Lehrer Show. He wrote an op-ed piece for the New York Times and an article in Foreign Affairs— all heavily critical of the junta. You think the Greek government doesn't keep track of Senator Tolson? The Colonels hate him. *Tha ton evnouhisei.*" He was talking about castration.

Mrs. Giannou was so shocked to hear her son use such a word that, if he were still a boy, she would wash his mouth out with soap. "Who taught you to talk like that? Certainly not me."

"Sorry, Mom, but it's true." He did not bother to tell her that an officer close to the Greek Colonels once said, shoot the motherfucker—meaning Pappandreau— because he is going to come back and haunt you.

But Mrs. Giannou was not ready to give up without one last try. "You have a government friend in Athens. Maybe she can help."

"You mean Sally Haggarty?"

"*Nai, teen Americanitha.*" Being an American woman was anathema to Mrs. Giannou because she feared her son might marry one, but she could forgive Sally even for that if invoking her name would convince Marcus to go to Greece.

"Mom, Sally works for the USIA. She has no political clout. And she is not in Athens, she is in Sparta."

"Close enough."

At least his mother was right about being close enough—Sparta was the capital of the District of Laconias where Kremasti was located, albeit a two-hour drive over inhospitable mountain roads.

Sally Haggerty ran the American Library in Sparta, a coveted assignment for a career officer of the US Information Agency. She and Marcus had a thin but hopeful relationship inasmuch as she spent most of her

Theophanes' Virgin

time abroad while he was landlocked in DC. They met during his first year in Washington. Sally was finishing an immersion course in the Greek language, making their meeting at The Church Key, an after hours hangout for government people on K Street, more than casual once she heard his last name.

"Are you Greek?" she asked.

"One hundred per cent."

"*Steen efharisti thesi na sas gnorisoumai*," she said. Pleased to meet you.

Marcus was impressed. "Didn't you say your name was Haggarty? That sounds Irish."

"One hundred per cent," she responded.

"Your Greek is better than mine."

"I learned it at the Foreign Service Institute."

"I learned it listening to my parents."

They laughed, having flattened the learning curve associated with first impressions. It was only later that he found out Sally was a Radcliff alumnae, ingrained in the virtues of noblesse oblige because her father came from old money, lots of it, while he had a BA in journalism from the University of Minnesota and his late father was a candy maker. The one thing they had in common: an interest in Byzantine art, her minor.

Now that his mother had mentioned Sally, a trip to Greece became more appealing. He hadn't thought of her in his calculus of dealing with the Kremasti Konspiracy, as he dismissingly referred to the letter from Caliope. Seeing Sally again, the Irish-Greek he called her in his infrequent telexes to find out how she was adjusting to her new habitat, reigniting their long-distance relationship—these thoughts began to intrigue him and whet his appetite. Once the nagging matters in Kremasti were settled—he imagined two or three days at the most—Marcus could escape the boredom of village life to rendezvous with Sally and cruise the Aegean Islands, Mykonos, Santorini, Rhodes, Crete—make a real vacation out of the trip. Sounds promising, he thought, more than promising, eventful. At the moment he did not realize how prescient those words were.

"Mom," he said, speaking with the assurance she wanted to hear from him, "I will ask the Senator if I can take time off during the August recess. If he says ok, I will telex Sally and ask if we can see her on our way to Kremasti."

There was a noise outside his cell door, the noise of metal wheels rolling on uneven concrete. The guard was delivering trays of food—breakfast, lunch, dinner—he did not know which because he did not know what time it was. There was no reference to the outside world. He did not even know how long he had been in here.

"Fagee!" The guard called out. Eats.

The narrow metal slot in his door slid open and a steel tray was pushed through onto a little shelf.

"Ella, ella," Come, come.

What he got to eat did not reveal the time of day either, as in eggs in the morning, chicken salad at noon and lamb shank with vegetables in the evening. The food was always the same, always cold, always congealed and always with little black things in it that could be maggots or currants, little black things he tried to spoon out just in case. He turned over the slop a couple of times, squinted his eyes shut, and ate.

2

The dozen-and-a-half landing gears dropped out of the belly and slowed the 747 to what felt like a baby's crawl, and then the flaps came down slowing the lumbering jet even more giving Marcus the unsettling sensation that they were actually suspended over the glassy Mediterranean. But the rugged coastline of Greece appeared beneath the giant wing, and Voula and Glifatha Beaches passing below reassured him that the giant plane was still moving.

He sighed to himself, going over in his mind the hectic days after his mother called. He had returned to the Senator's office to find that the meeting had broken up and the Senator was alone at his desk reviewing his notes.

"Get these typed up for Eyes Only," he said and handed the pad to Marcus. "By the way, how is your mother?"

Tolson disliked small talk, and so Marcus waded in. "Senator, I have to ask a favor." He cleared the restriction in his throat.

"You want the rest of the day off?"

"No, Jeff," he said, in the privacy of the office, the only time he called the Senator by his first name. "I want ten days off."

"You want *what*?"

Tolson remained silent while Marcus explained the essence of his mother's telephone call. The Senator's gray-black eyes seemed to be smiling even though his mouth was not, years of politicking had taught him this and Marcus was not sure what was going through his mind.

"So this man Kanellos, who is engaged to your cousin…"

"Eleni and I are not blood relatives," Marcus interrupted. "She is an orphan. All I know is that her mother died giving birth."

"So this guy she is engaged to is connected to ESA?"

"That's what my aunt thinks. She didn't back it up with any evidence. That is what I hope to find out when I get there."

Tolson became thoughtful. "Makes you wonder what else might be going on besides an engagement. I hope you are not getting into anything over your head."

"In a small village out of nowhere?"

"Nevertheless, do me a favor and check in at the Embassy first thing after you land."

"We plan to hire a driver and we can stop by before heading for Kremasti."

"Introduce yourself to Ron Constable, the Charge d' Affairs, a friend of mine. I'll telex him you will be checking in. Give him your schedule. Do you know if there is a phone in that village?"

"I don't know. But I plan to visit Sally Haggerty at the library in Sparta, and Sparta is not far from Kremasti."

Tolson smiled. "The Irish girl you are smitten with?"

"I hope there is time to take a cruise together and see some of the islands."

"Good. I want you rested because this fall you will be busy as hell. But remember," he added, waving a cautionary finger, "If you get into any trouble, Haggerty can't help you."

The landing gears screeched rubber on the runway and passengers leaned forward as the jet's reverse thrusters yanked it to an abrupt slowdown, changing what a moment ago had been a graceful gliding bird into a heavy hulking mass of metal and wiring.

Marcus stared at the scruffy grass bordering the concrete apron as the jet quickly decelerated and the hurtling became a leisurely roll. The 747, all 800,000 pounds of it, followed a Toyota pickup truck with a sign on its roof that read Follow Me, braking finally to a swaying stop next to a line of air-conditioned trailer-buses waiting to transport the passengers to the Athens International Airport Terminal shimmering in the hazy sun a few hundred yards away.

After traveling five thousand miles across the surface of the earth and twenty-five hundred years back in history Marcus was in his ancestral home. As he and his mother followed the throng to Customs, he yearned to have the freedom of the excited tourists around him, filled with the joyful anticipation of seeing classical wonders within reachable kilometers—Delphi and Olympia, the Temple of Sounion and the Tomb of Agamemnon. Alas, he could not think of sightseeing now, maybe a peek at the Acropolis as they drove to the Embassy—he had to deal with Kremasti first.

His mind thus occupied, he nearly stumbled into his mother who abruptly stopped to talk to the first Greek national she saw, a military policeman, an AK47 hanging from his shoulder, who looked for all the world as if he were constipated.

"This is my son," she said in the rapid Greek natives use on one other but not rapid enough for Marcus to miss what she was saying: "He is an important person in Washington, DC, the capital of the United States. His name is Marcus Giannou and he works for Senator Jeffrey Tolson. Maybe you heard of him. He knows a lot about Greece."

Marcus nudged his mother hoping she would get the hint that Tolson's name was anathema in Greece but she prattled on.

"Mom, let's go," he managed to say before he was swept along by the flood of passengers heading for the escalators to go through customs. At the top he stepped aside to wait for her. She came into view like a hot-air balloon rising from a valley, strands of white hair poking out here and there from under her blue pillbox hat, the skin on her right arm creased by the strap of her handbag, her cheeks flushed from excitement. He marveled at her. She was as indefatigable as when she boarded the plane in Minneapolis.

"There you are!" she called after her roving eyes found him. "Why didn't you wait for me?"

"That's what I'm doing up here, waiting for you." Marcus took his mother by the arm.

"You don't have to hold me so tight," she said, being pulled along by her son.

"I don't want to lose you again."

He escorted her to one of four lines queued up behind a row of glassed-in cubicles where grim-faced customs officers in light gray uniforms compared faces with passport photos and, once satisfied, thwacked the visa stamp on an open page.

As they waited in line Marcus leaned down and whispered in her ear. "We are not in America, Mom, so when you speak Greek remember that everyone can understand you."

"Did I say anything wrong?"

"For one thing you needn't broadcast my marital status and for another I would caution you not to mention the Senator's name."

"I am proud of you, Marcus. How many mothers have sons working for a Senator?"

"At least a hundred."

Before they knew it they were next, and Marcus suddenly found himself helping his mother fumble for her passport while the agent behind the glass glared at them as if thinking to himself, in Greek of course, you had all this time to get out your passport and only now you are searching for it?

Marcus found it and handed it over along with his. The agent compared the photo with the real Stamatina Giannou, stamped her passport and handed it back. Then he opened Marcus's passport and looked at it as though he was reading a novel.

"*Thouliah?*" he asked without looking up. Occupation?

"I work for the US government."

The agent reached under the counter and pressed a buzzer. Another agent sitting at a desk rose and came over. The badge on his shirt indicated an official rank of some kind. He looked at Marcus's passport.

"You speak Greek?" he asked in English.

"Conversational Greek."

"Your mother?" he motioned with his head.

"Yes, that is my mother."

He pointed to a security door. "If you please."

Marcus sensed curious stares from passengers wondering what kind of trouble he was in as he and his mother were ushered into what looked like an interrogation room. The small space held a desk and two chairs, that was all except for an ominous poster on the cream-colored wall: a black silhouette of a soldier bearing a rifle with a fixed bayonet standing at attention in front of an oversize eagle whose wings appeared as red flames. Above, as though being fed by these flames, were the letters ELLAS and along the bottom printed in reverse-color type was the date: 21 Apriliou 1967.

This was the first sighting of a poster Marcus was to see almost everywhere he traveled in Greece. It filled him with a sense of foreboding, not the best way to feel when entering a foreign country.

The official shut the door and motioned them to sit down. He perched on the edge of the desk. He was not tall, in fact he was rather short but by sitting on the desk he could look down on the pair with an air of authority his stature did not possess. He laid the two passports on the bare surface of the desk and pulled out a small notebook and a ballpoint pen from his shirt pocket, ready to take notes.

"Are you in Greece for business or pleasure?"

Marcus was unprepared for the question. He came to Greece to resolve a family crisis, not sight-see, although he hoped to do that as well. Both business and pleasure? So how should he answer?

Before he could, Mrs. Giannou took over, speaking in Greek: "We are going to Kremasti, the village of my birth, to visit my sister whom I have not seen in nearly 50 years. What could have more pleasure than that?"

His mother was doing a hell of a lot better than he was.

The official looked at Marcus. "You work for the US government?"

"I do."

"In what capacity?"

"Press Secretary."

"For your State Department?"

"No, a Senator, an elected representative by the way." Marcus emphasized the word elected to let the official know he was not happy with this grilling, which he found undemocratic.

The official stiffened slightly. "What Senator, please?"

"Jeffery Tolson, from the State of Minnesota."

The official made an entry in his notebook. "Will you be spending all of your time in Kremasti?"

"I hope to travel around a bit, perhaps take a cruise of the islands. This is my first visit to Greece."

If the official was sympathetic he did not show it. "Will your mother accompany you?"

"She will remain in Kremasti."

"So you will be alone?"
"I hope to connect with a friend."
"Greek?"
"American."
"Name please."
"Name?"
"The name of the man you plan to connect with."
"The name is Sally Haggerty."
"Sally? A woman? Sally what? Spell it, please."
Marcus did.

As he wrote her name in his notebook, the official asked, "*Kopellara?*" and winked

Marcus looked at his mother to translate but she lowered her head in embarrassment.

"*Kopellara?* What does that mean?" Marcus demanded of the official, his temper rising.

The official stood up. "That will be all. Return to the window to have your passport stamped."

He went to the corner sink with a faucet that constantly dripped, another cause of sleeplessness, the steady drip drip drip, to wash the meal down using his cupped hand as a drinking glass. The brown brackish water coming out tasted as if the pipe had been diverted through a sewer line. Under the sink was a small metal bucket he used to wash away his stools after squatting over the hole in the opposite corner. All in all it was not Conrad Hilton. Whatever was in the metal tray he ate because he was hungry, so goddamned hungry he could eat the leather off his shoes. He looked down at his Hush Puppies he bought especially for the trip, comfortable, ideal for travel, soft leather also suitable for chewing. But the shoes were filthy and not at all appetizing. The laces were gone, probably because the guards were afraid he'd try to garrote himself. They let him keep his shoes but there was nothing else to tell who he was— no passport, no driver's license, no credit cards.

3

Marcus's cheeks burned as he walked with his mother to Baggage Claim. He knew he had been insulted, demeaned even, by this pint-sized bureaucrat. He wondered if her conversation with that soldier outside the terminal about her son working for a Senator critical of the Greek rulers might have triggered the grilling. Marcus recalled that the soldier had a Walkie-Talkie strapped to his belt. He could have called the immigration officials upstairs to alert them.

He now had good reason to believe this trip to Greece would be anything but pleasure, having got off to such a bad start.

They discovered that the luggage conveyor was on Greek Time and joined the other passengers who were still waiting for their bags to appear. Around them was a happy confusion of relatives talking Greek incredibly fast. The sounds were almost meaningless to Marcus in spite of the fact that he was familiar with the language. Would he be able to communicate left to his own devices? But it was still exhilarating to share, even vicariously, the happiness spilling over him.

They did not expect anyone to meet them at the airport which was not the case for many of their fellow travelers, and so the welcoming of happy tears and noisy kisses would have to wait until Marcus and his mother reached Kremasti, and that would take another half-day with a hired car and driver.

As he watched, a train of suitcases began to emerge from a chute on the far wall and travel toward them on the conveyor, he felt an itchy sensation crawl up the nape of his neck and tickle his ears, the kind of feeling you get when you think someone is watching you. He turned his head and looked over his shoulder. Near the busy exit, a pair of dark, brooding eyes belonging to a thin, sharply featured man connected with Marcus's eyes for a brief moment and then shifted a millimeter to focus on his mother. Marcus could swear the man was checking them out.

His mother sensed his tension. "What is bothering you?"

"Were you expecting someone to meet us?"

"No, why?"

"Well, don't look now."

If he expected her not to look he was hugely mistaken. She spun around as if she were standing on a lazy susan. "Where?"

"You would make a great spy," he said and gestured toward the exit with his head. It didn't make any difference to be subtle any longer. The person looking at them by now realized he had been spotted. He abruptly dropped his gaze and busied himself lighting a cigarette.

"See that guy by the main doors with a cigarette, the thin one in the brown suit and straw hat? He was staring at us."

She took a half step back and peeked around her son's body. "Who is he?"

"If you don't recognize him, how in the world would I? Maybe he was assigned to tail me. If so, he better look for another line of work."

"Your imagination is too wild."

"Really? Have you forgotten the treatment I got in that interrogation room?"

"That official was just doing his job."

"Oh yeah? What does *kopellara* mean?"

She shrugged noncommittally. "A bouncing girl, like when you bounce a baby on your lap."

That was not the image Marcus had in mind. "Sure, Mom, sure." He chanced another glance at the thin man who had shifted his position and was now standing closer to the large automatic doors. For a moment Marcus thought he was going outside but instead he stopped and talked to one of the porters wheeling luggage to waiting taxis.

Marcus spotted their bags coming down the chute and became preoccupied with grabbing them off the belt, stacking them at his mother's feet. Before he had a chance to hail a porter one was already piling their luggage on a four-wheel truck. Marcus realized he was the same man who was talking to the stranger.

The porter walked away without a backward glance, pushing the truck across the lobby and out the door.

"Our luggage!" Marcus called out helplessly and followed the porter as best he could in the crowded terminal with his mother in tow.

As they neared the exit the thin man came toward them and removed his hat.

"Kyrie Giannou?" he asked Marcus's mother.

Marcus stared in surprise. The man knew her name. "Where is our luggage?" Marcus asked in his best Greek.

"Quite safe," the man replied in Greek.

"*Pios eisai?*" Mrs. Giannou asked who he was, irritation propelling her voice.

"Kanellos," he said, bowing slightly, his hat over his chest. "Kostas Kanellos."

Marcus looked him over with unadulterated curiosity. So this was Eleni's betrothed, this skinny character with dry, dusty eyes, sun-browned skin pulled tightly over sharp cheekbones, black hair that seemed to grip his scalp rather than lie on it. The man Caliope feared most was meeting them at the airport. How thoughtful.

"We were expecting no one, Kyrio Kanellos," Mrs. Giannou replied.

He replaced his hat. "I apologize. There was no way to contact you. Kremasti is a remote village."

"You do not have to remind me," his mother said, "I was born there. Tell me," she asked, her voice betraying concern that this was the reason Kanellos was meeting them. "Dimitri, is he all right?"

Kanellos nodded but his face was lined with doubt. "His lungs... you know about his illness?"

Marcus thought his mother was going to break into tears. "And Caliope?" she asked, pressing her fingers to her mouth.

"With the exception of stiffness in her hip, she is well."

A sigh of relief escaped through her fingers.

"And Eleni? I am looking forward to meeting my niece for the first time."

"A grown, beautiful woman." Kanellos humbled himself with a bow.

Bouncing on Kanellos's knee? Marcus was thinking.

"When I learned you were coming," Kanellos said, "I told your dear sister and brother-in-law that I would be most pleased to offer my services and meet your flight."

"You did not have to bother," Marcus said. "We were going to hire an overland taxi."

"An unnecessary expenditure of drachmas when I have a car at your service."

"You are very thoughtful," his mother replied politely.

"*Perimenai,*" Marcus said, hold on, but his Greek was too rusty to complete his thought. He looked at his mother. "Tell this goody-two-shoes we have to stop at the American Embassy before we head for Kremasti."

Mrs. Giannou raised her eyebrows. "It is a good thing he cannot understand you," she admonished. "Why do you have to stop at the Embassy?"

Marcus sighed in frustration. He had forgotten to tell her. "Senator Tolson thinks the Embassy should have an official record of my presence in Greece."

"Is he worried about you?"

"Just a precaution, Mom."

She nodded and then spoke Greek to Kanellos, "Do you mind if we stop at the American Embassy on our way?"

Kanellos smiled as though it was an effort. Marcus wondered if he was close to his daily quota. "Mrs. Giannou, I would be more than happy to oblige but Athens traffic is very heavy and we have a long trip ahead of us. Some of the roads we will travel on are hardly more than donkey trails."

That settled it. "*Then berazie*," Marcus said, never mind.

Kanellos led them outside. Immediately the hot air imposed itself on their skin.

"I still feel this is too much trouble," Mrs. Giannou said as she fanned her face with her hand.

"How would Dimitri and your sister feel if I returned in an empty car? Then, dear lady, it truly would be an imposition. Besides, Kyrie Giannou, since I soon will be a member of the family it is my obligation to be of service in any way I can."

However self-serving his comment was, Kanellos made a point. Old World custom demanded that you made whatever effort was required to help out a family member. Anything less would result in hurt feelings.

"Of course, Kyrio Kanellos. If I seemed ungrateful I apologize."

Kanellos held up a bone-gnarled hand. "There is no need to apologize."

They tagged along to a string of cars parked at the curb and stopped by a two-door Simca, so dust-covered the white finish appeared gray. Kanellos opened the trunk to show that their luggage had been safely delivered by the porter. Stuffed in the rear next to the spare, Marcus caught sight of a camera case and next to it a leather satchel about the size of a two-pound box of candy.

"*Toh aftokinito sas?*" Marcus asked. Your car?

Kanellos seemed embarrassed by the question. "It is borrowed, but," he added, his face brightening, "I expect to own one soon." With that he slammed the trunk lid and opened the passenger doors. Trapped heat poured out of the car.

"You will be comfortable after I start the engine," Kanellos said as Marcus climbed into the confining rear seat while his mother sat in front. "This car has air-conditioning. He pointed to an add-on system clamped to the underside of the dash.

Marcus looked at his mother who was waving her handkerchief in front of her face. Droplets of perspiration were clinging to the tiny hairs of her upper lip.

"Well, Mom," he said in English, totally disregarding his earlier admonition to be careful what you say. "This guy may have the personality of a desert cactus but at least his car has air conditioning."

Kanellos looked at Marcus in his rearview mirror as he started the engine. "Mr. Giannou," he said in a way that Marcus had no trouble understanding. "I neglected to tell you that I am fluent in English."

He sat on the bench that doubled as a cot, biding time. He rubbed his fingers along the sackcloth material of his prison garb. He had never seen sackcloth before let alone wear it—the coarse fabric of the imprisoned, at least in Greece. It was rough on his skin and made him itch. It was also dense and trapped the hot air against his body. He read once that in Biblical times sackcloth was a sign of submission.

The shirt was a pullover and the pants had an elastic waistband, no cord or belt, crucial if one is contemplating suicide. Funny that preventing suicide was a major concern. Maybe after interrogation they give you a belt as well as a handy beam when you are of no further use to them. He didn't know, since he hadn't been interrogated yet.

He rubbed his chin and felt another kind of coarseness, the stubble from his beard. Can't shave either, razor blades great for cutting wrists. Why was he fixated on dying? He wasn't ready yet, not by a long shot. But these past days, how many he could not tell, had worn him down and weakened his resolve.

4

Smarting from embarrassment, Marcus looked over his shoulder, the airport terminal and his self-respect falling behind as they drove away. What a stupid mistake, not only humiliating himself but also his mother whose sweaty cheeks turned a bright crimson. She did not have to turn to show him one of her stares, he could feel it. Meanwhile Kanellos, after his display of perfect English, reverted to perfect Greek as if nothing had happened, commenting on the sights they passed along the busy National Highway, a very good asphalt freeway not unlike those in America. Since the airport was south of Athens, they followed the Mediterranean coast, too far south even to see the elevated Acropolis, no matter how vigilant Marcus's gaze. He was disappointed but took comfort in the hope that, once things settled down in Kremasti, he would hire a driver, pick up Sally and together spend a day in Athens before going on their cruise.

He would also keep his promise to the Senator to check in at the Embassy and introduce himself to Ron Constable, but for now this, like his gaze, was out the window.

Marcus sighed inwardly. Time to apologize, as difficult as this was. He could no longer let his impolite statement hang in the air like a stale smell.

"Kyrio Kanellos," he said in English, "please accept my apologies. I am sorry."

Kanellos raised his hand in a forgiving gesture but, even so, Marcus knew he was at a distinct disadvantage with this unpleasant man. Well, he thought glumly, leaning back into the cushion, the air conditioning fighting valiantly to keep the Simca's interior cooler than the outside air, he already had one bad experience in the airport's interrogation room, so why should this one be any different?

Talk about getting off to a bad start. Athens and the Acropolis, Lycavittos, the Roman Agora, the archaeological museums—all disappearing behind him at a steady 70 kph. On both sides of the highway his eyes instead were accosted by ugly sprawl: factories and warehouses, refineries, tall chimneys belching acrid smoke and, in the fouled harbor of Pireaus, cargo ships whose rusted black hulls and stained white superstructures reminded him of the seafaring novels of Howard Pease he read as a child.

Not until they passed over the Isthmus of Corinth, the narrow, hand-hewn canal connecting the Gulfs of Corinth and Saronikos that Marcus rediscovered his vocal chords.

"Incredible," he said, straining to see the deep chasm cut into solid rock a century ago.

"Do you wish to take a closer look?" Kostas asked, slowing the car.

Marcus glanced at his mother who shook her head, anxious to see her sister. The only sightseeing she was looking forward to was in Kremasti.

Nevertheless Kostas braked the car. "It will only take a moment, Kyrie Giannou, I need gas anyway."

Ahead was a small shopping strip with a filling station, gift shop and restaurant. Kanellos pulled into the roofed lane of a gas pump providing welcome shade. The Isthmus was a popular tourist attraction, although at this early hour Marcus seemed to be the only tourist who was attracted. He got out, slammed the door behind him and walked across the road to the gorge. He looked down. If one had vertigo this was no place to be. Hundreds of feet below was a channel of water, so narrow it looked like a blue ribbon.

On both sides were rough-hewn cliffs of rich geological layers in gray, tan and amber plunging almost vertically.

Bisecting the gorge was a metal foot-bridge which attracted Marcus not because of its quaint pattern but because of the large metal sign attached to it: the jarring silhouette of the soldier he had seen in the poster in the interrogation room at the airport. As warm as the air was, his blood nearly congealed. The life-size figure was brazed out of metal and riveted to the triangles of steel supporting the bridge, not unlike a railroad trestle. Below it was the infamous date also cut out of metal: ZHITO 27 APRILIOU 1967, a grim reminder of the day the democratically elected government of Greece was overthrown in a quick and bloodless coup by a military junta.

In a gesture of impotent defiance, Marcus lifted his arm high and gave the sign of the middle finger, jamming it in the air several times to make sure he made his point. He didn't give a damn who saw him, he was that upset. He walked back to the car, angry that this beautiful scene was desecrated by Fascist propaganda. Have these colonels no sense of honor, no respect for Greece's great tradition of democracy?

Kanellos was closing the trunk of the Simca when Marcus approached. Was he checking their luggage?

"Your mother is in the restroom," Kanellos said.

Marcus decided to do the same. He went inside and passed his mother coming out. "I'll wait for you," she said.

Upon his return she motioned him to join her between shelves packed with evzona dolls, plaster casts of the Parthenon and other touristy items almost as tasteless as the sign over the Isthmus. They were alone except for the cashier at the front of the shop.

"*Paithee mou.*" My son, what she called him when she was concerned about something.

"What is it, Mom?" he asked.

"*Aftos.*" Him. She motioned with her head at Kanellos leaning against the car fender smoking a cigarette. "He took your picture."

"He what?"

"I watched him through the window. He went to the trunk and took out a camera. I didn't know he had one."

Marcus nodded. "I saw a camera case next to our luggage."

"He thought I was in the bathroom but I stopped to look at souvenirs, and then I saw him pointing the camera at you. What were you doing?"

"Making a statement."

"Well, whatever it was, he got a picture of it."

He yearned to sleep but the incessant pounding on the metal door with a billy club kept jarring him awake. He tried leaning against the damp concrete wall to see if he could doze off for a few seconds, anything to relieve his sleep-deprived state. Even with his head nodding he mercifully managed a brief respite. Moments passed and suddenly his eyes snapped open. He was wide awake again, wary, cautious. Something had changed. What was it? He looked around the confines of his cell as if the answer lay before him. Nothing visible had changed and yet the atmosphere was different. His mind struggled to make sense of why he felt this way. And then it hit him. No screams. They had stopped. Is this the break he was hoping, praying for? Were they becoming compassionate after all?

5

Kanellos traveled the National Expressway a few more kilometers and then exited onto a winding dirt road, leaving behind the urban sprawl of Athens and the seaport of Pireaus. They drove through the village of Corinth, the gateway to the Peloponnese, its shaded square surrounded by open-air shops, including gift stores, a restaurant and a grocery.

Behind a grove of gnarly olive trees, Marcus could see the ancient temples of Corinth with their restored columns and Corinthian capitals, hence the name. These treasures suddenly disappeared behind a row of whitewashed houses crowding the road, their exteriors dust-covered from passing traffic. There was no sidewalk and an occasional villager on foot or riding a donkey suddenly hugged the walls as the Simca, going too fast for the existing circumstances, swept by.

Leaving the village, the road became asphalt again, cutting through a stunning countryside of rolling hills dotted with white farmhouses sheltered by stands of cypress trees, deep green and shaped like arrowheads.

Marcus tried to focus on the pink and yellow flowers growing on bushes along the road but Kanellos was driving so fast they passed in a blur. He was racing along, cutting curves and passing with reckless abandon. Marcus wondered if this was his way of driving or the way Greeks generally attacked roadways. After a few more kilometers he realized the latter was true: Greeks drive as fast as they can, using horns frequently and passing at will. Heaven help you if you are a timid driver.

Marcus's mother was gripping the door handle as though her life depended on it. In a way it did as her body bounced back and forth in cadence with the jerky motions of the car. She had managed to hold her tongue until Kostas tried to pass a crowded bus with an obnoxious exhaust, its springs and shock absorbers beyond repair, its roof carrier overfilled with suitcases and boxes, its interior packed with sweaty Greeks whose elbows hung out open windows.

Coming alongside the bus, Kostas leaned on his horn, warning the driver of his suicidal intentions, but the driver was having his own battle keeping his swaying, overweight vehicle on the road. The Simca seemed to be magnetized by the bus, whose tires were worn nearly smooth only inches from Marcus's window.

To the horror of mother and son, instead of pulling back into his lane—better to kiss the bus's rear than your life goodbye—Kanellos threw in his clutch and shifted down, hoping the lower gear would give the Simca's already whining engine more revs to pass.

"*Panagia mou!*" Marcus's mother cried out, invoking the Virgin Mary's assistance.

Kanellos looked briefly at Mrs. Giannou to assure her that God's assistance was not needed. While his eyes were off the road, Marcus's eyes were on it.

"Kostas!" he shouted. "There's a car coming!"

Kanellos faced the windshield and, with a quick nod, confirmed Marcus's warning that the glinting silver object hurtling toward them was indeed a car but, to Marcus's horror, instead of hitting the brakes, Kanellos pushed harder on the accelerator, the odometer approaching 150 kph, more than ninety miles per hour! The modest engine was flat out, straining its pistons and beating its valves. Marcus felt a curious and unexpected wave of relief pour over him as he was now convinced they would all die in a fiery crash, and he would no longer have to worry about anything, not his mother, not his job, not his future…

But Kanellos, staying cool under his straw hat, ruined all that. In the split-second between uncertain life and certain death, he managed to squeeze between the bus and the braking Mercedes whose Michelins left smears of black on the lane the Simca had just vacated.

As Kanellos rode the galloping Simca down to a manageable trot, Mrs. Giannou smiled at him, her face shining with an angelic halo. Marcus knew what that meant, the calm before the storm. She was ready to explode and she did, right in Kanellos's ear. Marcus did not think his mother was capable of such expressive Greek. Kanellos probably didn't either. He wilted under her barrage, his reed-like body seeming to slice into the seat cushion. He tried turning his head to apologize, but the force of her withering harangue was like wind on a beachball.

Her anger finally depleted, Marcus' mother leaned back into the corner where the seat cushion met the door. What the near-death experience had not taken out of her, her denunciation of Kanellos's driving had, and she became silent, staring moodily out the window.

Marcus broke the thickening silence when he saw a sign pointing to Mycenea. "Isn't that where Agamemnon's tomb is located?" he asked.

"Yes," Kanellos replied, happy to change the subject. "The famous Lion's Gate is three thousand years old. Mycenae is one of Greece's earliest civilizations."

"Too bad the present does not match the past."

They entered Argos, a dreary village of several thousand, interesting only for a citadel built by the Venetians in the Middle Ages. Protected by crenellated parapets, it sat on a hill overlooking the dry valley they were driving through. Once across the valley they began climbing. Kanellos shifted into low gear to accommodate the steeper grade. They came around a curve and entered a construction zone. A pair of Caterpillar bulldozers, their yellow and black markings obscured by cloying dust, lifted boulders and clots of dried clay clawed from the mountainside into waiting dump trucks. Kanellos was forced to slow down, a welcome relief from his racecar impersonation of Barney Oldfield, and he carefully picked his way along the rock-strewn roadbed.

As they approached the construction site, a workman ran toward them shouting, *"Theenaimeetai! Theenaimeetai!"*

Kanellos hit the brakes and threw the gears in reverse. As he was backing up, an explosion spewed rocks into the air, and the Simca bounced like an empty tin can. In that instant Marcus understood what the workman was yelling: Dynamite!

Mrs. Giannou did not even have time to cross herself when the concussion swept over them. All she could do was grip her ears. As the dust settled, what had been part of the mountain wall was now a pile of rubble and the dozers moved in to continue filling the trucks.

Damnit!" Marcus shouted, his bubbling anger finally boiling over. "Where were the flagmen? We could have been killed!"

"The man warned us," Kanellos said in defense of his fellow countrymen.

Marcus stewed in silence as Kanellos turned on the windshield washer to clear the layer of dust and maneuvered the car around the heavy equipment. After a few kilometers they were back on asphalt, the terrifying experience still resonating and reminding them how close they came to being swept off the mountain road along with the debris.

They drove through Tripoli, a picturesque village except for a huge Big Brother image of George Pappathopoulos, the repressive prime minister of Greece, hanging in the square between two lampposts. This time Marcus kept his counsel and made no disparaging comment although he certainly felt like it.

He looked at his watch. Almost noon. "How about stopping for something to eat?" he asked Kanellos.

"We will stop in Sparta for lunch," he announced as though this was part of his route plan.

"Excellent," Marcus said. "I can visit the American library."

Kanellos looked into the rearview mirror. "Why do you want to do that?" The expression on his face was one of guarded concern.

"The person who runs it is a friend."

"I don't think we will have the time."

"We're stopping for lunch, aren't we?"

Kanellos fell into a troubled silence. Something was eating him. Marcus wished now they had turned down his offer and hired a driver. He and his mother would have had the advantage of being in control, directing the driver rather than the driver directing them. He glanced at her. At least right now she was doing better than he. She had dozed off and her head was bobbing with the rhythm of the moving car. This was an arduous journey even without having nearly been blown off a cliff.

South of Tripoli the terrain leveled off, as if nature's hand had scooped away the tops of mountains and kneaded them into rounded slopes. The road followed a shallow valley and they quickly made up the time lost crawling up and down the mountain roads behind them. As they neared Sparta the road separated into double lanes. Marcus was impressed to see a modern city unfold before him. Running down the main thoroughfare was a beautifully landscaped boulevard of sparkling grass, palm trees and subtropical shrubs.

Kostas pulled up in front of a café called the Kipris Estiatorio and cut the engine. The sudden silence roused Mrs. Giannou from her slumber.

"*Pou eimastai?*" she asked. Where are we?

"Sparta, Mom," Marcus said. He got out, stretched his legs and opened the front door for her. "Very cosmopolitan," he said, looking around.

Kanellos joined them on the sidewalk, smiling. He finally heard something positive coming from the American who was speaking in English.

They chose a table under the shade of a large awning and the waiter was quick to help Mrs. Giannou into her chair. Waiting for their order, Kanellos began talking like a tour guide. "Sparta has a population of 30,000, the largest city in the southern Peloponnese. It is quite modern."

Marcus nodded. "Like an American city."

"In image only. Greece is a poor country." He lowered his voice as though ashamed to admit it. "What Americans earn in a month we earn in a year."

"Would you rather live in America?" Mrs. Giannou asked.

"Of course."

"Take my word for it, this is better," Marcus said.

Kanellos looked in astonishment at Marcus. "Really? You would trade Greece for America?"

"I would trade for the simpler life."

Kanellos laughed sardonically. "That is what keeps us lagging behind the West. But we are changing."

"In what way?"

"We have a no-nonsense government that is cleaning up corruption and graft."

To Marcus no-nonsense meant Fascism.

The waiter brought their lunch, *horiotico salata*, a village salad of tomatoes, cucumbers, onions and feta cheese for all to share with large slices of coarse bread washed down with iced tea. They ate with relish because the food was excellent and they were hungry.

When they finished Marcus asked the waiter for directions to the American Library and was pleased to learn it was close enough to walk; no need for a taxi.

"May I suggest waiting for another day to visit your friend?" Kanellos said. "I don't want them to wait for us."

"Them?" Marcus asked, wondering who "them" were.

He stammered, "Your family, of course."

"I will be gone only a few minutes. This will give me the chance to make up for not checking in at the Embassy. Sally can send a Telex to Athens and let them know I'm in Greece."

"Sally?" Kanellos inquired.

"The friend I was telling you about."

"A woman, then?" he asked, as though relieved. "In that case, one must not keep her waiting." He even winked, making Marcus fear he might use that pejorative term, *kopellara*, in which case, Marcus was ready to punch him.

"Kyrios Kanellos and I will share a dessert," Mrs. Giannou said, sensing her son's displeasure. She did not want another confrontation. "What would you prefer, baklava, thieples, galaktoburiko?"

The American Library was housed in a one-story, spread-out building set on a manicured lawn shaded here and there with cypress trees. The grounds were protected by a knee-high metal fence rusting at the weld joints. A gate opened to a flagstone walkway that led to the entrance, a double wood door with glass sidelites. The architecture was typical government-issue, without distinction or character, the more anonymous the better.

He went inside, the interior warm but not uncomfortable, and looked around. He was in a large room typical of branch libraries back home with bookshelves along the wall, a card catalog, and a rolling truck with books waiting to be re-shelved. There were only two patrons, one sitting at a table reading a newspaper and another scanning the shelves for something to read. The front desk was manned, or should he say womaned, by a person in her forties. She looked at him curiously. He obviously did nor resemble a local person.

"*Meilatai Englezika?*" he asked.

"Of course," she said, her English enriched by Greek inflection.

"I am here to see Sally Haggerty."

She smiled knowingly. "You must be Marcus Giannou."

Marcus nodded. "Passing through, on my way to Kremasti."

"First time in Greece?"

"Yes, but hopefully not my last."

"One never says farewell to Greece, only *Sas thoumai.*" See you later.

Their voices drifted through the open door to an office on the left.

"Marcus, is that you?" came a voice, and then Sally emerged, smiling broadly. "*Kalos Eirthatai,*" she said, and came over to embrace him, kissing him first on one cheek and then the other as was Greek custom.

She was dressed casually in an ecru satin blouse and a pleated skirt of subdued Scottish plaid with plenty of overlapping material to hide wrinkles common in the Greek climate. Like most buildings in Mediterranean countries, the library was not air-conditioned and the windows were wide open to let in air, warm yes but undeniably dry. One did not perspire unless forced to, a condition Marcus did not expect to find himself in although he had no way of predicting the future.

After introducing Marcus to her assistant, Maria, Sally escorted him into her office, tidy and spare: gray metal filing cabinet, typewriter, desk blotter, a glass vase with fresh flowers and, on the wall over her desk, a framed photograph of Secretary of State William P. Rogers.

She joined Marcus, sitting in a guest chair next to him rather than at her desk.

He hadn't seen her since she left Washington five months ago, where her American ways still dictated her style. Now she had been in Greece long enough to be comfortable, even her English had a Greek cadence, a rolling of the Rs and a softening of the consonants.

It delighted him. "You look different."

"In what way?"

"More Greek."

"I'm Irish."

They laughed because her comment helped explain why she could pass for Greek: she had hair the color of pitch and her eyes were dark brown. Even though she was as fair as most Irish, her time in Greece had browned her skin. Her grasp of the language and local custom did the rest.

"If I didn't know you, I'd swear you were born here."

"Thanks for the compliment," she said and got down to business. "I overheard you telling Maria that you are on your way to Kremasti."

He nodded.

"I've been there."

"Really?" he said, surprised.

"I travel around Laconias, visiting villages to introduce myself and talk about the library. It is rare for villagers to visit Sparta. Few own a car and, if someone does, more often than not it's a Toyota pickup used for farming. It occurred to me that if the villagers can't get to a library why not bring the library to them? So I am working on a proposal for USIA to fund a bookmobile. It would break new ground in the way we provide services especially in rural areas the way we do it in America. Most of our patrons live here in Sparta but the Greeks I want to reach have limited access to the outside world. This does not mean they are ignorant. Village schools do a great job teaching kids to read and write. And there are retired Greek-Americans who moved back to their villages and tutor the kids in English."

Marcus was impressed with her enterprise and the uniqueness of her idea.

"There is a fly in the ointment though," she said, lowering her voice. "ESA. They are trying to control what Greeks read." She looked out her door to make sure they were not being overheard. "Did you notice a man walking around looking at books?"

Marcus nodded. "When I came in he was your only customer except for someone reading at a table."

"He is one of those self-appointed vigilantes who checks book titles to make sure there isn't anything subversive printed about the government. A retired Greek from New York used to come in every day to read the International Herald Tribune but he stopped coming because he was warned by that guy not to read American propaganda or he would be reported. It's like Big Brother watching over us."

"We need a counter-revolution."

"What I need is support. Do you think Senator Tolson will back my project?"

"I will make sure he does."

Sally stood. "I'm forgetting my manners. May I offer you anything? Something cold perhaps? Iced tea?"

"I have to go. Mother is waiting for me at Kipris Estiatorio and she is anxious to meet her sister."

Sally looked out her window. "You walked over? Did you hire a car?"

"We were met at the airport by the man who is engaged to my mother's niece." Marcus went on to tell Sally about the disturbing incident when Kanellos took a picture of him giving the finger to the image of the soldier suspended over the Isthmus of Corinth.

Sally shook her head. "Not a good idea, Marcus. You have to be careful. The colonels who run this country are not only ruthless, they are also paranoid."

"I'm an American. What can they do to me?"

"You may work for a US Senator but you do not have political immunity as I do. The man who took your picture, the one who is engaged to your mother's niece, what is his name?"

"Kostas Kanellos."

She jotted it down. "I'll contact the Embassy and see if they have a dossier on him."

"Also would you let the charge d'affairs know that you saw me? Jeff Tolson asked me to check in at the Embassy as soon as I arrived but we didn't have the time."

"Gladly. We are in a kind of cold war with Greece. I am concerned about you."

Marcus shrugged. "I'll be tucked away in a small village. What could happen to me there?"

"A culture of spying has even reached the villages. People turn one another in for criticizing the government. I doubt if there is a telephone in Kremasti but even if there is one I wouldn't risk talking to you because telephones here have party lines. If I find out anything about Kanellos I will drive down to see you."

Marcus was concerned that he revealed too much and would make her worry needlessly. "I don't see myself spending more than two or three days in Kremasti. Once mother is settled, I will be a fifth wheel, so what I would really like to do is see some sights. Can you take time off and be my tour guide?"

"That would be different, an Irish girl showing a Greek his home country. I'll come see you as soon as I learn anything about Kanellos and then we can visit some local attractions. Monemvasia is a picturesque village and so is Gythion. We can take a boat ride in the Diros Cave, incredible stalagmites and stalagtites, and we can do all that in one day. In the meantime," she added, moving her finger across her lips in a zipping fashion, "be careful."

Marcus walked back feeling really good, things were looking up after all. When he got to the restaurant he found his mother sitting alone at the outdoor table and Kanellos inside talking on the telephone.

"Who is he talking to?" Marcus asked his mother as he joined her.

She shrugged. "I don't know. He said he had to make a call. He must know the owner because he let Kostas go behind the counter."

Marcus heard only muffled tones through the open door as Kanellos talked with his back to them, but as the conversation went on, he became agitated and his voice carried into the open air. Marcus was able to piece together some of the conversation in rapid Greek but he knew he would hear the rest from his mother later when they were alone.

Kanellos was talking to a man he called Janos. And the conversation included Marcus and his mother, referred to as the Americans.

"I have the Americans with me," he was saying. "Why would a single day make any difference...be reasonable...let me handle this...don't you trust me?"

When he hung up, Mrs. Giannou looked at her son. "How much did you understand?"

"Enough to know Kostas is in trouble of some kind."

Marcus paid the bill and they were ready to climb into the Simca when a taxi with a black shield on its door pulled up behind them. Marcus paid no mind till he noticed Kostas' face blanch, then turned to see what was getting his attention. Two men got out, one tall and thin, the other short and overweight, reminding Marcus of Mutt and Jeff. The tall man who paid off the taxi driver was casually yet smartly dressed in a maroon sport shirt and gray slacks. He looked out of place, even in an apparently cosmopolitan city like Sparta. He would be more at home on a yacht at anchor in Mykonos.

The other man was the antithesis of the well-dressed man: beefy, uncomfortably red-faced in the bright sun, and his clothes in need of dry cleaning. He stood in the shade of a street pole and lit a cigarette, the slim shadow made by the pole too narrow to be of much good for his protruding belly.

"Ah, we caught you before you left," the dapper man said in perfect, although curiously accented, English. Marcus could not place it.

"Aren't you going to introduce us?" he said to Kostas who seemed to have lost his tongue.

"Of course," Kostas mumbled, out of synch in the presence of these strangers. "May I present Kyrie Giannou and her son, Marcus." He hesitated a moment and added, "From America."

Before he could shift gears and introduce the strangers, the dapper man took over, further embarrassing Kostas, enough so that Marcus was actually feeling sorry for him.

"I am Janos Drovich, and the gentleman with me is Ernst Weber." He pronounced the W as a V. He extended his hand to Mrs. Giannou and when she held hers out he brought it to his lips and kissed it lightly.

She was taken aback by the unexpected courtly gesture and blushed.

"You are not Greek," Marcus said, not suggesting that Greek men lack chivalry but rather, simply, that he was not Greek.

"I am Yugoslav," Drovich said, bowing slightly, "from Zagreb, a pleasant city not unlike Sparta but without the palm trees." He smiled at his small joke. "Have you been to Yugoslavia?"

This was clearly a patronizing question since travel to East Bloc countries was highly restricted.

"I am still waiting for an invitation from your benevolent dictator, Marshall Tito," Marcus replied.

Drovich's face soured while Kostas reacted as if he had swallowed a nail. And Marcus's mother? Better not to ask.

Drovich forced a smile, ending the standoff. "Shall we have coffee? It will give us time to get acquainted." He called to his partner, "Ernst, we are having coffee."

Weber dropped his cigarette, snuffed it out with his toe and walked over. He sat next to Drovich, not meeting anyone's eyes but rather looking down.

Drovich signaled the waiter who came over. "*Kafaithes, parakalo, Turkiko.*"

Marcus was surprised and, if he was willing to admit it, impressed that Drovich spoke good Greek, probably better than his. He swallowed what was left of his pride.

At least he was familiar enough with the East Bloc to know that Drovich had to have a high position in the Communist Party's *nomenklatura* to travel in the West. He also knew that they travel in pairs so one can keep an eye on the other. Perhaps that is why this silent, overweight man was along.

"What brings you to Greece?" Marcus asked.

"Byzantine iconography, my specialty," Drovich said. "You may not be familiar with the fact that many village churches as well as homes contain treasures that even your Metropolitan Museum in New York would steal for."

Marcus wondered if adding New York was meant to be gratuitous. "Not to mention the Hermitage in St. Petersburg," he said returning the volley.

Drovich smiled indulgently, letting Marcus know that he did not have to be reminded that the Hermitage was in St. Petersburg.

"Speaking of the Hermitage," Marcus added, "isn't it easier for you to travel in Russia rather than in the West?"

"The Russia you speak of has been the Soviet Union since 1918. But, to answer your question, I travel extensively there as well."

Just then the waiter came out with a tray of demitasse cups of black coffee, rich and steaming, reminding Marcus that Kostas had made a phone call from inside the restaurant. "On the telephone a few minutes ago," he said, "Kostas was talking to someone named Janos. So that was you."

Kostas froze from the sharp look he got from Drovich. Marcus was eavesdropping or Kostas was talking too loudly. Either way he was overheard.

"And the Simca is your car," Marcus said, the confusion beginning to clear.

Drovich bowed stiffly in acknowledgment. "Kostas asked to borrow my car so he could pick you up at the airport. I was only too happy to oblige."

I'll bet you were, Marcus thought. "So what brought you two together?"

"Kostas is my guide in the Peloponnese, including Kremasti."

"Oh?" Marcus raised his eyebrows in surprise. "You are heading there, too?"

"That is why we are here. We are joining you on the drive to Kremasti."

Marcus looked at the Simca, its gray metal shimmering in the sun.

"All five of us?"

"It is only forty-five kilometers," Kostas said, trying to make the best of a bad situation. He looked down at his shoes.

Mrs. Giannou wiped her brow with a handkerchief getting more and more damp.

"*Panagia mou*," she said, all too often now it seemed.

6

From passersby there were smiles of mock humor, as if witnessing clowns climbing out of a toy car, but in this case people, not necessarily clowns, were climbing into a real car. Whatever went through their minds, the sight *was* a circus: Kostas at the wheel with the tubby man next to him, and Mrs. Giannou, Marcus and Drovich in back as the overfull Simca pulled away from the curb—not only sardined with humans but also weighted down by a trunk full of suitcases, its air conditioner whining doggedly but still losing to the heat produced by bodies struggling to cool off.

Inevitably windows were rolled down. At least now there was air blowing in, however warm. The narrow asphalt road they were on followed a valley between twin mountain ranges, so there was no grade to strain the overworked Poissy in-line four, and they drove at a steady 50 kph. If they got to Kremasti, a tribute would have to be paid to Societe Industrielle de Mecanique et Carrosserie Automobile, the French automaker for which Simca is the acronym.

Drovich sat between Marcus and his mother. They occupied themselves looking out at the flat, arid landscape interrupted here and there by scruffy grass and grazing goats. There was little if any traffic and a few goats wandered onto the road oblivious of a car horn beeping at them. No one seemed to be tending the animals and

Marcus wondered if they were feral. The scene reminded him that Greece was a third-world country, the result of four centuries of Ottoman rule that prevented it from flourishing during the Renaissance as did the rest of Europe.

The thought made him feel vaguely sad and he began to wonder what kind of relationship this Slavic stranger he was squeezed next to had with Kostas, Eleni's betrothed. Was he the problem Caliope wrote about in her letter to Marcus's mother? It was obvious Kostas was unnerved by Drovich's presence. Marcus decided to ask a few questions.

"Have you known Kostas very long?"

"Even though we are of different nationalities, we share common values. Both of us were young idealists during the Greek Civil War, the first stand-off of the Cold War, you might say. Your country supported the Greek government while mine, Yugoslavia, supported the partisans."

"You were insurgents." Marcus knew enough about the tragedy following World War II when Greeks fought one another, sometimes brother against brother, while neighboring countries like Yugoslavia took up the cause of the military branch of the Greek Communists.

Drovich smiled an inscrutable smile. "We were supporting a noble cause."

"Blood flowed for nothing, Mr. Drovich. Your side lost."

"We did not lose, Kyrio Giannou. Isn't the Greek government more allied to the Soviet Union than it is to the United States?"

Marcus had no answer for that and looked instead at the back of Kostas' head. He wanted to ask the driver with the crumpled, sweat-stained hat what side he was on. He didn't have to ask, he could guess well enough.

Kostas turned off the asphalt road and followed a windy, unpaved lane heavily shrubbed along its borders with flowering bougainvillea. Marcus wondered how the purple blossoms managed to be so plentiful in this arid climate.

Behind the stand of shrubs Marcus spotted the tip of a white obelisk, "What is that?" he asked.

Kostas glanced at Weber who was staring straight ahead. "That is Monodendri," he said, "a monument to the war."

"What happened there?" Marcus mused aloud, looking out the rear window at the receding granite object pointing to the sky as his question hung in the air like a disturbed ghost.

The terrain flattened into a large plain and they drove through a village whose sign identified it as Niata. Marcus noted something he had not seen since leaving Sparta, a series of light poles along the road. He mentioned this to Kostas.

"Niata is the first village in our area to receive not only electricity but a telephone. The poles come from Spain as there are not enough trees in Greece to supply the wood."

A large church dominated the village with twin bell towers and a tiled dome. They passed three men sitting in the shade of grapevines hanging from an arbor and drinking who knew what in this heat. They waved and everyone in the Simca waved back.

After Niata the road worsened, turning into what can only be described as a dry riverbed. They escalated through two other villages, one named Skala and the other Elos, each with a whitewashed church and campanile, not nearly as impressive as the one in Niata. Marcus realized that village churches commanded their surroundings not only because of their spiritual presence but also because they were sited on the highest elevation.

Drovich noted the attention Marcus was paying to the churches, prompting him to say, "We should put aside our political differences, don't you think, and share what we may have in common: an interest in the Byzantine arts?"

"All right," Marcus said.

Drovich beamed. "I have a passion for all things Byzantine, not only architecure but also the decorative arts—icons, chalices, patens, Bible covers. I have found that the naive art in homes and churches of these isolated villages is more interesting than the mannered work one sees in the cathedrals of Athens. Many of these homes, stone hovels hundreds of years old, have miniature altarpieces and icon paintings, equally old, of the Mother and Child that are unique treasures."

"So what do you do with these so-called unique treasures? You can't take them home with you." Marcus laughed at his little bit of humor.

"I photograph them." Drovich pointed over his shoulder. "In the trunk I have a 35 millimeter Minolta SRT 101, a fine slide camera with a Fresnel lens for sharp close ups. State of the art."

So it was Drovich's camera Kostas used to take the compromising photograph at the Isthmus of Corinth. Marcus leaned back against the cushion, the ramifications swirling in his head. Inside that camera on a roll of film of Byzantine icons was a single exposure of an American jamming his defiant middle finger high in the air at the black silhouette of the soldier symbolizing ESA, the repressive regime now controlling Greece. How could he have been so foolish? His mother warned him to be careful and now he was a marked man.

He stared at Kostas driving with both hands gripping the steering wheel as he maneuvered the steaming Simca on a narrow road strewn with rocks, some the size of soccer balls that had to be carefully circumnavigated. Why did he take the photograph? For blackmail to use as a threat in case Marcus tried to interfere in Kostas' plan to marry Eleni? He hadn't even met her and already he was embroiled in an intrigue whose consequences he did not understand nor fully appreciate.

He stared in dismay at a landscape so dry and barren it was not even worthy of a painting. How can

Greeks cut a living out of this rock-infested dirt, he asked himself, trying to put his troubled thoughts behind him. He leaned forward to check his mother sitting on the other side of Drovich. She was waving her handkerchief to ward off the dust coming through the open windows. Even though she was bone tired there was excitement in her eyes because each passing kilometer brought her closer to her sister.

"Does this road look familiar, Mom?" he asked, assuming this was the route she took when she left Kremasti for her long, as well as long ago, trip to America.

"No, son," she said. "I went the other direction, on a donkey to Kiparisi, and from there I took a ferryboat to Piraeus where I boarded a steamship for America."

She looked out the window as they bounced and jounced over the rocky path barely making 25 kph. This road was never meant for an *aftokinito.*

"Is this how Sparta got its reputation for toughness?" Marcus asked of no one in particular

Kostas glanced over his shoulder. "I am sure what you see here is no match for the verdant fields in Minnesota. But we still grow olives and figs, and wheat in the winter."

They drove over a roughly made stone bridge, old enough, Marcus thought, to have carried chariots, if the Greeks indeed used those conveyances in ancient times. Under the bridge ran a ravine that looked like a dry riverbed. "So it rains here after all."

"So heavy sometimes that streams overflow. Every home has a cistern to collect water. However, Kremasti, as you will soon see, is very fortunate. Natural mountain springs irrigate the land."

"Where you grew up," Marcus said to his mother.

She nodded, tears forming in her eyes.

Over the next rise, they saw it: Kremasti, the village so-named because it appeared to be hanging from the mountain slope. Marcus heard his mother inhale sharply when the clay-tiled roofs and whitewashed stone walls came into view, a breathtaking scene because the houses were surrounded by lush green, like an oasis in the desert. Above the tiled roofs dominating the village, was a single campanile, weathered gray and leaning like the tower of Piza.

Mrs. Giannou pointed to it and dabbed at teardrops running down her cheeks. "That is what is left of the original *eklisia*." Behind it was the new church, sparkling from a fresh coat of whitewash, its dome covered in orange tile. A new campanele stood beside it, a proudly straight replacement of the original.

Kostas braked the Simca, its engine hissing, and parked under a eucalyptus grove bordering the square. Immediately a cluster of villagers swarmed the car, among them boys in short pants fighting each other for the privilege of opening the doors for the Very Important Persons. Kostas shouted at them in Greek to stay back but they paid no attention. This was a special occasion.

As Marcus rounded the car to help his mother, he was surrounded by the boys who wanted to touch him as if he were a movie star. His mother was already climbing out in her excitement to see her sister, but the bumpy ride had stiffened her muscles and it took a few seconds for her to stand erect. She looked around the square, calling up a wellspring of memories only she would remember.

"Caliope," she asked. "*Pou einai?*" Where is she?

"We did not know the time of your arrival," said a villager, his silver hair in sharp contrast to his darkened skin. "Do you remember me?" he asked, continuing in Greek. "I am Theodoros Apistothelis. I was twelve when you left."

Mrs. Giannou nodded appreciatively although it was evident her memory of him was hazy.

"I saw one of the boys running down the path to the house. Come, let us follow him."

"The luggage," Marcus said.

"There are many helpful hands to carry your bags. Do not worry."

Marcus worried but for another reason. "What about Drovich and that man Weber?" he asked as they followed a steep dirt path cut between houses and chicken coops. "Where are they staying?"

"There is a pistachio nut farmer outside of town who puts up travelers."

"How long will they be here?"

"A day or two, long enough for Drovich to take some slides."

Marcus wondered if he could get hold of that Minolta and expose the negative of him giving the finger. But if he managed, what then? Drovich's precious shots would be ruined and Marcus would be suspect number one. Either way, he thought grimly, he was cooked.

"Marcus!" Mrs. Giannou was waving at him. "Catch up!" It was as if she had shed sixty years. She was almost running in her excitement to meet her sister. He had never seen her so full of energy.

"Coming mother," he shouted, mimicking Henry Aldrich on the radio show he listened to as a kid.

As they followed a path with Kostas in the lead, women in black scarves and gray dresses and men in white shirts with sleeves rolled up shouted greetings and waved like people watching a parade. Permanently squinting eyes and missing teeth seemed to be the norm for both genders.

These villagers had an unhurried and uncomplicated existence, to be sure, tending animals and raising crops, aging cheese and curing yogurt, napping in the afternoon and drinking homemade wine at dinner— still this was a life of subsistence, not sufficiency. They were poor. Their stone-built homes consisted of three small rooms, one for sitting, one for sleeping and one that doubled for cooking and dining. In back was a wood-burning oven, a pen for lambs that baaed at the newcomers, and an outhouse.

And yet, paradoxically, the simple lives these Greeks led provided far more space for happiness than the hectic one Marcus left behind in Washington.

Suddenly there was a shriek so piercing he thought for a moment his mother had stumbled and hurt herself. She had rounded the corner of a house and was out of his view when the shout occurred. He turned the corner just in time to see her break into a run and join a trio of persons standing in a small yard of packed dirt. He stopped short to watch the reunion, letting his mother have her moment alone with her sister, Caliope, brother-in-law Dimitri, and a young woman shyly looking on who was so pretty she almost took Marcus's breath away. She had to be Eleni, the adopted daughter around whom the trip to Kremasti pivoted.

Mrs. Giannou and Caliope embraced and dug their faces into one another's necks reasserting a bond, although separated by nearly half a century, that was never broken. They had parted as teens and now they were aging sisters from starkly different backgrounds. Marcus could see the difference in what they were wearing: his mother in a factory-made dress, purchased on clearance at Dayton's Downstairs Store, but still a Christian Dior compared to Caliope's homemade peasant dress, undoubtedly her Sunday best but of a coarse material Marcus could not identify.

Aside from what she was wearing, a matter of greater concern was her physical well-being. Marcus noted that her right hip jutted out, misshaping the hang of her dress so that the hem was uneven, and as she hugged her sister Marcus saw pain etching her face from the pressure of the embrace. Caliope was small and worn, as if peasant life had shrunken her. Nevertheless she was happy beyond description, tears of love and joy streaming down a face creased by a lifetime of outdoor labor.

Dimitri waded in, his arms across the backs of both women to form a trio of huggers. He was wearing a dull-green sweater over a printed shirt. The sweater looked familiar. And then Marcus remembered that it was one he had worn in his teens and shipped to Kremasti in a box along with other hand-me-down clothing he had outgrown.

The sweater, pilled from constant wearing, fit Dimitri loosely because he had lost weight, not because he was smaller than Marcus. A few years ago, when he still had his health, a photograph showed him to be fit and well-built. Now he was stoop-shouldered, and his eyes were too small for their sockets.

His vision blurred by tears, Marcus had trouble focusing when Caliope released herself from her sister's arms and sucked him into the vortex of unbridled emotion. Trapped in a whorl of embracing arms, he tried to concentrate on Eleni who was staring at them a few steps away. He wanted to smile at her, even lob a greeting over the heads pressed against his, but before he could do either of these he was strong-armed around his neck and hauled down to receive a fiercely planted, moisture-laden kiss.

"Poulaki mou!" Caliope shouted in his ear. My chick! She released him and reached for Eleni's arm, pulling her over. It was now her turn. Eleni embraced her visiting relatives shyly, unaccustomed probably to wild displays of emotion. His mother grabbed the slender girl by her waist and hugged her so tightly Marcus was concerned she might get hurt.

"Mom," he said. "Take it easy. You'll break a bone."

This was the first English spoken since the reunion began. It sounded out of place but his mother did as told and then it was Marcus's turn to embrace his cousin. As he did so, he had the distinct impression that everyone stopped whatever each was doing to watch.

He bent slightly and touched his cheek to hers. It was cool even in the warm air. His cheeks for sure were hot—maybe it was the contrast that affected him. In any case, the sensation was pleasant. But what he reacted to next was unusual: a smell tingled his nostrils, an aroma of skin, totally foreign to frequently washed and deodorized Americans who have been programed to find body odor offensive in others and fearful in themselves.

Here, in a Greek village, where in-door plumbing and running water were luxuries if they existed at all, there was this unfamiliar smell of the body, not unpleasant, just different.

And yet the smell of Eleni *was* different. There was a faint but noticeable odor, perhaps heightened by the excitement of the moment and it touched his nostrils in a curiously sexual way.

They separated and Marcus ventured in Greek, "You are pretty, prettier than I imagined," knowing that he could never get his tenses straight.

He detected proud smiles. Marcus was not afraid to try his *Ellenika*, however hesitant.

Eleni blushed as though on cue. Her skin was not as dark as the others and the pink coloring on her cheeks came through. She was uncharacteristically thin for a village woman, having what appeared to be a model's figure hidden under her printed peasant dress, too long to be stylish, too loose to be revealing. Her hair, lustrous from a fresh washing, was more reddish-brown than dark like her Greek counterparts. But what he liked most were her eyes—lively, even mischievous.

She surprised him by saying in English, although heavily accented, "Welcome to Kremasti. We are very happy to see you."

"You speak English," Marcus said.

Everyone beamed, especially Kostas.

Marcus understood. "You taught her, didn't you?"

"Eleni is a good pupil. She learns quickly."

No one could have been more delighted than Marcus. With Eleni's help he would have less problem communicating. What a relief not to depend on his mother, who frequently got short with him for his fractured Greek, or failed to rescue him when he foundered.

Caliope listened to the brief exchange in English and, not understanding became frustrated, a condition not different, except in reverse, from what Marcus went through.

"Ti lenne?" she asked. What are they saying?

"Eleni ehi miala," his mother replied. Eleni has brains.

Everyone laughed and Eleni blushed appropriately. The interruption gave Marcus and his mother the opportunity to greet other well-wishers surrounding them, including Athena in whose home Marcus would sleep while his mother stayed with her sister. Athena was introduced simply as *ei hira*, the widow.

"How old is she?" Marcus asked Eleni of the widow who was now departing for home.

"Thirty-four."

Marcus shook his head. Only a few years older than Eleni, who was also destined to be a widow before her time if she married Kostas Kanellos. Sadly, Greece was full of these young women since the custom was for men to take wives half their age. They wore widow's weeds—black dresses and black scarves the rest of their lives, more as martyrs than as mourners.

"Athena will marry again," he said hopefully.

"A widow with a small child?" Eleni replied, as though describing damaged goods.

The crowd began to disperse, time to let the Giannous be alone with their relatives. Mother and son stepped onto a porch with a metal table and chairs, freshly painted for company, and entered a house of thick stone walls and plank flooring. The windows lacking frames, panes or screens were simple rectangular openings protected by wood shutters now pulled shut against the sun.

The parlor was sparsely furnished with a dresser, a table and four chairs with square backs and a sofa with pillows. Shelves on one wall displayed a variety of notions and food: thread, needles and yarn, as well as cans and jars of preserves, honey and olives. Uncle Dimitri, Marcus discovered, ran a general store out of his living room.

A doorway led to the bedroom and a curtain separated the parlor from the kitchen, which was nothing more than a counter and open shelves for dishes and pans. In the corner was a fireplace and in the center a table and chairs. A backdoor opened to a small patio with a stone oven and a galvanized iron washtub. Stone steps led down to a lower level of the house, probably the stable.

That was it, his mother's birthplace and the home of Dimitri, Caliope and Eleni Stathos.

They packed into the small parlor while Dimitri fetched a demijohn of homemade wine from the kitchen and filled glasses to overflowing.

Marcus cautioned him in Greek. "That is a lot of wine, Theio," he said, calling Dimitri uncle.

Dimitri smiled. "Village wine will not make you drunk like wine in bottles."

As they sat around the crowded table raising glasses that resembled jelly jars, Marcus felt himself going through a spiritual metamorphosis, from moth to butterfly, his soul spreading wings to soar into a glorious new experience. He had the overwhelming feeling that he, as well as his mother, had come home.

7

They toasted one another till the bottle was empty. Dimitri was right, the homemade wine did not make Marcus drunk but it certainly made him sleepy. After all, he and his mother had traveled through seven time zones to reach Kremasti. He watched her for signs of fatigue but he might as well as have watched a racecar going for the finish line. She was indefatigable.

It was Eleni who came to his rescue. "Is it true in America you do not rest in the afternoon?" she said, speaking English

"We don't have the time," he said, an illogical syllogism if there ever was one.

The two young people laughed. Caliope looked questioningly. "*Yiati gelas?*" Why do you laugh? Eleni translated, and then there was laughter all around.

Marcus looked over the limited space of the small house. Assuming his mother would sleep on the sofa and there was only one bedroom, he could not help but ask Eleni, "Where do you sleep?"

The directness of his question brought conversation to a halt and an uneasy stare from his mother, but Eleni shrugged it off with a disarming smile. "I will show you," she said and led him outside through a back door and down stone steps.

There was a small pasture penned in with chicken wire. Lambs and goats grazed while chickens ran between their hooves. A skinny horse stood under a fig tree, his flanks worn smooth from brushing off flies with his tail. Eleni watched Marcus taking in the scene.

"The goats are for milk, the lambs and chickens are for meat."

No need to expound further, Marcus thought. For him milk came in cartons and meat came shrink-wrapped from the supermarket.

Eleni opened a wood door to a bedroom under the main level, a space that once must have been the stable. The room was spotlessly clean and Marcus felt like a voyeur peeking in but Eleni clearly wanted him to see it, perhaps to reveal more about herself. The dirt floor was so hard-packed it looked like concrete. Her bed was neatly made with fresh sheets. A small dresser held a washbasin and a mirror, and next to it was a wood hook for a towel. In the corner was a hope chest. He wondered what was in there, a trousseau, needlework, linens? It irked him that Kostas would be the one who sees the contents on her wedding night. Marcus turned his attention to an icon above Eleni's bed of the Virgin Mary, about eight by ten inches, simple yet profoundly magnetic, his eye drawn to it as though the image compelled him to pay attention.

"That is beautiful," he said.

Eleni smiled appreciatively.

"It looks old. Where did you get it?'"

"It was always here. I pray under it every night."

Marcus returned to the upper level to find his mother unpacking her things and putting them in the dresser.

"Nap time, Marcus," she said and pointed to the sofa in the parlor.

Marcus looked around. "Where do I go?"

"Athena's house. Your luggage is already there."

Whispering to her, he described Eleni's bedroom. "Where do you suppose Kostas sleeps?"

"I do not know and I do not ask."

"They can't be living together. That bedroom is her sanctuary. I don't see her sharing it with anyone, let alone Kostas."

His mother stared as though he had overstepped his bounds, and in a way he had. "That is not for us to talk about."

Yes it is, Marcus wanted to say. That is why we're here, isn't it?

Eleni walked Marcus to Athena's house, where he found his suitcase on a single bed in a small annex of the parlor. A wood table held a bouquet of flowers and a glass of water covered by a lace doily to protect it from insects.

Athena was looking in from her kitchen. Dressed in black she looked older than her years.

Marcus looked at her, filled with guilt from the special attention he was getting—the rich American taking over the home of a poor widow.

Athena blushed from Marcus's stare. She turned and stepped into the kitchen, her cheeks still rose-colored.

"I hope she is all right with my being here," he said to Eleni in English.

"She has not had a man in her home for two years."

"I hope she finds someone else."

Eleni shook her head soberly. "A widow with a small child is a burden no Greek man will take on."

If they didn't drape their bodies in black, Marcus thought, they would stand a better chance of remarrying. But that was Greek custom, eternally respecting the memory of a late husband.

When he awoke from his nap it was getting dark. Several seconds passed before he was able to orient himself. Then he realized where he was, in the widow's house, no electricity, just waning light from the sun's rays spilling over the tops of the Parnos Mountains, two thousand feet above him. He was more used to Minnesota, where the afternoon sun kept spreading across flat plains before dipping behind the western horizon.

He sat up and looked around. Something new had been added to the table as he napped, a large enamel basin chipped around the edges and filled with fresh water, a small bar of handmade soap and a towel to dry off with. Athena thought of everything. He wet the soap and cleaned his upper body with it, then rinsed and wiped himself dry, totally refreshed. He had stripped down to his shorts for his nap, and now he dressed again. The air was so dry he did not sweat. His shirt and pants were fresh enough to wear one more time before digging into the suitcase.

He had to go to the bathroom and found the privy behind a grove of trees, hidden from the house by a small arbor covered with grapevines. The last time he used a latrine was at boyscout camp when he was eleven. As he relieved himself he expected an offensive odor but there was none, just a pungent sweetness. He wondered what Athena used for freshener, certainly not Air Wick.

Marcus followed the path to the home of Dimitri and Caliope. As he neared the house he expected to see his mother and her family on the porch, enjoying the approach of evening. But instead he saw three men: Kostas, Drovich and that nondescript Weber sitting around the metal patio table drinking a milky liquid. As he neared, Dimitri appeared at the front door and waved. He did not seem very happy, as though he had just discovered termites in the rafters.

"Ah, there you are," Drovich said, rising from his chair to greet him. "Please join us. I trust you napped well. Greek hospitality is second to none. Would you like a glass of ouzo? It clears the palate for dinner."

"No thanks," Marcus replied and sat down, wondering what he and Weber were doing here. It would not seem likely that Caliope invited them. Surely she would want the first dinner with her sister and nephew to be a family affair, not meant to be crashed by Drovich and

Weber. Their first evening as a family reunited and they could not enjoy it alone. Something fishy was going on. He could see it in Dimitri's eyes and in the unpleasant atmosphere that permeated the table where he now sat.

"Where are the ladies?" Marcus asked in Greek.

"In the kitchen preparing dinner," Dimitri replied.

Eleni showed up with a tray of plates and utensils to set the table. Weber stared at her as she leaned over and her dress opened enough to show her breasts filling out. His eyes were taking their time.

She pretended not to notice, but her cheeks gave her away. She glanced briefly at Marcus, reading in his eyes that he, too, was offended. There was a brief brush of her hand across his, letting him know how much she appreciated his support.

When Eleni finished putting the plates down, Marcus counted five. "Aren't we all eating out here?" he asked.

"Only the men," she said and went back in the house, leaving Marcus alone to ponder the old-world treatment of women as servants.

Presently, Caliope and Mrs. Giannou emerged with trays of food: souvlaki, cucumber and tomato salad heavily coated with olive oil and liberally sprinkled with oregano, thick-sliced bread, and yogurt. Right behind them was Eleni carrying a demijohn of wine and fresh glasses. Once served, the three women disappeared into the kitchen where they had their dinner.

Marcus had forgotten how hungry he was and ate with gusto, stuffing himself with the marvelous tasting food. Very little was said as the men ate until Drovich leaned back in his chair and belched into his hand. The food and wine seemed to mellow him. He pulled a cigar from his jacket pocket and lit it, circling the tip till it glowed evenly. It smelled masculine.

Dinner over, Caliope cleared the table of the dirty plates. She reappeared with a tray of demitasse cups and a copper pot with a long handle full of rich, steaming coffee and poured the rich brew, grounds and all, into the cups.

"My compliments to Kyrie Stathos," Drovich said to Dimitri. "You are fortunate to have such a great cook."

Dimitri smiled as if on cue but said nothing.

Drovich turned his attention to Marcus by blowing cigar smoke in his direction. "My American friend," he said switching to English, "by now I am sure you appreciate village life—simple pleasures without pressure, unhurried, contemplative, a life expectancy that exceeds that in America."

As he said this, Weber lit a cigarette from a package labeled *Samum* with an illustration of a Bedouin smoking on his camel. He held the cigarette between his lips, letting the smoke curl up his nose and irritate his eyes.

Well, Marcus thought, if Weber smokes those potent Arabian cigarettes he will likely nudge life expectancy down a bit.

"What is your take on this, Mr. Weber?" Marcus asked. He had yet to hear from him.

Kostas looked at Drovich warily while Weber remained absorbed in his smoking.

Drovich leaned forward as if to interrupt Marcus's line of vision. "Herr Weber, I have to say, is a mute. He does not speak."

So that was why Weber kept to himself, leaning against the lamppost in Sparta, as well as staring resolutely at the road on the trip to Kremasti. "Sorry," Marcus said, surprised as well as apologetic. "Is he deaf?"

"No, nor is he dumb."

"Of course not," Marcus was quick to add, feeling slightly embarrassed. "You refer to him as Herr. Is he from Germany?"

Drovich bowed slightly, his method of showing mock respect. "He is from Switzerland but born of German parents."

"Is he your body guard?"

Drovich laughed indulgently. "What an odd word, as though you think I may need someone to guard, as you say, my body."

"Just wondering."

"You Americans are direct, but no matter. By the way," he said changing the subject, "have you seen the icons that adorn the Stathos home?"

"Only one," Marcus replied, raising Drovich's eyebrows.

"But through the eyes of an expert?" Drovich said.

"Yours, I presume?"

"I have not been as lucky as you to have seen at least one icon but with the kindness of your uncle, perhaps he will let us examine them together. Then tomorrow, again with his kindness, I would like to take photographs."

Drovich laid his cigar on the stone ledge and stood. "Kyrio Stathos," he said switching to Greek, "would you kindly let your nephew and me see your *ikones*?"

Putting it that way, Dimitri had no choice but to nod assent. Marcus followed Drovich into the parlor.

Dimitri pointed to the bedroom which Marcus had not yet entered. Hanging from the rafters, darkened by age, was a votive light. Flickering through a filigreed brass bowl was a wick floating in oil, burning quietly. Next to it were two icons on a narrow shelf, the size of large picture postcards. They were of wood with edges painted in gold to simulate frames. The Byzantine images on the icons were dark from candle soot.

What does Drovich see in these? "Who are they?" Marcus asked. Other than Jesus, there were two he did not recognize.

"St. John the Baptist and St. John of Chrisostom, lovingly painted by devoted artists using simple materials, egg tempera on wood. There is a mystical spirit about them, don't you think? These saints, although stern and aloof, nevertheless are absorbed in contemplation of the Savior."

Marcus was surprised by the expressive words Drovich was using. "I didn't think Communists spoke so reverently about anything, let alone art."

Drovich sniffed as though smelling something unpleasant. "My dear Kyrio Giannou, I appreciate art for art's sake, and furthermore my country is not Communist it is a Socialist Republic."

Close enough, Marcus wanted to say but this time held his tongue.

Drovich smiled, regaining his composure. "These small icons are merely objects to whet the appetite for something even more special. From what Kostas has told me, there is another one that is of great personal interest to me. I would also like to see it, but it is hanging in the bedroom of Kostas' betrothed and I hesitate to..."

"Are you talking about the one in Eleni's bedroom?"

Drovich's eye lighted up with anticipation, perhaps even jealousy. "Ah, so that is the one you have seen. You have the advantage over me because I have not. If only I could just..."

"... look at it?" Marcus said, finishing Drovich's hope-filled sentence.

"Do you think it is possible?" he asked eagerly.

Eleni came out of the kitchen.

"Ah, there you are," Drovich said obsequiously. "You must have overheard us talking about the icon in your bedroom. Is there any way at all that I might look at it? With your permission, of course, inasmuch as I would be invading the private quarters of a pretty young woman." All the stops were out except kissing her hand.

Eleni looked helplessly at Marcus. It was clear she did not want this oily person to go into her bedroom. She would feel violated.

"Why don't I get it," Marcus said. "It is just hanging on the wall."

Eleni nodded, relieved that he rescued her.

"But handle it carefully," Drovich cautioned.

Marcus went out the front door and passed Kostas and Weber still sitting at the porch table. Weber looked his usual sullen self and Kostas was staring down at his hands folded across his lap as though divorcing himself from the proceedings. This is not my battle his posture seemed to be signaling. Marcus walked around the house to the lower level and entered Eleni's bedroom. Even with her permission he felt like a trespasser.

He leaned over the bed and looked carefully at the icon. The image of Mary seemed to stare back at him, her face sympathetic, almost lifelike, entreating Marcus to hold her reverently. Then he carefully lifted the icon off its hook and brought it upstairs.

"Highly expressive, wouldn't you say?" Drovich commented when Marcus handed him the icon. "Observe the restrained pallet, the subtle orange-brown and silver-blue, the clear dynamic lines. The work conveys a spiritual message to worshippers who could not read or write but who were able to perceive the subtleties of their theology through the skill of the painter. What you see here is art for the masses."

Art for the masses? A Marxist term if ever there was one, Marcus thought. And why not? Drovich came from a Russian satellite country so why wouldn't he spout party doctrine.

"Seeing it firsthand, the icon has to be the work of Theophanes the Greek," Drovich continued, "one of the most famous icon painters of the Byzantine Era. Although he was born and educated in Constantinople, he emigrated to Moscow where all of his known works were completed. The story goes that his work in Greece did not survive but if this icon we are looking at is genuine, we have a treasure of immense value. Can you imagine—Theophanes' Virgin hanging in the bedroom of a peasant girl?"

Describing Eleni as a peasant girl did not ride well with Marcus. "So you believe it is genuine?"

"Yes, but the Virgin has to be evaluated by respected authorities. Where could such a person be found around here?" he questioned dismissively.

"I know a respected authority on Byzantine art, and she is close by, in Sparta."

Drovich stared.

"She can drive down and look at it."

"A woman drive to Kremasti?" Drovich snorted. "You saw for yourself, the road is barely passable."

Marcus gave Drovich a smile of one-upmanship. "You don't know Sally. She has already been here on a tour of villages in the area."

"Sally..." Drovich reacted as though tasting something to determine its flavor. "She works in the American Library?"

Marcus nodded. "Sally Haggerty. You have met her?"

"No, no, just the name, that is all."

"Sally is planning to drive down in the next day or two. I will show it to her. If she agrees that it is genuine, it should be moved for safe keeping, don't you agree?"

"Moved?"

"A precious work of art hanging, as you say, in the room of a peasant girl?"

"Do not react hastily, Kyrio Giannou." Drovich seemed almost on the verge of panicking "After all it has remained perfectly safe in Eleni's room for many years."

"Unknown and anonymous, but now that you told me of its potential value, I won't stop worrying. What if someone tries to steal it? I will never forgive myself. No, it has to be put away," he said, looking at Eleni for confirmation. She nodded.

Drovich was almost shaking. His face was mottled and he kept swallowing as though phlegm had stuck in his throat. Marcus felt no compunction to feel sorry for him. It was Drovich after all who told him the icon was precious, so what else was Marcus to do but assure its safety, to protect what belonged to Eleni? So let him stew. He did not trust Drovich anyway. He might even try to steal it himself. Marcus now felt responsible for the icon. It should be out of here, maybe even tonight, he was that concerned.

Caliope began moving about the house lighting kerosene lamps. Drovich made no overture about leaving. It was Marcus's mother who sensed that her sister was too shy and reticent to speak up.

"You must be as tired as we are, Kyrio Drovich. We won't keep you any longer."

Drovich took the hint. There was nothing else for him to do. He had regained his composure. "Of course, dear lady," he said. "Time to call it a night, as you say in America." He stepped out to the porch and signaled Weber who stood like a soldier awaiting orders. Drovich picked up his now stale cigar and put on his hat.

"With your kind permission," he said to Dimitri, "I will return first thing in the morning to photograph the icon before it is removed." He was speaking to Dimitri, but he was looking at Marcus as though challenging him to contradict his words. But Marcus remained silent. Then, his confidence returning, Drovich added, "After that, we will be out of your hair. Another Americanism, right, Kyrio Giannou?'

Marcus smiled politely, happy to be rid of them. Till now he and his mother had not spent a moment alone with the family. He was looking forward to visiting with Eleni and finding out more about that icon.

Drovich and Weber bowed, made their way down the steps and waved. Their goodbyes over, Kostas joined them. Marcus wished he could follow and listen in to what they were saying.

Everyone sat quietly until the only sound coming through the window was the rustle of leaves moving in the evening breeze.

In fact it was so quiet, so typical of village life, that Marcus could hear Dimitri's labored breathing.

A troubled expression sagged the skin under his uncle's eyes. "I will be happy when they go," he said.

"Kostas meets strange people in his line of work," Marcus said to his mother in English.

"I do not like them. Did you see the way that dirty old man looked at Eleni?" After she said this, she realized Eleni understood her. "*Signomie,*" she said.

"Do not worry, Theia Stamatina. I welcome your concern."

Caliope wanted to know what they were saying and her sister translated, but toned it down so as not to add more worries to her already full plate. Nevertheless, Caliope's brows were knitted with worry.

"*Tee tha canoumai?*" she asked more to herself than to her sister. What are we to do?

Eleni looked at Marcus. "Let us go outside," she said in English. She led the way to the porch and sat at the table where the men ate their dinner.

"I am very happy you left your busy job in Washington to visit us." She looked down at her lap. "There are more important things to worry about than our little problem."

"We are family," he reminded her.

She looked up. "Family, yes, but we are not from the same world."

"Your world is my world, too," he said. "Ever since I arrived in Greece I felt this is where I belong. Even though I was born and raised in America, *to psihee mou einai etho.*" My soul is here.

She touched his arm in appreciation. That was all, even though Marcus hoped it might mean something more.

"You know more about me than I know about you," he said. "Tell me about yourself."

She sighed recalling memories. "What is there to tell? Stories mixed up in my head. Made-up stories full of adventure to make me feel good about myself. Growing up, I wanted to believe that my true mother and father were heroes, resistance fighters captured by the Germans who died in front of a firing squad."

"You imagine this?"

"Yes, and then the Nazis burned our house down."

"Why?"

"To erase my family's existence." Eleni sighed. "I am the only one left."

Marcus almost shuddered at this distorted make-believe story of Eleni's parents who died trying to free Greece from Fascism. Eleni imagined them in order to give herself status that she felt she did not have or even deserve. The emptiness of her childhood was so deep she had to fill it with this idealized, heroic story to give it heft and meaning, however imagined. It was sad and also ironical because Fascism was ruling Greece again, and Marcus and Eleni were both in the middle of it.

She was so vulnerable, Marcus wanted to take her in his arms but, paradoxically, the gesture seemed backwards. She was actually much braver than he. What had ever happened to him that would test his character growing up in America? Nothing.

Marcus thought a bit. "The icon of the Virgin Mary in your bedroom, the one Drovich is interested in."

"What about it?"

"Do you think that it might have anything to do with why Kostas wants to marry you?"

She looked surprised. "*Yiati?*" Why?

"Because if it is by the Byzantine artist Theophanes, it is extremely rare. It could be worth many thousands."

"Drachmas?"

"No dollars."

Eleni crossed herself, surprising Marcus. He thought only the old ones did this but then Eleni was raised in the Orthodox tradition, so why should she not cross herself over shocking news that what was hanging in her bedoom could be worth a fortune.

"I'd like to confirm the value of that icon." He was thinking about Sally Haggerty. She could research it for him. "Is there a telephone?" he asked.

"The nearest is in Niata."

An hour's drive over inhospitable roads, and how would he get there anyway, hitchhike? He'd have to wait till Sally drove down as she promised, or hire a taxi and drive to Sparta. The latter made more sense. He felt he had no time to waste.

"I'd like to show it to a friend at the American library in Sparta."

Eleni raised her eyebrows. "You mean Miss Haggerty?"

Marcus stared in surprise. "You know her?"

"She visited a month ago to tell us about a special *aftokinito* library she hopes to bring here. She calls it a bookmobile."

Marcus was amazed. Two separate entities in his life had intersected by pure chance in a remote village in Southern Greece. Sally and Eleni. He could not get over it.

Eleni was trying to analyze the expression on his face. "She is a friend?" she asked. There was a hint of inevitability, perhaps of jealousy as well, in her question.

"We knew each other in Washington."

"She is very pretty," Eleni said resignedly.

"Not as pretty as you," he said as convincingly as he could without sounding patronizing. He might have added, hoping to reassure Eleni, that Sally was also Catholic. No Greek in his right mind would become interested in a Catholic.

"I would like to show the icon to Sally," he continued. "She studied Byzantine art and knows scholars in America as well as experts at the Library of Congress. If only I could get a taxi."

"There is an overland taxi that comes two times a week."

"When?"

"Tuesdays and Fridays."

"Today is Wednesday," he said, frustrated. He was foiled at every turn. He wished he could just borrow Drovich's Simca, he thought ruefully. Sure—he'd have as much chance of succeeding in that as removing the incriminating portrait of himself in Drovich's camera.

8

The only light came from flickering kerosene lamps. Caliope noticed Marcus yawning. "*O yios sou fenetai kourazmenos,*" she said to her sister. Your son appears tired.

Mrs. Giannou examined her son as if the possibility of getting tired was as remote as her bed back in Minneapolis. "Young people wear out like cheap shoes." She was clearly in her element—her birthplace, where she grew up and where she now owned the town. She was taking every advantage of it.

"Mom," Marcus said, "you napped in the car."

"So?" she replied, twisting his remark to suit her own purpose. "You should deny your own mother a nap?"

He was in no mood to take her on. He had other things on his mind that were also making him tired.

Eleni, alert to every nuance, stood. "I am tired, too. I will walk you to Athena's house."

This was all Marcus needed or wanted. He hugged everyone and went outside. He was surprised by the intense darkness, but lamplight coming through the windows of the houses showed the way. However the path was pitch black.

"Don't you need a lantern?" he asked Eleni who had taken him by the hand.

She answered by sure-footing her way along the path with Marcus right behind. They got to Athena's house and stood on the tiny stoop before the door, their shoulders touching.

Theophanes' Virgin

Suddenly she embraced him. It was unexpected and what happened next was even more unexpected. As they stood, her arms around his waist, he turned her toward him and she looked up. Even in the dark he could see her eyes shining. She reached up suddenly and kissed him on the mouth, her lips warm and inviting. He wanted more but just as suddenly she pulled away and ran off in the dark.

A minute passed before Marcus was composed enough to tap on the door. Athena opened it and ushered him into the shadowy parlor, the only light coming from the ubiquitous kerosene lamp—electricity, if it ever came to Kremati, was still a generation away.

He looked into the room where he was to sleep, set up as it was for his nap, the drinking glass covered, the enamel pan with fresh water and a fresh towel, as well as the bar of soap. But the atmosphere was different—an afternoon nap was not the same as going to bed for the night and, as they stood facing each other, the unspoken thought was on both their minds, a single man and a widow sharing a house alone. But they were not alone, he realized with relief.

Marcus asked in Greek, "Is your daughter in bed?"

She nodded.

"Where?"

Athena looked down, embarrassed to answer, and then it came to him that the little girl was probably sleeping in the manger with the animals.

"*Signomi,*" he said. I am sorry.

She looked at him questioningly.

He wanted to say, I should be sleeping in the manger, not your daughter. She understood what was on his mind.

She smiled. "Do not feel bad. It is an honor to have you share my little home."

He left her wondering how to pay her back. Dollars left on the dresser would be patronizing. He fell asleep thinking about how he could do this without making it look like welfare. Perhaps a trust fund to help educate her child. He would consult his mother about that.

He awoke with pain searing his midsection. His bladder was screaming for relief. He had forgotten to empty it on the way over. Damn, it would have been awkward in any case with Eleni coming with him. When she left him at the door, he should have taken the opportunity to urinate then but how could he remember something so mundane when his head was still spinning from the memory of her impulsive kiss?

He rolled over and sat up, the pressure even worse in a sitting position, and he quickly stood, nearly doubling over from cramps. He opened the door and peeked into the parlor. The kerosene lamp was out but there was a votive candle clearing away enough darkness to see Athena on the sofa, her back to him, covered by a thin blanket. The soft wavering light helped him reach the front door as he tiptoed across the plain wood floor.

Eerie darkness met him outside. There was no moon, only stars pulsating the sky. He had used the outhouse before and knew how to get there, but not as easily in the dark nor with stabs of pain hitting his groin with each step. His bladder as solid as a bowling ball, he followed the path by the retaining wall and the rows of neatly piled firewood to the squat, square structure with sheet metal for a roof, and opened the door.

The heavy smell slightly disguised by lime told him he had reached his destination. He dropped his shorts and groped for the enamel toilet seat. Just like home. He let go with blessed relief. His bladder was so tight it seemed to take the better part of a minute to empty it, and he nodded off listening to the steady hissing sound under him. Somewhere a braying donkey interrupted his solitude. The animal made an unhappy sound: three short blasts and then a long, mournful honk. My sentiments exactly, Marcus thought, but he was feeling a lot better as he rose and pulled up his shorts. He unconsciously felt for the flush handle and laughed at his immaculate conditioning.

He was ready to open the door and heard footsteps. Someone on a similar errand to another outhouse, he assumed. He hesitated, not wanting to be seen in his shorts and waited for the steps to recede. But they got louder. Someone was walking along the path from the other direction but in an angry mood. He was stamping his feet on the hard dirt. This was not someone on his way to an outhouse. With one eye, Marcus looked through the space between the door and the strip of wood to which it was loosely hinged. An unidentifiable silhouette was heading in the direction of Dimitri's house. Marcus came out and followed, curious to see what he was up to. The figure climbed the porch of Dimitri's house, now better defined against the whitewashed wall—a fedora and a lean physique told Marcus it was Kostas. He whistled softly and the door opened. Dimitri stepped out on the porch and shut the door.

What in hell are they up to? Marcus had to find out. He crept closer so he could hear them. The two men were whispering, but coarsely so that their Greek words carried across the night air.

"You are asking too much of me," Dimitri was saying.

"You speak bravely now that your American relatives are here."

"Even it they weren't here I would not help you with your crazy scheme."

"I warn you, do not tell them anything. I cannot promise their safety if you do."

"Leave us alone!"

"You stubborn fool. Do you realize you could be signing your death warrant?"

"Better to die proudly than live ashamed."

"All right then, suffer the consequences."

Fuming with frustration, Kostas turned and crossed the porch. Marcus ducked and hugged the wall of the house as he came down the steps in one long stride and walked by Marcus so closely he was certain Kostas sensed his presence, but the lone figure gave no indication and charged down the path out of sight.

Marcus waited a moment until he was sure Kostas was gone and then stood and looked around. It was deathly quiet. Dimitri had gone back inside. Marcus climbed the steps and approached the door, debating whether he should whistle as Kostas had done and see if Dimitri came to the door, but decided to wait till morning. There was a lot to talk about and with his limited Greek he decided he had better have his mother with him.

He began to walk back to Athena's house. Get some sleep, he thought, as elusive as that might seem. He retraced his steps and was following the path next to the wall when he heard the sharp sound of stone disintegrating, as though someone had struck the wall next to him with a pick—so unexpected and alarming that he jumped back instinctively. Bewildered, he looked around, wondering if Kostas was out there in the dark. Marcus moved his hand along the wall, poking his finger into an indentation about the size of a quarter. He knelt and moved his hand on the dirt path and found chips and bits of stone scattered below the hole.

What was going on? As he wasted foolish time thinking about it, a tiny explosion went off by his head. Chips and powdered stone struck his face and pricked the skin on his shoulders.

Bewilderment was replaced by understanding and then, in rapid order, anger and fear. Someone was shooting at him! And, since the only sound he heard was a bullet hitting the wall, the shooter was using a gun with a silencer. Marcus instinctively dropped to his stomach, making himself as flat as possible, and wriggled along the cold dirt toward the house. Above him there was another tiny explosion, more like a plink. He rose and ran like a startled gazelle to Athena's house, bounded up the steps, opened the door and slammed it shut. The abrupt noise was startling and so was his panting.

Her body covered by the blanket, Athena rose from the sofa like a figure levitating. Her face was semi-lit from the votive candle, light and unfocused, as she came out of her sleep.

"Kyrio Giannou?" she asked. "*Tee eginai?*" What happened?

She got up with the blanket wrapped around her body and raised the wick in the lamp on the small table by the sofa, bringing more light. Then she quickly ran her fingers through her hair, aware that in the larger light she was being stared at by a man dressed only in jockey shorts. Try as she might to be modest, she was also staring.

Just then there was a tap on the door and Marcus tensed, certain whoever shot at him was going to finish him off right there in Athena's parlor. The door opened and his mother walked in. Marcus sighed with relief.

"I was in the *apohoritirio* and heard running. Was that you? You probably woke up half the village." She stopped talking as she took in the scene, her son in his shorts and Athena with a blanket wrapped around her body. "My god, what is going on?"

"I just got shot at."

"In your underwear?"

"Let me explain…"

"Get some clothes on. This is ridiculous."

"It isn't ridiculous," he said from the bedroom, hauling up his pants and sliding his shirt over his shoulders. He returned tightening his belt. Athena was in a state of shock. It was obvious nothing like this had ever happened to her before.

"I am not joking. Someone took a shot at me."

"The only thing I heard was the door slamming."

"Whoever it was used a silencer."

His mother stared. She didn't know what that was.

"It is what you put on a gun so it doesn't make any noise."

His mother shook her head. "Why would anyone shoot at you?"

"I overheard Kostas threatening Dimitri."

His story was getting weirder by the second and his mother was beginning to wonder if her son had not gone mad.

"Let me backtrack, Mom. I saw Kostas walking toward Dimitri's house. He whistled and Dimitri came out and they talked on the porch. Kostas threatened him. I am not making this up."

"What was Kostas threatening him about?"

Marcus shrugged. "I don't know. Kostas called him a stubborn fool and said he was signing his death warrant."

Athena, not understanding a word, was jerking her head back and forth as she followed the decibel level if not the meaning of the bewildering conversation between mother and son.

"Not only that, Kostas also said that if Dimitri said anything, Kostas could not guaranty our safety—you and me, Mom."

His mother was still doubtful. "Then what happened?"

"Kostas was really angry. He stomped off and practically bumped into me as he rushed down the path."

"Did he see you?"

"No…" Marcus said, and began to wonder. "Maybe he did, maybe that's what the shooting was about."

"What are you thinking?"

"That his guarantee for our safety did not last very long."

"Nonsense."

"Mother, that is the only explanation that makes sense. Kostas did see me. He probably wanted to stop me before I talked to uncle Dimitri who would tell me the very thing Kostas warned him not to do. So he panicked and shot at me."

Theophanes' Virgin

"Where would Kostas get a gun?"

Marcus recalled looking in the trunk of the Simca and seeing the leather satchel along with the camera equipment. There easily could have been a gun stashed in it.

"Maybe he borrowed it from Drovich the way he borrowed the Simca."

Even in the semi-dark, Marcus could read the doubt in his mother's eyes.

"You don't believe me do you?" He pointed to his scalp "Look at the bits of stone in my hair. After the first shot I ducked down and the next bullet shattered bits of stone and they flew all over me."

Mrs. Giannou worked her way through his thick, dark hair with her fingers. "Hold still."

"Do you have to be so rough?"

Out of the corner of his eye Marcus noticed Athena leaning toward them, curiosity devouring her but propriety requiring that she not make a move unless invited to, and his mother was so wrapped up in his scalp she wasn't paying attention. She looked at her fingers, rubbing particles of stone between them. "Well, it isn't dandruff."

"Now do you believe me?"

"It could have happened."

"I'll show you the bullet holes."

"Tomorrow when it is light you can show me." She was far from the hysterical old woman who could be stampeded by an overly excited son.

Marcus gave in. He was drained. "Let's go to bed. Do you want me to walk you back?"

"I grew up here, remember?"

Before leaving, Mrs. Giannou took the time to calm Athena down by varnishing his story so that it had a shiny finish to it. "He heard noises which frightened him," she related in Greek. "You understand—first night in a strange place."

9

He fell into bed again, exhausted but not sleepy. He lay on his back, convexly curved to fit the dip in the old mattress, and folded his hands behind his head, staring at the hand-hewn rafters holding up the roof. Everything seemed surreal, the lumpy bed, the rough-plastered walls, the simple furniture. Perhaps his mother was right. He was suffering culture shock in this foreign land, this third-world country where emotions were raw and unpredictable. Scarcely two days ago he was in familiar Washington, saying goodbye to the Senator and the staff. Now he lay terrified in a strange house, wondering why Kostas shot at him. Was he afraid Marcus might steal Eleni away from him? The mere thought of her comforted him somewhat but also emphasized the delicate role he was expected to play.

He began brooding again. Can this really be happening? He squeezed his head between his fingers, feeling the stress translate itself into a muscle spasm at the base his skull. He was getting a headache for sure.

The longer he thought about the shooting the more it seemed like a dream, the result of too much homemade wine. He hoped it was a dream, that there were no bullet holes in the wall to remind him that he nearly lost his life. But the bullets did miss him by a fair margin. Maybe it was only a warning…

He dozed off only to awaken again in a cold sweat. Suppose it was not a warning, just bad aim? Suppose Kostas tried again? He knew where Marcus was sleeping, right by an open window. All he had to do was reach in and shoot at point blank range, not missing this time. He sat up, shaking, fully expecting to see Kostas leering at him, the barrel of a gun pushed against his cheek. He shook his head, trying to clear these inane images from his muddled brain. He got up and pulled the shutters closed, hauled the mattress and bedding off the creaky springs and laid everything on the floor where at least he had a fighting chance. As he settled down he realized how much more comfortable he was lying on a flat surface.

Surprisingly it relaxed his neck muscles and he began to feel heavy with much-needed sleep. Finally he slept dreamlessly until someone rudely began shaking his shoulders.

He jerked his eyes awake and stared up from the floor. Athena was bending over him, in the pre-dawn darkness more an apparition then human. Her eyes were wide open, the whites outlining the black spots of her irises.

"*Kyris Giannos, ei meitera sou hreiazetai!*" Your mother wants you!

Having done her duty Athena ran out of the room, no doubt concerned about propriety.

Marcus got up, his head at war from being woken up so abruptly. It was a wonder Athena did not trip over him on the floor, no doubt expecting him to be on the bed. She also was probably wondering what she had got herself into, renting a room to this crazy American.

Marcus cleaned up but did not bother to shave, a smart decision he was to discover soon, and dressed in fresh slacks and shirt from his suitcase. He came out of his room. There was no sign of Athena. Probably hiding her daughter, not knowing any longer what to expect. He laughed to himself. And why shouldn't he—a cool breeze lifted his spirits as well as his hair when he stepped outside. Nevertheless he stopped where he had been shot at and ran his fingers on the rough stones to reassure himself he was not dreaming. He did not feel any holes! He bent over and looked more closely. Those bullets had dug out sizable chunks from the wall. They had to be here. He examined the path. No dust, no chips. Everything swept clean. He stopped at the privy one more time, puzzled by what he saw or, rather, by what he did not see, evidence of bullet holes.

When he reached the house Caliope had already set out a breakfast of kasseri cheese, bread, honey, goat's milk, and sliced meat that resembled headcheese.

He said good morning and even though he received kisses from Caliope and Dimitri, the air was heavy with concern. He sat at the place made for him at the table.

"Mother," he said in English, "did you notice the wall? It's been repaired."

"Speak softly. We do not wish to worry Eleni."

Marcus cut some of the cheese and placed it on a piece of bread. He munched thoughtfully. "Where is she?"

"In her room."

"Still asleep?"

"No, she is not asleep," his mother said. "Do you have to ask so many questions?"

"Yes, and I have another one. Who fixed that wall?" he said this in Greek to make sure he got an answer other than from his mother.

Dimitri's stricken expression gave him away.

Marcus looked around. "What is going on?"

"That is what we have to talk about," his mother said.

"I could use some coffee."

"It is coming. Stop complaining."

"I have every reason to complain, Mom. I was shot at last night. Instead of talking we should be contacting the police."

The word police was familiar enough for Dimitri to understand. He shook his head in futility. "The police? Not the police! They are ESA!" he cried out in Greek.

Marcus thought, in America we dial 911. "Ok, so we can't contact the police. What do we do, then, just forget about it? Pretend it didn't happen?"

"We cannot alarm the village."

"Is that why Uncle Dimitri cleaned up the wall?"

His mother nodded

"Was it Kostas?" Marcus asked in Greek.

Dimitri shrugged. "Maybe Drovich."

That effete, Marcus thought, a gunslinger? "Don't forget Weber—the man who can't shoot his mouth off might have shot at me," Marcus said in English.

"What do you mean he can't shoot his mouth off?" his mother asked.

"Weber can't talk, he is a mute. Remember, Mom, when we drove down from Sparta? He never said a thing. But why was I shot at? Was it a warning? I could have been picked off easily. Think of it, I was walking along a white wall, like a duck in a shooting gallery. But what were they warning me about?"

"You must have said something, which doesn't surprise me."

"I did use some strong stuff on Drovich when we were in Eleni's room."

Mrs. Giannou's body tightened visibly. "What did you say to him?"

Marcus related his conversation, ending with Drovich's near panic when he threatened to hide the icon for safekeeping.

Mrs. Giannou listened intently, her eyes unblinking. When he finished she took a deep breath. "Marcus, listen to me. This is important. We came to help Eleni. I thought we had a few days but after what happened last night we have to act now. We have to find a way to get Eleni out of Greece. We have no time to lose…"

Caliope brought the coffee pot and poured strong, steaming coffee into his cup. Marcus drank almost greedily. It tasted good and he really needed the caffeine.

"Mom," he said, draining his cup and getting a refill, "let me get this straight. You want to get Eleni out of Greece? How do you plan to do that? Smuggle her in a piece of luggage or have that official at the airport give her a ticket?"

Caliope put the pot down and sat next to her husband. The two could not understand the fast-talking English coming from Marcus but they could follow the imperative sound of his voice. They exchanged glances with Mrs. Giannou.

"Marcus," she said, "as crazy as this sounds, it can be done but only with your help."

Marcus stared at his mother as he would a stranger. What she was saying was downright scary. "You know a lot more than you're telling me, don't you?"

"We don't have much time. You must take Eleni away from here as quickly as possible, right now, this morning!"

Marcus looked at Caliope and Dimitri. They appeared stricken. "*Êinai Eleni kinthinos?*" His grammar was awful but he knew the word for danger.

Caliope blanched.

"Don't make matters worse, Marcus. You are frightening Caliope."

"You said I have to take Eleni away from here, but where?"

"The American Embassy so she can apply for a passport."

He was dumbfounded. "Wait a minute, Mom. You think someone in the American Embassy can wave a magic wand? She's a Greek national."

While he was talking, Uncle Dimitri rose from the table and went into the bedroom. Marcus heard a dresser drawer open and close and Dimitri returned with an old, legal-size manila envelope frayed at the corners. There were crease marks that made it appear it once contained something thicker. Dimitri opened the envelope and removed a baptismal certificate and a US passport. He handed them to Marcus.

Marcus opened the passport to the first page. The inked entries were made by a broad-tip pen typical of another era. The official photograph was of a dark-haired woman, born February 12, 1920, in Wheeling, West Virginia, USA. The issue date was June 10, 1939, and it was made out to Anna Maria Koulouris. Her photograph revealed a handsome woman with dark eyes, thin features, a pronounced jawbone, and a straight, slender nose. The face bore a resemblance to Eleni.

Marcus looked up. "*Eleni's meitera?*"

Dimitri nodded, tears welling in his eyes. Caliope was wiping hers with a napkin.

"So her mother was an American citizen."

Marcus then looked at the baptismal certificate, a half page with elaborate markings of Angels with feathered wings, Christ and John the Baptist with golden halos, and a yellow sun in the center radiating beams of light in sanguine splendor. It recorded the baptism of Eleni, first name only, on February 1, 1942, in Kremasti, district of Parnon, Greece.

He read on: The mother was Anna M. Kouloris. The priest officiating was Father Christos Nashopoulos and the sponsors were Dimitri and Caliope Stathos. The child's father was indicated as "*Agnostos.*"

Marcus looked his mother. "*Agnostos* means unknown, doesn't it?"

She nodded.

"No wonder Eleni felt she had to make up a story."

"What story?" his mother asked.

"Last night she told me that her mother and father were executed by the Nazis."

Mrs. Giannou gripped her throat. "Oh my god, she said that?"

Even though Mrs. Giannou was speaking English the concern in her voice made Caliope look in from the kitchen expectantly as if someone had called her name.

Mrs. Giannou quickly changed her tone to be more upbeat. "Put a smile on your face."

"Ok, Mom, but I want to clear up something. Sponsors are godparents, aren't they?"

She nodded.

"So that means Eleni isn't legally Caliope and Dimitri's daughter."

Dimitri recognized his name and asked what Marcus was talking about.

Mrs. Giannou translated.

Dimitri looked worried. "But we raised her as our own."

"But they have no legal relationship to Eleni. She could be taken away from them." Marcus replaced the documents in the envelope. "Why was her mother, an American citizen, in Greece during the war?"

"She was a student doing research. The war broke out and she was trapped here. It was impossible even for Americans to leave."

"What happened to her?"

"She died giving birth to Eleni. Her remains are in the bone house next to the church."

"Bone house? You mean ossuary?"

"Greek villages do not have enough ground for cemeteries. They are buried till what is left becomes a skeleton. It is dug up and placed on shelves in the bone house."

"How do you tell them apart?" It was a lurid question but he had to know.

"The names are painted on the skulls."

"Thanks, Mom."

"You asked."

But it made sense as he thought of the vast plots of real estate in America reserved for the dead whose memory probably is lost after the next generation dies off. At least in Kremasti your remains are remembered.

"What is most important is that Eleni is an American citizen because her mother was born in the United States." Mrs. Giannou pointed to the envelope. "The proof is in there. You must get Eleni to the Embassy so she can apply for an American passport. That will give her protection."

"All right, Mom, you think you have it all figured out, but you forgot one thing."

"What is that?"

"Eleni told me there is no taxi out of here till Friday."

"Taxi? You can't take a taxi. You have to hide out."

"Hide out?" He motioned with his hand. "Where can we hide out around here? Anyone can find us in a minute."

"Not here. Niata."

"Niata? That village we passed on the way up here?"

"Yes."

"How do you expect us to get there?"

"Walk."

Marcus could not believe what he was hearing. "Walk?"

"Over the mountains. Eleni knows the way."

Marcus sighed with resignation. "There is a phone in Niata. I can call Sally Haggerty. She can pick us up and drive us to Athens."

"Do not contact her," Marcus's mother cautioned. "That is too dangerous. It will identify you as an American. You have to blend in. Pretend you are Greek."

"I'm already Greek," he said wryly.

"I am serious. You cannot bring attention to yourselves. Do not take any chances, Marcus."

"Being an American is dangerous? In that case how will we get to Athens?"

"By bus, traveling with other people. Blend in, act like a married couple."

Finally his mother said something that appealed to him.

"Eleni has contacts in Niata who will take care of you." It was beginning to lighten up outside. "Finish your breakfast. It is time to go."

Marcus looked at his mother. She did not at all resemble the mother he knew. She was different now, strong, in charge. "But how do I know you will be ok, Mom?"

"An old woman? They aren't interested in me. It is the icon they want."

"Theophanes' Virgin?"

"Our insurance policy."

"What do you mean?"

"You will take the icon with you. It will guarantee our safety."

"Is that what Kostas and Dimitri were talking about last night?"

His mother looked sharply at him. "Never mind."

"What do you mean, never mind? I was shot at, remember?"

"The icon is very important, more than I imagined, more than I understood. It is rare, yes, but there is something else…" Her words trailed off and then she took his arm. "You must get ready."

"I have to pack."

"You cannot wear American clothes. Athena has clothes her dead husband wore. You have to look like a villager. She will pack extra things in a shoulder bag. Not much. You need to travel light. And you need to leave right away. You have to be well on your way up the mountain or they will find you. Eleni will carry the icon. It is very important that you protect it."

"My god," he said, suspicion growing that he was entering into real danger and even more mystery. "But how can I contact you?"

"Do not try. We will be safe as long as you have the icon. Caliope has packed food for you."

"You have money?" Dimitri asked.

"We exchanged drachmas in America before we left."

"Then you are ready. Eleni has her documents. Do not forget your passport."

Marcus chewed down the rest of his bread and cheese. "I'll change in the bedroom."

His mother grabbed him and hugged him as if this might be the last time she would see him. "Practice your Greek. You will need it."

Eleni led him along a brambly path even a donkey would have trouble navigating. The path took them in a direction opposite from the one the Simca took to Kremasti. They climbed. The going was hard and eventually they were far enough away and high enough to look back down on the village that stood out like a white flower surrounded by green leaves. It was a picturesque scene worthy of a painting but they did not take time to admire it. They pushed on.

Marcus was wearing black pants printed with a small gray grid, baggy at the knees, a shirt of rough wool and a sailor's hat. On his back was a large bag containing their food, which bumped against his waist as he walked. The only clue to his real background were Hush Puppies on his feet but they were getting so scuffed they too were blending in. Walking was arduous and he was breathing too heavily to talk although he had a million questions to ask Eleni. Aided by a walking stick broken from a tree, she trudged doggedly in front of him, obviously stronger and in better shape than he. She was wearing a peasant dress, a jacket more like a man's than a woman's, a gray scarf over her head, and heavy shoes for mountain climbing. In addition to her backpack, she also carried a shoulder bag containing the icon of the Virgin Mary wrapped in a woolen shawl.

Theophanes' Virgin

Although Marcus did not have the energy to talk, at least he could think. He realized his mother knew much more than she was letting on, even from the very beginning when she called him from Minneapolis to read him the letter from Caliope. Perhaps something that harkened back to her youth that she had never shared with her son. And now she had to enlist his aid without telling him why. Maybe Eleni knows something. They would have to stop and rest before he could talk to her.

Ahead was an outcropping of rock, like a stone bench, a place to catch their breaths. It looked almost like a bus stop, Marcus thought, wishing that a bus would indeed stop and pick them up, he was that tired.

He pointed to it as they approached and Eleni nodded. They placed their shoulder bags on the ground and sat. Eleni pulled out a bottle of water and offered it to Marcus.

"You first," he said.

"Speak only Greek," she reminded him, taking a swallow and handing the bottle to Marcus. "Even if you make mistakes, speak only Greek. I will help you with words."

"My grammar is terrible."

"You must try."

"My mother...oops...*Ei meitera mou*," he said, and so began his odyssey in the Greek language, syntactically awkward and vocabulary-starved at first but, with Eleni's gentle correcting, he improved quickly. He did not realize how much was buried in his synapses waiting to be plumbed until he was forced to speak exclusively in Greek. He did not realize at the time how much he was to depend on his freshly unearthed skill, even to the point of saving his life.

What he said to Eleni, and he did so while struggling to find words, was the change in his mother since arriving in Kremasti, as though he was meeting her for the first time.

Eleni listened, nodding occasionally, helping him with a hesitant word, correcting tenses and sentence structure. "Maybe she is the same person but you are the one who has changed."

"Changed? In what way?"

"You are more aware. You no longer see your mother as you have in the past."

"You mean I haven't grown up as far as my mother is concerned?"

Eleni thought about that for a few seconds and then said, "Maybe."

He changed to English because he could not express himself well enough in Greek: "That is known as arrested development."

Eleni did not know what he meant and so Marcus explained, in Greek now, that sometimes it is easier to stop growing up, that he wanted his mother always to be the way he knew her as a child.

"Sometimes we see what we want to see, what makes us feel comfortable," she said.

He smiled. Eleni made a lot of sense, and she was able to be critical without hurting his feelings. What a remarkable woman, and he only met her yesterday.

"Even so, my mother knows a lot more than she is telling me." If Marcus expected a reply he did not get one and let it drop, for now at least.

Eleni stood. "It is time to go. We have to be halfway to Niata by nightfall."

"Where will we sleep?"

"There is a shepherd's hut along the way."

The idea of spending the night in an abandoned shepherd's hut kept Marcus going, reenergizing his tired body, his aching legs and feet. He had never before trekked along a mountain trail and if someone had even suggested it before leaving Washington he would have laughed uproariously at the absurdity of the idea.

They walked an hour and rested ten minutes, a repeating schedule better meant for fit persons such as

Eleni but not for an out of shape thirty-year-old American who spent most of his time behind a desk. But Marcus was not going to admit he could not keep up with a woman. The scenery helped keep his mind off his aching body, the farther from Kremasti the more barren and arid the land became. The only green, perked up by bright pinks and deep reds, was from shrubs of bougainvillea. Otherwise the flora consisted of sagebrush and tufts of grass that sheep, if they saw any, gnawed on.

It was music to his ears when he heard Eleni say, finally, "the sun is going down and we will stop at the shepherd's hut."

The path they followed presently widened and became almost like a road packed down with hard dirt that appeared to have hoof marks stamped on it. "What are these?" he asked, pointing.

Eleni smiled teasingly. "I see you don't know much about farm life. Those are the hoof marks of sheep."

"But where are they? I haven't seen any."

"It is growing close to autumn and the sheep are being moved to lower altitudes."

To Marcus the lack of sheep struck him with a sense of emptiness, as though he had missed a once-in-a-lifetime opportunity to see the natural life of Greece. There was probably a lot of truth in this because he would never come along this path again. But then, if sheep were here, there would also be a shepherd and that would create problems. Nevertheless, he felt the same way he felt when the leaves fell back home and the days grew shorter.

They came upon a pasture enclosed by a low stone wall. In the center was a domed hut, roughly circular, also built of stone.

Eleni was keeping an eye on his reaction. "These have changed little since ancient times except that there was wood to make the roofs. Greece once had a temperate climate and there were more trees. There were even deer, I am told."

"Amazing," Marcus said. "The stones get smaller at the top to make the dome."

"You use what you have," Eleni said, "and here we have many stones."

He looked through the opening. The floor was covered with matted sheep's wool and, against the wall, was a stack of sheepskins neatly folded.

"It looks more comfortable than my bed back home," he said and meant it. But what they did not talk about was the confining space they would have to share.

They sat on the wool padding and opened their backpacks. Time for dinner, and Marcus had no idea what he had been carrying all day. Caliope had put together what looked like a feast: a jar of Kalamata olives, dried figs, slices of bread wrapped in coarse paper that reminded Marcus of how meat was wrapped in the butcher shop when he was a small boy, *kasseri tiri*, the dry, hard cheese he was so fond of, and a small demijohn of wine. Caliope had even remembered a cloth to spread their food out on, as well as cloth napkins.

"Is that all?" he asked kiddingly, but Eleni took that as criticism. Her stern look told him so and made him realize that Greeks probably take things literally and she thought he was critical of Caliope. He did not know how to explain in Greek, or even in English, to make her understand that in America sometimes a contradiction applied unexpectedly is meant to be humorous.

She smiled politely because she did not understand that he was making a joke, and reminded Marcus how delicate his relationship with this incredibly interesting woman truly was.

Nothing more was said of his faux pas and, after finishing their meal, they repacked their backpacks and used them to lean on as the sun fell behind the mountain range. It was not only getting dark, it was also getting chilly. He folded his arms against his chest.

"Cold?"

He nodded.

Eleni reached for a sheepskin and put it around his shoulders. He warmed in an instant not only because of the sheepskin but also the attention he was getting.

"It is so dark we can hardly see each other," he said. "We could use a flashlight."

"It would not be a good idea. A light, even a small one, can be seen a long way."

"I guess you are right. We will have to talk in the dark." He let his mind wander. "Tell me, Eleni, what do you think about?"

"You mean right now?"

"When you are alone. What do you think about?"

Natural light was almost gone and he could only see the outlines of her face. He was trying to imagine what kind of expression she was wearing as he waited for her answer.

"I think," she began, "of what it would be like not to live in fear."

The answer surprised him not because he was unaware of the danger she was in but because she seemed so vulnerable when she said it, so different from the strong self-assured image she presented up till now.

"Is it Kostas you fear?"

"I fear for the power he has over my family."

"You don't have to marry him."

"I have no choice."

"Caliope would not have written mother if she thought you did not have a choice."

"Father is frightened that if I marry Kostas something terrible will happen."

"Like what?"

"I do not know."

They fell into a mutual silence. Finally Eleni said, "We should get some sleep. We have to reach Niata by tomorrow night."

"Where is the bathroom?" Marcus asked idly.

"Outside, wherever you want it to be."

They laughed. Taking turns, they went outside. While it was Eleni's turn Marcus could not help but wonder what it would be like to share life with her, to be so comfortable with one another that modesty had no place in their relationship—what she looked like naked, her thinness totally exposed, how delicate her breasts, how sinewy her thighs, how round her buttocks. He was almost ashamed of himself having these thoughts, and even looked away when she returned to the hut.

"Now it is your turn," she said, feeling for a sheepskin and bumping his leg. It sent tingles through him.

He went out into the dark, the sky atwinkle with myriad stars but no moon, feeling his way until he came to a clump of sagebrush and used it for his toilet. When he returned Eleni was lying down. She was so still he thought she was already asleep but as he lay beside her she moved, not much but enough to feel her thigh brushing his. He wanted to think this was intentional, shifting to accommodate someone else in a tight space. Marcus recalled the old canard about shepherds and sheep. This was probably the first time in the history of this hut that a man and a woman shared it together. Perhaps not, but the main thought was, can he do anything about it?

This prompted him to say, "Eleni?"

"*Ti?*" What?

He reverted to English: "Let's not speak Greek right now."

"Yiati?" Why?

"Well, for one thing, I can express myself better in English for what I want to say and, for another, if we speak English, just for now, in this moment, in the dark of a secret place where no one knows where we are, we can start fresh, like we just met each other for the first time."

"But my English is not as good as yours."

"Please don't think I am doing this to take advantage of you. I want us to be free of our conventional roles. I feel that by speaking in English we are not restricted by a relationship that puts a wall between us. Does this make any sense?"

"I don't know…"

"What I am trying to say is, can there be more of a relationship between us than just cousins? If that is possible I thought that by speaking English we pretend we are two people on a blind date."

"Blind? You mean they cannot see?"

"No, no, it is a term to describe two people who meet for the first time, and they have dinner together, go for a walk, see a movie."

"A movie?"

"A film, a cinema."

She laughed. "I have a lot more to learn about English. A movie is when things move on a screen, is that right? Some day I will go to a *movie*." She wriggled against him, animating the word.

Marcus was delighted. "That will be our first date, a movie." He hesitated a moment, searching for the right words. "Eleni, what I am trying to say can't be expressed in Greek. I am not fluent enough. I don't want to think of you as a relative but as a woman I just met and want to know better. I find you very attractive, and so I thought that if we speak English it will give us a fresh start."

In the dark, everything was still, too still it seemed to Marcus. He felt he had gone too far too soon.

"Maybe I am assuming too much, but after we kissed last night…"

Suddenly she turned her body and pressed against him. Relieved, he wrapped his arm around her and they clung together, uncertain how to proceed but still willing to take the chance.

The pressure of her body against his spread warmth throughout his system and his senses swam in a sea of newfound impressions—skin cleansed by handmade soap, breath mingling olive oil and honey…

As delirious as he was getting, he pulled back. His growing desire for Eleni was diffused by sudden, guilt-ridden memories of one-night stands in Marriott Inn bedrooms, the blinding-bright bathroom walls, the vinyl-topped nightstands, the Walter Keane print above the dresser...

Feeling his abrupt change in mood, Eleni lifted her head to look at him, perplexity arching her eyebrows. She was blaming herself, wondering what she was doing wrong. He could read the hurt, her crumpling self-assurance as a lover. Does my body smell? Will the hair under my arms offend you? Am I too simple for your worldly experiences?

She whispered in his ear, "I am only a village woman, Marcus. That you speak English to me now makes me hope you look at me in the way you would look at a...a sophisticated woman." The word came together syllable by syllable because she was unused to long words. "I wish I felt more strong—is that the word?"

"I think you mean confident." He realized now that his reluctance only made her feel uncertain. He kissed her hair and, when she lifted her face, her forehead, her eyelids, the tip of her nose. "Eleni," he whispered, "you are beautiful, a gift of God."

"You act one way and speak another. You are a strange man."

"Not strange, unformed."

"You?" she asked, surprised to hear such an unlikely admission.

"What do you really know about me?"

"I know you are a kind person, willing to help others even if it is dangerous."

"These are special times. If you saw me under normal circumstances you probably would think differently."

She shifted her body, half turning away from him. "Why are you saying these things? It is as if you want to hurt me."

He reached around and lifted her hair from her neck and let it fall across her shoulders. How can he explain the contradiction and hypocrisies of a life that Eleni had so forcefully brought into focus? She was a woman who never slept between starched sheets, did not know what a Do Not Disturb sign meant. Love to her would be this hut they were sharing, laying on musty sheepskins, inhaling the smell of dung, feeling the crisp mountain air.

Everything concerning him was clinical by comparison. What did he know about life, about *zoi*?

"Maybe I fear that if you knew me intimately, the mystery would be gone," he whispered.

"You talk as a man uncertain of himself rather than a man of experience who has enjoyed the attention of many women."

"I cannot say that I am proud of it."

"Like a hunter who displays animal heads on a wall? Is that what I might be to you?"

"No!" he shouted but even as he denied her charge, he realized that she had unlocked his attitude toward women. He was cynical and insensitive. He had never taken the time to examine himself in such harsh light because he had never met someone who truly mattered to him.

Eleni was right. Pride had everything to do with him, typical male Greek pride. His ego was in charge, informing him that it did not matter how he got his pleasures, just so he got them. She was no target for such a shabby, selfish goal. She might make love, he felt, but would do so on her terms as an equal partner, not as another trophy. She would think not of the momentary pleasure but of the long-term consequence of giving herself up to him, that there was a future between them. The idea frightened him. He felt inadequate, inferior. How could he measure up to her worthiness?

She read the concern in his eyes but she misrepresented it. "I have said bad things that hurt you. I am truly sorry."

"Do not be sorry, Eleni. I needed to hear them."

They became engrossed in their inner thoughts, lying quietly, not moving, each waiting for the other to make a decision. It was Eleni who decided. She inched close to him and whispered in his ear. "I am not like American women. I have not experimented. It is not something to be ashamed of, I know, yet I yearn for experience. Teach me the secrets of love, Marcus. Please be my first and only lover."

The dark neutralized whatever uncertainty they still might have felt. If this were happening anywhere else it would be impossible, of course. This could happen only in the dark of night in a shepherd's hut on a mountain in Greece.

11

Marcus was awakened by a stroke on his cheek, now getting scratchy from the stubble of his beard, the words of his mother hearkening back as he came out of his slumber— don't shave, look like a peasant. That part was easy, but acting like one was something else, his entire adult life dictated by an office environment.

At first he thought the touch on his cheek was a fly and he was ready to brush it away but as he came awake he realized that it was the back of Eleni's hand stroking him.

He sat up disoriented, and rubbed his eyes. The pitch dark that enveloped their sleep was now dusky gray but still not light enough to see clearly.

"What time is it?"

"Time to go.'

"It is still dark out."

"Kostas knows the mountains as well as I do."

Her touch rekindled the excitement of sleeping together and made him want to linger, kiss her good morning at least, but Eleni was already on her feet, picking up her backpack and her walking stick.

"Let's go," she ordered.

They began their trek on level ground as the sun rose above the peaks to illuminate another day. The sunrise at this height was breathtaking, the shadows created by the craggy outcroppings made more acute as the sun moved higher in the sky until the shadows became vertical pencil lines and finally disappeared as the sun crested. The scene made him appreciate the rugged beauty of this land, and he wondered if the Greeks appreciated it as much as he, or even could they, having to scratch out a living on this hardscrabble landscape.

An hour later they began descending and Marcus assumed the going would be easier but he was mistaken. Walking downslope was even more difficult than climbing, straining his calves and creating a reverse pull on his Achilles tendons. Climbing up or down, he decided, was not for him. Level ground was where he belonged.

"I don't see any path," he said to Eleni ahead of him, his breath coming in spurts.

"There is no path. I don't want anyone to see us."

They stopped once long enough to eat the last of their provisions. He hoped his next meal would be a hot one.

By nightfall, they reached the outskirts of Niata, laid out on the flat, arid plain he remembered when they drove through it only two days ago. Approaching on foot from the opposite direction gave the village a whole new dimension as though seeing it for the first time.

"Niata is the municipality of Agios Dimitrios," Eleni told Marcus. "Larger than Kremasti but it does not have spring water as we do. Olives and honey are all they produce. We cultivate everything else," she said proudly.

They walked around a hill that provided a natural boundary and entered the village behind the church, its size and grandeur once again reminding Marcus of the power and authority of Greek Orthodoxy.

Niata was dotted with lights coming through open windows. They followed a path between the church and a row of houses, stepping carefully so as not to draw attention. They stopped at the rear of a taverna. Eleni opened what appeared to be a delivery door and they walked into virtual darkness. Marcus strained his eyes to see a few wood tables and chairs, a bar, a tiny bandstand just large enough for a bouzouki player. There was the distant smell of lamb fat.

As they adjusted to the dark, Marcus saw someone behind the bar. "*Kalos eirthate*," the man said—welcome—as though he was expecting them.

Hanging in the window was a neon sign that read *Taverna Omikron* and under it *Kleista,* Closed.

Eleni noticed Marcus staring at the electric light.

"Niata also has a telephone."

"Where?"

"In front by the entrance."

"Here in the Taverna?"

"Yes, it is centrally located."

Everything is up to date in Niata, Marcus thought.

Eleni nodded to the bartender and, to be friendly, so did Marcus. She led him to another door next to the bandstand that opened into a narrow hallway. A disembodied voice greeted them. It was melodic, as though trained to sing the ancient chants of the Orthodox *Litourgia.*

The man with the finely tuned voice embraced Eleni, kissing her on both cheeks. He was squat, powerfully built, as dark as the walls around him. His face had a brooding quality as if weighted by the sum of all the problems in the world.

He led them down the hallway to another door that opened into a kind of dayroom, half as large as the bar area in front. There was a table with folding chairs occupied by men playing casino, a card game Marcus recognized because his father played it. The men were puffing on Greek cigarettes, making the air heavy with smoke. They nodded to the new arrivals. Another man sitting in a chair leaning up against the wall was softly strumming a mandolin, eliciting from the frail wood a sound so poignant it made Marcus ache from an undefined sense of loss.

Hanging on the wall above the musician was a framed sampler, very like those his mother embroidered when her eyes were better. The message also made him ache, this time from a defined sense of anger:

> They were cast into iron and into flame.
> Who dares to tell why half are found beneath
> the soil, the other half locked in iron.
> Yiannis Ritsos

Ritsos was well known in the Senator's office, his anti-government poetry had put him in a prison camp.

The brooding man led Marcus and Eleni to a second table where they sat.

He asked, "*Eisai peinazmenos?*" Are you hungry?

Famished, Marcus wanted to say but he did not know the Greek word for it. It did not matter. Within a minute, the man who was behind the bar came with a tray of cold lamb, feta cheese, pita bread, a *horyiotiko salat*a of tomatoes, cucumbers and onion, and of course the ubiquitous bottle of Retsina.

The man with the melodic voice joined them at the table. "I am Haralambos," he said in Greek. "First names only. The men playing cards are Panaioti and Nickos. The bartender is Kleftis."

"That means Thief," Marcus said.

Haralambos laughed. "A nickname." He settled back in his chair. "You work for the great Senator Tolson."

Marcus was impressed that his boss's reputation had reached a small village. "You know the Senator?"

"He is a hero to us. He freed Andreas Papandreou from prison when that malaka, Pappathopoulos..." he spat the name from his mouth "...stole our country."

Marcus had met Papandreou, a professor of economics at the University of Minnesota, before he returned to Greece and embroiled himself in the nation's politics.

Marcus wasn't sure what malaka meant.

"Masturbator!" Haralambos shouted in English and everyone laughed robustly. The mandolin player struck a loud chord.

"Does everybody understand English?" Marcus asked.

"That word, yes," Haralambos said.

"Haralambos speaks English," Eleni said, "but he has to be careful not to use it."

"I lived in Detroit for fourteen years," Halamabos said. "I moved back after the coup to save my country."

The bartender returned with shot glasses of ouzo, and a carafe of water.

"Time to celebrate!" Haralambos shouted, returning to Greek.

Marcus was not so sure he was ready to drink ouzo on top of retsina but he could not refuse the gesture of solidarity.

Haralambos poured water into the shot glasses, turning the ouzo into a milky white, and passed them around to everyone except Eleni. Drinking ouzo was men's work after all. She gave Marcus a smile of encouragement. If he passed out, which was not beyond the realm of possibility, she would take care of him.

"Drink, drink my friends! We celebrate our new-found compatriot and friend of the great Senator!"

While the others downed their shots, Marcus sipped his out of sympathy for his throat. Even with water, ouzo had a kick to it, the sweet flavor notwithstanding.

"You must inform Senator Tolson that while we cannot show our faces we are many, and Greece will one day breathe again the air of freedom. This is our promise. Tell him we make it with our blood!"

The others shouted approval.

"Now then," Haralambos said, wiping his mouth with the sleeve of his shirt, "we understand that you need to reach Athens."

"Yes," Marcus replied. And looked at Eleni. "I am concerned for her."

"We all are, my friend. She cannot be arrested. The jails are wicked places and the men who run them are ruthless perverts. They care nothing for justice and laugh at the agony of their victims. Have you heard the name Theodoros Theophylianakos?"

Marcus knew who he was: a major in the Greek Army who was head of the ESA's Interrogation Unit of the Greek Military Police.

"He keeps a collection of fingernails in his desk drawer that he pulls from the fingers of his victims. A real sweetheart, yes?"

"But Eleni would not end up in a place like that."

"Oh no?" Haralambos closed his hand over his worry beads and shook the defiant fist in the air, trembling with emotion.

Eleni placed her arm along his broad shoulders. "Do not worry about me. You must not waste energy on fruitless conversation. Save it for the liberation."

Haralambos smiled ruefully. "I will cut out his heart!" He uncurled his fist and made a twisting motion with it. "When that day comes, Greece will be free...*free!*"

Marcus knew Greeks were hot-blooded and this was a perfect example of it.

Shouts of "*Yiasou! Yiasou!*" filled the room.

This called for another round of ouzo and the mellowing process began. In moments Marcus was swept into their aura, becoming part of their cause, championing their cries for freedom.

"Does anyone ever escape interrogation?"

"Unless we save them. That is what we specialize in, escape."

"*Pios?*" Marcus asked. Who.

Haralambos swept his hand before him. "These heroes." He leaned forward conspiratorially, "I have a story of just such a...what you call on American television, a caper, is that right?"

Marcus nodded smiling and he too leaned forward, waiting for the story.

"I will tell you about the time we broke a fellow freedom fighter out of Aegina Prison, right under the noses of the prison guards! We had a clever plan: his relatives brought him a plant to decorate his cell. Do you know what kind of plant it was?"

The *compatrioti* began to laugh as they waited for Harlambos to answer his own question. "A dieffenbachia."

"What is a dieffenbachia?"

Haralambos stared as if Marcus had come from another planet. "Don't you have dieffenbachia plants in America?"

Marcus shrugged.

"Hey, Kleftis!" he shouted to the man at the bar. "*Feretai toh fito.*"

Presently Kleftis came into the room, bent at his waist and dragging a large houseplant by its pot. He wiped his hands on his apron. "It is a house plant with big leaves. It is also called dumb cane," he said and walked out as if upset that he had been bothered.

Marcus recognized the plant. They were everywhere in public buildings, in lobbies and offices. "Of course," he said. "I just didn't know its name. What makes it so special?"

"I will tell you," Haralambos said. "Something stupid guards do not know about. It is poisonous."

"That harmless plant is poisonous?"

"If you bite the leaves, they make you sick with loss of voice and a heaving stomach. My friend in prison broke off a leaf and ate the stalk where most of the poison is. His mouth burned, he screamed from pain. He could not talk." Haralambos slapped his thigh and dust flew up. "The guards thought he was dying. They rushed him to the hospital in a paddy wagon. And we were waiting in the street with a getaway car. The rest was easy."

"I hope you never have to do that again," Marcus said, not realizing how prophetic his words were.

12

When Marcus awoke his skull felt like fine crystal that someone was tapping with a spoon to hear the delicacy of its ring, but inside his head, the ring had the percussive effect of timpani. He groaned and opened an eye.

"*Kalimaira.*" Good morning, Eleni was saying to him from somewhere nearby.

He opened his other eye and looked around. "Where am I?"

"Remember," she said, "Greek only."

"*Pou eimai?*"

"Haralambos's house, next door to the Taverna."

"How did I get here?"

"You were carried."

He groaned.

"Ouzo has a kick like a donkey. Americans should not try to keep up with Greeks."

"Were the others carried, too?" He pulled himself up on an elbow, a Herculean effort it seemed. The room was Spartan, a dresser, a chair, a chamber pot. "You are more involved than I thought, aren't you?"

"Why do you say that?"

"The men I met last night—you are very close to them."

"They are my friends."

"More than friends, *compatrioti*."

Eleni nodded.

"Is that why Haralambos is concerned about that torturer, Theo…"

"…phylianakos. I am not afraid of him."

"Don't say that." He sat up, it was hard but they had to get moving.

They ate breakfast in the back room, bread, cheese, yogurt and coffee, lots of coffee. His head was clearing. "I'm sorry if I let you down."

She stared. "You did not let me down."

"Getting drunk is not exactly a way to build confidence."

She laughed and touched his arm. "Last night was a way to bond with my friends. You did very well, they all like you and now you are family. If you get in trouble, they will be here to help you."

All for one and one for all, he thought as he sipped his coffee, strong and robust. "We have to think about getting to Athens."

"A local bus will take us to Sparta. From there we take another bus to Athens."

"When does the bus arrive?"

"If it is on time, one in the afternoon. We will wait here till then."

"I wish I could walk around. Niata looks interesting, much bigger than Kremasti." Marcus went to a window where he could see the church. "That is truly impressive."

"It is named after Taxiarchis, the patron saint of the Aegean."

The church was painted a peach color. "Why isn't it white like the church in Kremasti?" he asked Eleni.

"Because it is head of our Diocese."

The colonnaded entrance was at the end of a long flight of stone steps and flanked by twin bell towers. Large white crosses were displayed on the wood doors.

He pushed the window wider and leaned out for a better look. He could also see the square where a few cars were parked, even a donkey tied to a hitching post. The contrast amused him. He was ready to close the window when he leaned out again and looked at the line of cars. One was troublingly familiar.

"Eleni, come here."

She joined him looking out the window.

"That car, the white one. Do you recognize it?"

She pulled back, suddenly tense. Fear clouded her eyes as she nodded.

"The Simca," Marcus said. "The car we drove to Kremasti in. They must have guessed we would come to Niata. We have to get out of here."

Eleni was trembling. "We cannot run. They will catch us."

"But we can't stay here." Marcus thought a moment. "One of your friends must have a car."

"No, they are poor like the rest of us."

As if on cue, Kleftis came in to clear the breakfast dishes. Seeing him in the light of day, he did look like a thief, eyes that shifted rather than looked at you directly, sensitive fingers that could determine the combination of a bank vault, and a wiry frame good for springing away after a robbery.

"Kleftis," Marcus said, "there is a car parked outside, a Simca. The man driving it is looking for us. Can you find out where he is?"

Kleftis grinned, clearly delighted to be part of a clandestine operation.

Marcus and Eleni sat at the table with nothing to do but wait. Marcus grew frustrated. He had always lived a life of action, looking forward to doing something and getting it done. Sitting around like this was not only anxiety producing it was also boring. Now he understood what twiddling your thumbs meant. He set his mind to formulating a new plan of action, given the renewed threat.

He could not let events dictate their goal—reaching Athens and the US Embassy.

Kleftis returned in fifteen minutes. "I have news."

"What is it?"

"The owner of the car is here to study the icons in St. Taxiarchis."

"That is what he may be saying, but he is looking for us."

"One more thing," Kleftis said. "He is traveling with another man. Fat and sweaty."

Marcus and Eleni exchanged concerned glances. Drovich and Weber. "Anyone else? A skinny man with a hat?"

"Just those two."

"We have to get out of here," Marcus said.

"But how?" Eleni asked.

"We can't take the bus. They will see us. Damn it," he added in frustration, "if we only had a car."

Kleftis stared as though deep in thought, his eyes unblinking, the raw intelligence of his brain showing through.

"*Toh eho*,' he said. I have it.

"Have what?"

He put the tips of his thin, expressive fingers close together and made a zapping noise with his tongue. Then, he brought his fingertips together and made a whining sound followed by a purring sound.

Marcus thought Kleftis had lost his marbles. "What is all this?"

He grinned. "I will hot-wire the car."

"What?"

"Easy. I have done it before."

"Sure," Marcus said, not taking Kleftis seriously. "What car do you have in mind?

"That one." Kleftis pointed to the Simca shimmering outside in the sun.

Eleni stared, not understanding.

"I can start a car without the key, Eleni," Kleftis said. "I will do that late tonight and you will drive to Athens in it."

Eleni could only shake her head over the craziness of his plan.

Marcus was getting enthused. "We will be in Athens before Drovich even wakes up."

"But a stolen car," Eleni said. "We could be arrested."

Kleftis was listening intently. "Eleni, you cannot stay here much longer, another day at the most. If you are caught, Haralambos and I will be arrested for protecting you. I know I can get the car started."

"What if it is locked?"

Kleftis laughed. "In Niata? Car windows are always down."

Eleni was still unconvinced. "Who will drive us? You?"

Kleftis shook his head. "I cannot. I must stay in the Taverna tending the bar. If I am not where it is familiar to see me, questions will be asked—where is Kleftis? It will cast unnecessary suspicion. We cannot take that chance."

"But starting the car is taking a chance."

"Do not worry," he said reassuringly. "That man, Drovich, will simply assume Marcus did it. We will help by spreading the rumor that we saw someone we did not know, an *Americanos*. And they will not see the car is stolen till morning. And you will be in Athens by then."

The rest of the day, sitting in the private backroom of the Taverna, was a test of patience that Marcus had never before experienced. He stopped drinking coffee after the third cup because it was jangling his already tense nerves. Lunch and finally dinner were eaten mostly in silence, with Marcus and Eleni each deep into their own thoughts. After clearing the dinner plates, Kleftis returned with Haralambos and they sat at the table to lay out the plan for their escape. A lone lightbulb hanging from the ceiling by its cord was the only illumination.

As Kleftis talked, Haralambos interrupted to translate into English so that Marcus could understand fully the details of their flight. He would need to be proficient not only driving at night in Greece but also in how to handle a hot-wired car.

"Listen carefully," Kleftis began with Haralambos translating. "There are three sets of wires for the battery, starter and ignition. The wires are red for ignition, brown for battery, and green for starter. Do you understand me so far?"

Marcus nodded. "I think so. Where are the wires?"

"Inside the steering column. I will open the cover to expose the wires, cut them free and reconnect them so the car will start without a key and the lights will come on. The red wires are the only ones you have to think about. I will splice the ends. Place them together and the car will start. There is a wire nut in the cup holder. Use it to hold the wires in place. When you arrive at the Embassy, just separate the wires and the engine will turn off."

"And when I want to start it again, I reconnect the red wires?"

"That is correct."

"What about fuel?" Eleni asked. A good question Marcus had not thought of.

"I will fill the tank to the top so you can drive all the way to Athens without stopping. I will leave a flashlight and road maps, one for the Peloponnese and a street map of Athens."

"You think of everything."

He smiled appreciatively. "The rest is up to you."

Marcus expected Niata to close down like Kremasti but Niata had a later nightlife enabled by electricity. The tables outside Kleftis' Taverna stayed busy. Marcus and Eleni could hear the sounds of laughter and conversation through the window of their self-imposed prison. And all they could do was sit in the gloom and listen to the fun other people were having. Would they ever be able to do this themselves?

At midnight Kleftis closed the Taverna Omikron and, one by one, the houses went dark. The residents of Niata were finally going to bed. At one a.m., carrying a small tool bag and, of all things, a demijohn he walked across the square as though he was heading home. Marcus and Eleni looked out the front window of the darkened bar to watch Kleftis, but they lost sight of him. Only by focusing on the Simca did they finally see him, a furtive figure crouching beside the car. The first thing he did was lean through the window and reach for something on the headliner.

"What is he doing?" Eleni asked.

It finally dawned on Marcus what Kleftis was doing. "He is switching off the dome light before he opens the door."

Then Kleftis unscrewed the gas cap poured the contents of the demijohn into the tank. So that's what was in the demijohn, not wine but gas! A clever ruse Marcus would not have thought of.

Now Kleftis was ready to hotwire the Simca. Marcus and Eleni watched with apprehension as he opened the door and bent down out of view. No one would notice him under the dashboard, but what if Drovich, on a late night stroll, decided to check his car or look in the trunk to make sure his camera and film were safe.

Film!

Marcus suddenly remembered the negative of him giving the finger to the silhouette of the ESA soldier at the Isthmus of Corinth locked in the Simca's trunk. He smiled with relief. An unintended consequence of his car theft—once they got to Athens he could destroy the negative. He was in so deep now—stealing a car belonging to Drovich—that ruining a role of his film seemed like a prank. At least he would no longer worry about getting in trouble with the Greek dictatorship.

Ten tense minutes later Kleftis was finished, mission accomplished. He climbed out of the car, gently shutting the door and walked toward his home nonchalantly, with his tool kit and the empty demijohn, as though he was going to do a repair job and restock his wine supply. Now it was up to Marcus. With their backpacks, and dressed as they were on their trek over the mountains, he and Eleni left the Taverna and walked along the perimeter behind the cars to the Simca and climbed in. Eleni flicked on the flashlight and held her hand over the beam to contain its spread while Marcus checked the wiring. The wires were dangling beneath the exposed steering column, the brown and green wires spliced together, the two lead wires hanging free, ready to connect. It looked so simple and straightforward, yet Marcus stiffened with fear as he held the two wires. What if it doesn't work? What if the starter makes so much noise it will wake someone up? What if the car backfires? What if, what if! He had to get control of himself. He held his breath as did Eleni and he connected the wires. The starter turned and the engine sparked to life. Quickly he groped for the wing nut to tie the ends together when he dropped it on the floor. Eleni re-aimed the light beam and it seemed forever to find the nut and twist it around the wires.

And now Marcus had to remember how to drive a stick shift. He hadn't done that since college. Would he kill the engine? He had to force these fearful thoughts from his mind. He put the gears in reverse, let out the clutch slowly. There was a slight shudder as he released the clutch but the engine held. He backed out and put the car in forward gear. Without lights they drove through the empty village to the main road. In the dark of night they were on their way to Athens.

13

They parked on a side street near the American Embassy. It was five-thirty in the morning and Athens was barely waking up. Marcus disconnected the wires and the engine died, a metaphor for how he felt. Not literally dead but exhausted beyond feeling. He looked at Eleni. As indefatigable as her spirit was, she also showed fatigue. She could barely keep her eyes open.

Their journey in the middle of the night was the reverse of Marcus's journey with his mother. The highway was largely empty of traffic and they made good time with Eleni reading the map, but they still felt as though they were being pursued and only the sanctuary of the American Embassy would make them safe.

He looked at the impressive edifice as the sun came out to blanket it with light. Marcus knew something about the Embassy designed by Walter Gropius, the eminent architect who founded the Bauhaus School in Weimar, Germany, after World War I. The structure embodied the familiar elements of ancient Greek temples, but reinvented them in twentieth century terms. Slim, unadorned columns held up a narrow portico. Sheets of glass rose from the marble floor to the roofline.

Marcus got out to stretch his legs and walk to the Embassy entrance to find out what time it opened. As he approached he saw the sign: HOURS 10 am to 4 pm. Closed Saturdays and Sundays. Still four hours to go. He returned to the car and found that Eleni had fallen asleep, her body resting against the doorpost. He decided not to wake her and carefully got back in the car so as not to disturb her. It did not take long to join her in slumber.

A sharp rapping on the car door jarred them awake, so startling Marcus jumped and bumped his head on the roof. He was ready to curse the person responsible for this rude awakening when he realized that a police officer was staring at him, the sun at his back outlining his body like an aura. He was swinging a billy club by its leather strap.

"*Ksipneistai!*" he barked. Wake up! "No sleeping in a car!"

Fortunately, in his laid-out position, Marcus's knees covered the loose wires hanging beneath the steering column. He slid up to a sitting position careful not to shift his legs. If the cop saw those wires they would be arrested for stealing a car and trace the ownership to Drovich.

"Where are you from?"

The question reminded them both how they must look dressed as they were, and Marcus with a three-day growth of beard. "We are from Kremasti," he said.

The cop tapped the club against his thigh as though he was making up his mind whether or not to arrest them.

"You can afford a car?"

"It was loaned to us," Eleni answered quickly, taking over for Marcus. "So I could come to Athens to buy a wedding dress. I have been saving for a year."

Marcus had to smile. Eleni was a born con artist.

"Who are you?" he asked Marcus but it was Eleni who answered.

"He is my cousin. I cannot drive. We did not want to spend our money on a hotel and decided to nap and then shop for my dress. We will drive back this afternoon."

Eleni sounded so convincing and the look on her face so innocent that the cop's demeanor softened.

"You are not in a neighborhood for shopping. And you do not want to go to expensive shops in the Plaka. Go to Halandri. Do you know the way?"

Eleni held up her Athens street map and waved it.

The cop leaned over so he could address her directly. "Be on your way, then. Remember no more sleeping in the car, *kai evtihismenos gamos!*" Happy wedding! He saluted her with his billy club and walked away.

Marcus followed the officer's receding figure in the rearview window and breathed a huge sigh of relief. "You were brilliant."

Eleni put her hands to her face. Her fingers were trembling. "I cannot believe I just did that."

He gripped her wrists. "Everything is fine. He has gone away. We are safe." After she composed herself he looked at his watch. They had napped almost three hours.

14

After parking the Simca in a nearby garage, they walked through the front entrance of the Embassy and were met by a significant drop in temperature. Carrying their backpacks and in their village clothes they were also met by significant stares from crisply uniformed marine guards who moved their eyes if not their military-erect bodies as the couple walked across the shiny marble floor to the receptionist.

Unaccustomed to air-conditioning, Eleni shivered and rubbed her upper arms.

The interior, Marcus discovered, was an atrium supported by columns of Greek marble in various shades from white to gray to black. There was a center court with plants surrounding a fountain. Marcus wondered if the people he saw were here to cool off or had business in the Embassy.

The receptionist was also a marine, a captain, who sat behind a desk by the elevators. His hairline was immaculately trimmed, as were his fingernails and the hairs of his nostrils. He was an interchangeable part of a system where individuality was a common enemy. Over his pocket was a plastic nametag that identified him as Capt. R. Hendershot, and on his belt was strapped a holster with a .45 caliber revolver, the gun of choice for marines as well as a show of force in a military-controlled country.

He regarded Marcus and Eleni with curiosity edged with humor. He did not know whether to take them seriously.

"I'd like to see Ron Constable, Charge d' Affairs," Marcus said. His authoritative English surprised the Captain who had assumed that Marcus was a villager like Eleni. The disguise was working all too well. His mother would be proud. He pulled out his passport and showed it to the now attentive marine.

"Do you have an appointment?" he said with a Texas drawl.

"No, but Mr. Constable was notified that I am in Greece. I'm Press Secretary for Senator Tolson of Minnesota."

The marine probably wanted to ask why the Press Secretary of a Senator was dressed like this, but he was trained not to ask personal questions.

As he confirmed Marcus's ID, he said, "What is your business here?"

"My cousin wishes to apply for an American passport."

The marine punched a few numbers on his Centrex and spoke quietly into the receiver relaying the information supplied by Marcus. "Mr. Constable is not available but his office is referring you to Arthur Prager in the Consular's office."

He examined Eleni as if he were checking the bolt action on his .45. "Her name?" he asked Marcus

"Eleni Stathos," she interrupted, showing the officer that she understood him.

"You speak English?"

"A little."

A lot, Marcus wanted to say, but decided this was her show.

They rode the elevator to the second floor and, when the doors whispered shut behind them, so did

Greece. The carpeting, the wall hangings and furnishings were as typically American as a Howard Johnson's.

Prager's office was one of three sharing an anteroom and a secretary, a middle-aged woman who was too blonde to be Greek, probably a career State Department employee.

"We're here to see Arthur Prager."

She smiled politely even though she could not disguise the curious look on her face. She ushered them toward his office with a nod of her head.

Prager looked them over as they walked in. "Captain Hendershot told me expect to be surprised and he was right. Are you traveling incognito?"

"No, just traveling."

Prager laughed.

"We didn't have time to change," Marcus added by way of limited explanation.

Prager let it go. "Have a seat," he said, pointing to chairs facing his desk. He was older than Marcus but boyish-looking with curly hair and smooth skin, a likable person who, as it turned out, liked to ask questions. "Did you know Jim Elliot? He was at State for a number of years. We went to school together, Princeton..."

"So did F. Scott Fitzgerald. He was from St. Paul."

"Elliot, too. That's why I asked you."

Eleni listened patiently to what in America is known as small talk.

"How long have you been in Washington?" Prager asked.

"Three years."

"Like it?"

"It's ok," Marcus said. "All I do is work."

"We assume the pace of the country we serve, and in Greece everything is slower because of the climate."

"What difference does it make in here?"

"None, unless the generators break down." He leaned forward. "Tell me, know anyone at State?" Bill Patterson, Deputy Chief of AID?"

"No."

"How about Claus Ranzinger, he works the Desk."

"Sorry."

Prager shook his head. He so wanted to find someone they both knew, probably the result of living away from home much of his life. To know someone in common was a touchstone.

"How long have you been in Greece?" Marcus asked.

"Going on two years, my fifth tour."

It was Marcus's turn to ask, "Like it?"

"Great duty and why shouldn't it be? We love the Greeks and the Greeks love us." There was a hint of cynicism in his voice.

"Officially you mean?"

"Where I sit I wouldn't know the difference." He opened a cigarette box of hammered aluminum and offered it to Marcus who shook his head. Prager helped himself and lit a cigarette with a fancy Dunhill pocket lighter. He blew smoke ceilingward and then said, "What can I do for you?"

"I need a passport."

"For the lady?" he said, finally acknowledging Eleni who handed over the manila envelope with her documents.

"Eleni is my cousin," Marcus said as Prager examined the contents. "Those are her registration papers from the Periferia of Niata, her birth certificate, and her mother's passport. As you can see Eleni's mother was an American citizen."

He handed them back. "What about her father?"

"We don't know, but we assume he was Greek."

"Not married to one another?"

"Probably not."

"Ok. According to the Immigration and Nationality Act, a person born out of wedlock to a US citizen mother may acquire citizenship under Section 309 (c) if the mother was a US citizen at the time of the person's birth and if the mother was physically present in the US for a continuous period of one year prior to the person's birth. Looks like Miss Stathos fits the criteria. She will need to fill out a CRBA."

"What is that?"

Prager opened a file drawer and pulled out a multi-paged form and slid it across his desk to Marcus. "Consular Report of Birth Abroad. Fill it out and I will take it from there."

Marcus leafed through the application of seven pages. "How long will it take?"

"How long will it take to fill out the form or how long will it take to get the passport?" Prager smiled at his little joke. "I will see what I can do to expedite the process. Ok to talk to your boss?" he asked, almost as an afterthought.

"Senator Tolson?"

"If you were to name a Senator with the most clout on our side, he has it. I'll have my office get in touch with him. Any message you want to pass along?"

"Just one: Help!"

Prager laughed. "Your cousin will also need an exit visa from the Greek government and you know the Senator can't help with that, in fact mentioning his name on the other side would be the kiss of death."

"So how do we get an exit visa?"

"You apply for it just like applying for a passport."

Marcus was beginning to feel like a tennis ball.

"The Greeks are pretty fussy about who gets to leave their country."

Marcus looked at Eleni who was hanging on to every word spoken between the two men. "If she gets an American passport, why can't she leave the country like anyone else with an American passport?"

"Don't forget she was born in Greece which means the government still controls her fate. They won't let her travel abroad without a return date."

Everything was getting heavier, like someone adding rocks to their backpacks. "It sounds like Catch-22."

Prager expelled some smoke. "You're Greek aren't you?" he asked as if that explained everything.

"But this is an emergency."

"What kind?"

"Her freedom, her rights as an American citizen."

Prager interrupted. "Giannou, I hear that all the time in my business."

"But it's true. Eleni is being forced to marry against her will to a man named Kostas Kanellos. He is connected to ESA."

"Sounds more like a domestic matter to me. You need a lawyer not a diplomat." Prager paused. "Wait a minute, did you say Kanellos? There was a query about him from somewhere, let me think, oh yeah, the gal who runs the American Library in Sparta…"

"Sally Haggerty."

Prager looked in surprise. "You know her?"

"A friend. I stopped to see her on my way down to Kremasti. I asked her to check up on him but I haven't had a chance to get back in touch with her."

"Well, we have a dossier on Kanellos."

"I'd like to see it."

Prager smiled sympathetically. "Wish I could show it to you but you need Top Secret clearance. Just let me say that this guy is on our list and he's not exactly who you'd want to bring home to meet mamma."

"That is exactly what I am talking about. This is the guy Eleni is being forced to marry." He exhaled in frustration and Eleni had a look of trepidation. Things were not going well even if Prager was sympathetic.

"Look, Giannou, I'll do what I can and your Senator might be able to oil a few gears at the Embassy, but he is anathema to the Greek government as you already know. You have to be realistic that getting her out of Greece will take time and patience."

There was a moment of silence.

"There is another way," Prager said, speaking almost tentatively.

"What is that?" Marcus asked.

"Get married."

They both stared at Prager. "You mean Eleni and I...?"

"Hey, it's not like this is something illegal. It's done all the time. Eliminates an exit visa. Get married and, later, when she settles in the US you get divorced."

"Not me!" Eleni said sharply. Her uncompromising stare told them that marriage to her was a lifelong bond sanctified by God in the Orthodox Church and wasn't to be used as a means to a far less noble end, even if it meant getting to America.

Prager shrugged. "Ok, we'll do it the official way. Fill out the CRBA. But it would not hurt to pay a courtesy call to the Greek Consulate."

"Who do we see?"

"A guy named Panatoulis. I'll call to see if you can get an appointment." Prager picked up his phone but kept his finger on the plunger. "Be sure you don't mention the Senator's name." He held the receiver with his cigarette tucked between his fingers and made the call to Panatoulis office. He used pretty good, well-practiced Greek.

"You are set." Prager said after hanging up. "I told him you will come over after you fill out the CRBA. His office is at the north entrance on the right side of the Embassy as you face it."

"What should I tell him?"

"Be generous." Prager rubbed the tips of his thumb and forefinger together.

Marcus stared. "Give him money? Bribe him?"

"You want to get your cousin out of the country don't you?"

Marcus sighed. "If that's what it takes." As they were leaving he turned and asked Prager, "I wonder if you could do me another favor."

"Sure."

"Call Sally Haggerty and ask if she can get a message to my mother in Kremasti, privately of course. Tell her that we saw you. Maybe Sally can drive there and find out how she is doing."

"Are you worried about her?"

"Yes, I am."

Prager reached in the top drawer of his desk "Here's my card. Call me later today. Leave a message if I'm not around. Use the table outside my office to fill out the form. Leave it with the secretary and I will process it."

"Thanks."

"One more thing," Prager said.

"What is that?"

"Buy some new clothes. You stand out like a sore thumb in Athens, and from what you told me I don't think you really want to attract any added attention to yourselves."

15

Prager was right, of course. What had been Plan A, countrified on the road, was now Plan B, cosmopolitan in Athens. What they were doing was akin to improvisational theater, Marcus realized, invent as you go along—not easy, even Draconian, an appropriate word given the fact that it comes from Draco, the Athenian statesman known for his severe laws.

They sat at a table in the anteroom of Prager's office and filled out the form, pouring over it together with Marcus doing the writing. Like any government document it was loaded with instructions—two full pages in small type, reminding Marcus of doing his federal taxes back home. After they finished, they handed the form to the secretary, who made photocopies of Eleni's documents. The first part of their mission completed, it was now time to face a functionary of the Greek government.

Eleni was clearly weighed down. He could see it in the way she carried herself, not the usual erect, confident stride that was her hallmark on their trek over the mountains. He needed to reassure her.

"Eleni, things will work out. Don't worry." But he said this prematurely.

They followed the broad sidewalk to the Greek Consular Section on Kokkali Street and walked through the door. They were halted immediately by a tough-looking guard obviously more impressed with his uniform than Marcus was.

He motioned them to a desk in front of a pegboard with hooks for purses, bags and cameras.

"You have to leave your backpacks."

Marcus and Eleni exchanged concerned glances, wondering if the guard might search them and find the icon.

"Can't we take them with us?"

"Pick them up on your way out." He handed over a numbered ticket and directed Marcus and Eleni to another of his breed who sat behind a desk with a clipboard and a telephone. Lined up against a chest-high marble wall were metal chairs with well-worn, brown vinyl seats, some occupied by apprehensive Greeks who stared at the newcomers. The place was starkly quiet.

"We are here to see Mr. Panatoulis," Marcus said to the man at the desk. "Arthur Prager of the US Consulate sent us over."

"Names?"

"Marcus Giannou and Eleni Stathos."

The guard checked his clipboard "Sit down. I will call you."

A half-hour passed before they finally were directed down a bleak corridor appropriate for an asylum to door number 22. Marcus tapped on it and a voice from within called out, "*Ela!*" They walked into an office decorated with the Greek flag and a photo of Premier Pappathopoulos. A man behind a desk with a blotter and an in-basket filled with file folders was on the telephone. He waved at them to sit down while talking about a vacation cruise to Dubrovnik, bringing Drovich to mind. Marcus wondered what the Yugoslav was doing this minute, stewing no doubt, harboring revenge.

Presently Panatoulis hung up and settled back in his chair, folding his hands together. He had black hair on the backs of his fingers. He stared at them with round eyes, the irises solid black orbs. He spent a moment sizing up the American male and the Greek female dressed like farmers.

"*Yiati eisai ethoh?*" Why are you here?

"Do you speak English?"

"Of course. In my work, it is necessary," he replied and his chest expanded in self-congratulation.

"Good," Marcus said, reverting to English. "My cousin is applying for an American passport. Her mother, now deceased, was an American citizen. Mr. Prager said that she will need an exit visa and he directed us to you."

Panatoulis stared at Eleni, his eyes reflecting deep disappointment. "You want to leave Greece? Don't you like it here?"

"Of course," she said, unnerved by this bureaucrat, small of stature but large of ego. "Greece is my home."

He shrugged. "Then why leave it?"

"Let me explain," Marcus interupted. "Eleni has no wish to *leave* Greece. We just want her to visit."

"We?"

"My mother and I."

"I see. And where do you live?" he asked Eleni.

"Kremasti, District of Laconias."

"Ah, the land of the *Sparti*. Strong of spirit, valiant fighters, drank the blood of pigs." He gave Marcus a leering look. "Are you like your ancestors?"

"Not that part about drinking blood," Marcus replied, surprised, taken aback even, wondering where Panatoulis was going with this line of attack.

The Greek official rubbed his chin. "Well, your beard is a good start."

Marcus understood now that Panatoulis was making fun of his appearance, an American dressed like, what, a village idiot? "I always wanted to grow a beard and now that I am on vacation, I decided this is the time.

Come to think of it," Marcus, added, "you could grow a pretty good one yourself."

Panatoulis laughed it off. "But the clothes you are wearing," he continued, "Saks Fifth Avenue?" He probably was showing off his knowledge of New York as much as needling Marcus.

So far this interview was not going well. Marcus was thinking fast. He looked down at his flannel pants as though seeing them for the first time. "Oh, these," he said, improvising. "My uncle lent them to me. Our charter flight lost my luggage."

"I am happy to hear this was not the fault of Olympic Airlines." He laughed at his joke. "Your first trip to Greece?"

"Yes, and my mother's first trip since she left for America forty-seven years ago. We thought it would be nice to have Eleni visit us because my mother may not be able to travel again."

"I see. Well, your cousin's mother may have been born in America but your cousin is a still a citizen of Greece and will need permission to leave the country."

"That is why we came to see you. Mr. Prager said you could help."

"That depends. Does Miss Stathos own property?"

"No, but her father owns a home in Kremasti, and I presume she will inherit it someday."

"In the meantime, is she employed?"

Marcus did not think so but he looked at Eleni for verification. She shook her head.

"Then she falls into the category of immigrant class and there are quotas regarding such people." He said this with a smugness he could not disguise.

"But she will only be visiting."

"A person of immigrant class is not in a position to visit."

"Why not?"

"If she has no property and no source of income how can she pay her way?"

"I will pay her way."

"And once her visitor's visa expires, will you send her back to Greece?"

"Of course," Marcus said, and reassuringly patted Eleni's knee.

Panatoulis stretched his short frame so he could see over his desk at this gesture of familiarity, even intimacy. He settled back with a noisy rustle of his suit against the coarse fabric of the chair and padlocked a smirk on his face. His heavy beard turned the creases around his mouth into black lines, making him appear for all the world like an actor in a Greek tragedy, perhaps an American one, too, a tragedy about an obsequious functionary who controlled Eleni's future.

Marcus knew the meeting was coming to an end, even a dead end, and so it was time to put Prager's advice to the test. He took out his wallet and revealed the contents of the bill compartment.

Panatoulis leaned forward like a dog on a scent, staring at the bills Marcus was showing him—four fifties and five twenties, three hundred dollars, all the money he had except for travelers' checks and drachmas.

"Are you trying to bribe me?" Panatoulis asked huffily.

"Maybe I was a bit hasty." Marcus started to gather up the bills when Panatoulis reached across his desk with fingers shaped like sausages and slid the bills into the top drawer of his desk.

They walked across the lobby to retrieve their backpacks. Through the tall windows they could see that Athens had come to life—the bustle, the traffic, the crowded sidewalks—contributing to her unease and sense of strangeness. Marcus could tell she wished she were back in Kremasti, but there was no going back, at least for the time being. Their plan to escape Greece and therefore Kostas was on hold to assume the best, or dashed to assume the worst. She could get a passport and, if she did, getting that exit visa was in doubt even if it cost Marcus three hundred dollars.

Once outside she sat on a bench and checked her backpack to make certain the icon was safe. She unfolded the shawl it was wrapped in and looked at the serene image of Mary, the direct opposite of the expression on Eleni's face.

She was depending on Marcus to protect her as she was protecting Theophanes' Virgin. As he stared at Eleni in her homemade dress and flannel shirt, Prager's advice sprang to mind: buy new clothes. That's what they needed, something to symbolize a fresh start. At least they would no longer look like shepherds. Besides, there was no doubt in Marcus's mind that by now Drovich discovered his car had been stolen. He would not need a Philadelphia lawyer, even if there were one in Greece, to connect the fleeing pair with the stolen Simca.

His mind began to clear. "We can't drive the Simca any longer."

"Why not?"

"By now the police must be looking for it."

"But we need the car."

"We'll rent one. We'll leave the Simca in the parking garage. It will sit there for a few days before anyone notices it." Marcus hailed a taxi forgetting completely that in the trunk of the Simca was a roll of film with the incriminating photo of him making a rude gesture at the symbol of Greek authority.

Given their poor cousins look, it took several attempts before a taxi pulled over, the driver overcoming suspicion that the pair in homespun clothing might not have money to pay the fare. Nevertheless, the driver waited at the curb and eyed them in his rearview mirror until Marcus pulled out his wad of drachmas.

"I want to rent a car," he told the driver in Greek. "Can you take us to a rental agency?"

He nodded and drove them in a kind of bumper-car craziness through Athens traffic, dodging buses, other taxis of which there were many, delivery trucks, passenger cars and mopeds. In minutes they arrived at Constitution Square. The driver pointed in the general direction of Otto Street, named after the first King of Greece. "Car Rental, Hertz," he said, as Marcus and Eleni climbed out

Marcus gave him a generous tip, more as a sign of his affluence than a reward for his driving, which was frightening to say the least. They looked around, immersed in the cultural and commercial center of Athens for the first time.

They must have struck a singular image, looking like country bumpkins arriving in the big city and staring in awe at the throngs of people, the office buildings, the upscale shops.

"I'm hungry," Eleni said, reminding Marcus that they had nothing to eat since arriving in Athens.

They found an outdoor café and sat at a table under an umbrella nearest the wall to be as inconspicuous as possible. After a breakfast of fruit, cheese, toast and coffee, they investigated the streets off the Square, walking with their back-backs past small shops and markets almost shouldering each other for space in the narrow lanes. They came to a dress shop and looked inside. A well-tailored saleswoman was watching them through the open door.

"You need a new wardrobe," Marcus said. "Let's see what they have."

Reluctantly Eleni followed. "Everything is so expensive."

"I have a credit card." He approached the saleswoman. "*Melatai Englezika*?" he asked, hoping to dispel the notion that they were not serious customers.

"Yes," the woman said, surprised.

"We have been hiking in the mountains and just arrived in Athens. As you can see, my cousin needs a new outfit."

When he said this, the saleswoman looked him over rather critically suggesting that he too could use something new.

"Is there a men's store nearby?" he asked, picking up the vibes

"Around the corner."

Eleni took him aside. "Remember what the policeman said this morning? Go to Halandri where the prices are lower. Here they raise them because of the tourists."

Eleni was right. Marcus checked a sales tag. The dress was fifteen hundred drachmas, fifty dollars. He looked at her. She was far too pretty to walk around Athens in a rural housedress. "Let's look anyway," he encouraged her. Eleni did so, her eyes wide as she moved between racks of bright fashions. She took one off the hanger and held it to her body to see how she looked in a mirror.

The sales woman was beaming. "You are so pretty you deserve to wear something new and fresh." She was good at her profession all right.

"Try it on," Marcus encouraged.

Eleni disappeared into a fitting room and when she emerged she almost took Marcus's breath away. The transformation was from larvae to butterfly. Her slender body was flattered by excellent tailoring, her finally tapered knees visible for the first time, her breasts having definition for the first time. He finally could see how well-proportioned her figure was to modeling. With some training she could walk down the runway during Fashion Week in New York.

Her cheeks were flushed by the transformation she saw in the mirror.

"It fits her perfectly," the saleswoman said.

"Wear it," Marcus said. "My present to you."

Eleni looked at the price tag. "I will pay you back." She probably meant money she had saved for her dowry.

"Seeing you like this is payment enough," Marcus said and handed his credit card to the saleslady. There was no exchange of real money, creating the impression that charging something always does—the purchase wasn't so expensive after all. Eleni was also amazed at the ease and trust with which the transaction was concluded. All Marcus had to do was sign a slip of paper.

Now it was his turn. They followed the directions of the saleswoman to a men's clothing store named Davos on Ermou Street. A half hour later Marcus walked out wearing jeans and a polo shirt, giving his Greek sailor hat a sportive look. Seeing himself in the fitting-room mirror he decided to keep his beard, at least for now. It enhanced his image as a native Greek and he was beginning to like it.

They carried their old clothes in plastic bags with the respective store logos on them. If they were sought after based on their description when they left Niata, they would now go completely undetected. They looked like tourists rather than fugitives—but from what Marcus wondered, justice? He was not sure.

Next on the agenda was renting a car, but before that they decided to be tourists inasmuch as they now looked the part. They walked to various sights that heretofore had eluded Marcus as well as Eleni. In all her years growing up in Greece, she had never before visited Athens. And so they visited the archaeological museum, hiked across the National Garden to Hadrian's Arch and the Temple of Zeus. It was not only a heady experience, it was also a sobering one to see the splendors of ancient Greece firsthand and not out of picture books. To think that such a civilization existed to erect these monuments to democracy and dignity.

They decided to have lunch in the Plaka where Athens, hugging the steep walls at the base of the Acropolis, began its expansion outward. In the Giannou family album back in Minneapolis Marcus remembered a postcard sent to his father from Greece in the 1930s with a picture of Athens circling the Acropolis. It was not much more than a town then.

Marcus and Eleni negotiated the complicated labyrinth to the Plaka on streets so narrow that taxis brushed their legs as they managed the foot-wide sidewalks. Eleni was ahead of Marcus and he could observe the way she carried herself, so different from the hiker in the mountains with the walking stick. She was radiating self-confidence in her new dress, turning heads, especially Greek men who are known to ogle openly, touching with their eyes. Marcus was delighted to be her escort.

The Plaka's main street was not a street at all but rather a stone stairway of several hundred steps with landings every fifty feet or so. Off each landing were cafenios, tavernas, bistros—anything to attract tourists, most of whom it seemed were American. Tables and chairs were crammed together as though they were in storage. Marcus did not know how the waiters managed to serve customers but they did, with enormous zeal and a lot of yelling at each other.

Marcus and Eleni found a table in an alcove. Across the sidewalk at another café, a bouzouki band played with great fervor. As they enjoyed cold dolmathes, pita bread, a cucumber salad, and Amstel Beer, Marcus and Eleni forgot for the moment the delicate balance of their lives, how uncertain and inconclusive things were, not only what might befall them but the nature of their relationship as well. They were cousins, she a village woman he an urbanite, she with a grade school education he with a masters degree, she innocent he seasoned. They were thrown together by a crisis, and once that was over, what will they have in common, how will they bridge a chasm separating them culturally, temperamentally, physically?

"What are you thinking?" she asked, noting the frown of concern on his face.

"A number of things," he said, deflecting what was really on his mind. "Would you feel at home in America?"

"If I ever get there."

"Don't speak that way. You will make it."

"What if I do not? You heard the Greek official. He will not permit it." She sighed, "Maybe it is what fate has provided for me. I should stay and join the resistance against ESA, just like I imagined my mother and father fighting the German occupation in the war. One is just as bad as the other, the Greek colonels and the German Nazis."

"That sounds dangerous."

"Isn't what we are doing now dangerous?"

16

After lunch they looked for the Hertz Agency, which turned out to be a narrow office hardly wider than the cars they rented. Evidently the rental cars were stored in an adjacent parking garage. A man behind a tall wood desk and a runner waiting at the door made up the staff. Marcus signed up for an Auto Bianchi A112, a hatchback made in Milan, Italy. It had several thousand miles on it but all Marcus cared about were dependable wheels. He rented it for a week without knowing how long he would need the car or even where he would drop it off.

The runner brought the car around and parked it at the curb in front of the agency. Marcus and Eleni threw their old clothes and backpacks into the rear and drove off, merging into the heavy traffic of cars, buses, taxis and motor scooters spewing smoke out of their exhausts.

"Where can we go?"

He had been thinking about driving to Sparta and seeing Sally. She was his only help. But it was already mid-afternoon and he was very tired.

"We need to find a hotel, spend the night and in the morning we will drive down to Sparta." The prospect of spending another night with Eleni almost made him wonder if he decided this because he wanted to be alone with her. Maybe what happened last night on a mountaintop will happen again in a hotel room in Athens.

"Hotels here are expensive. Besides it is too noisy. The police officer told us to go to Halandri. We could find a hotel there and get some rest."

Eleni unfolded her city map and gave Marcus directions to Halandri on the northern outskirts of Athens. The center of the suburb was a landscaped square surrounded by three-story, cement-block buildings with shops at street level and apartments above. They found a hotel named Olympic on a shaded, tree-lined side street and parked in front. They were pleased to find a modest, neatly kept hotel with a small lobby and freeform plastic furniture, typical of what one sees in older American motels.

The young clerk spoke English and told them he had only two singles, one on the second floor and the other on the third. Marcus hid his disappointment that they could not at least have adjoining rooms. Still, he rationalized, he could easily navigate two floors.

"Only the room on the second floor has a bath. Floor three has a shared bathroom."

"I'll take the one on three," Marcus said.

Eleni challenged him. "No, Marcus, you take the room with the bath. I will take the other."

"I insist."

"I have lived my whole life walking to a bathroom." Her reference to the outhouse in Kremasti made them both laugh.

The clerk waited patiently, his pen poised to write down the room numbers on his registration pad.

"But I will be embarrassed," Marcus said.

Her eyes glinted stubbornly.

"All right, we will compromise. You occupy the room with the bath. If we stay another night, then we will trade."

Having accepted this arrangement, they climbed a circular staircase of black marble with their backpacks and two plastic shopping bags containing their peasant clothes while dodging a profusion of potted ferns whose long branches hung down the center well like a Tarzan jungle set. Marcus escorted Eleni to her room.

They agreed to rendezvous in the lobby at eight, when Athens awakened for the night.

"Now we will rest," she said to him before closing the door.

Marcus's room was small but comfortable. A pleasant breeze worked its way through the lattices of a metal balcony door that rolled up into a drum anchored to the ceiling. He heaved it up and stepped onto the balcony, which looked over a patio ablaze with flowers of every sort. Those he recognized were roses, calla lilies and azaleas. There were also clusters of shrubs and grape vines whose long twisty branches created natural arbors protecting the wrought iron chairs and tables.

Eleni was already waiting for him when he came down to the lobby at eight.

"Are you hungry?" Marcus asked her.

"Not yet."

He was still not used to the Mediterranean schedule for dining. "Let's go into Athens, see more sights and then have dinner."

Marcus decided not to drive the rental and asked the clerk for a taxi, who ran to the corner where there was more traffic and in a moment returned with a taxi following him. Marcus tipped him thirty drachmas.

Eleni chastised him. "Too much."

"It's only money," he kidded but she was not amused.

"You do not appreciate what you have."

They got out of the taxi at Constitution Square and strolled along the sidewalk, taking in the sights, the soft air, the pulse of the city, walking past the Parliament Building and its heavily wooded walled-in grounds, and followed Vassilisis Sofias, a wide thoroughfare also heavily tree-lined. To their left they saw a lighted dome high in the air, so high it seemed to float above the city.

"What is that?" he asked.

"I do not know."

Marcus leaned into the open window of a parked taxi and asked the driver what that lighted dome was, pointing to it.

"That is the Chapel of St. George on Lykavittos Hill," he said, "the highest point in Athens."

"I thought the Acropolis was the highest."

The driver smiled. "The Acropolis is grander, Lykavittos is higher."

"Can we go up there?"

"Of course. You can walk up or you can take the incline. I suggest the incline."

The driver never got his yellow cab out of second gear as he navigated through slow-moving traffic to a station at the base of Lykavittos Hill. Marcus and Eleni bought tickets for the next ride up, leaving in five minutes, and stood in a short line for the funicular car to trundle down the sloping tracks. They climbed aboard and sat in seats at a 45-degree angle to the ground. The car lurched into motion and they cabled up the steep hill while the counter-balancing tram car cabled down, passing each other midway. As they climbed, they saw Athens spreading out in all directions, a million lights, both stationary and moving, until they reached the summit, 900 feet above the bowl of the city.

They climbed out of the car and walked into a surreal world of dark and shadow. The focal point was the chapel of St. George, its dome brightly outlined against a starry sky by blinding arc lights mounted on the ground. They held their hands under their eyes to block the sharp light angling up and walked to the parapet. The night air at this height was cool and they clung together to stay warm.

"Look," he said, pointing, "there is the Acropolis."

In the distance they saw the illuminated columns of the Parthenon, majestic and timeless, beyond the reach of the gaudy and baubled lights at street level. Athens and its neighbor to the south, Piraeus, sprawled in every direction, stopping only at the foothills to the north, east and west and at water's edge to the south.

They stayed as long as they could, driven back down by the cool breeze. They huddled together for warmth on their wooden seat as the car took them back to the station.

"Tomorrow," he said, "we will visit the Acropolis."

Eleni smiled in agreement.

They dined in a small café off Syntagma Square, out of the way of tourists, and lingerd over Turkish coffee and *kourabiedes*. They hated to see the evening come to an end. Still, they were buoyed by the anticipation of another day, perhaps another night in Athens, as many as they could hope to have. Athens belonged to them, they felt, as they hailed a taxi driver who sped them along the darkened, after-midnight streets back to their hotel.

Marcus walked Eleni to her door, wondering if this memorable evening could somehow be extended in her bedroom. He tried to judge her manner as she unlocked the door and pushed it open. Then she reached for the light switch on the wall. The ceiling light came on to reveal a shocking sight.

"Oh my God!" she called out. "What happened?"

What happened stopped them cold. Eleni's bedroom seemed to have been turned inside out, like the sleeve of a garment. The two bottom dresser drawers were lying on the floor upside down. The top drawer was precariously hanging in its slot. The bedding was bunched in a large bundle by the wall and the mattress had been pulled sideways off the springs.

Fear trembled her thin frame. "Who did this? Who knew we were here?"

Marcus was shaking his head. "It had to be Kostas. But how could he have known we were in this hotel? He must have had help. Someone in Athens is responsible for this." Marcus snapped his fingers. "Wait a minute, that guy in the Greek Consulate, Panatoulis. He might have put a tail on us."

"Tail?"

"Someone secretly following us."

"But why would they break into my room? What were they looking for?"

And then it hit Marcus. "The icon. Where is it?"

"Inside my bag."

He stepped over to the closet and opened the slatted door. Eleni's backpack was lying empty on the floor, the zipper torn open. Her old clothes, the peasant dress and shirt, the stockings, the old shoes lay in a heap.

"I wrapped it in the shawl with my papers." She rummaged through the mess, finally finding it in the corner. "Here it is." She let out a sigh of relief. But then she began rummaging again. "The envelope with my papers was here, too, but now I can't find it."

Trembling with anxiety, Eleni again went through the scattering of her clothes, looking around in confusion. "My papers...my documents, they are gone!"

"What?"

"I can't find them anywhere," she said helplessly.

Marcus joined her in another search, which proved to be futile.

"I don't understand," he said. "Your papers were stolen but the icon is left behind. It doesn't make any sense."

He walked out on the small balcony overlooking the garden illuminated by a spotlight hanging from the roof. It would have been a simple matter to climb one of the thick vines and jump over the railing onto the balcony and through the open door. And he assumed they were perfectly safe!

"We have to get out of here."

"Right now?"

"Yes, whoever turned this place upside down may come back. They may even be waiting outside somewhere in the dark."

"But where can we go?"

Marcus thought a moment. He considered the Embassy but only he, an American, could ask for protection. They could return to Niata and hide out with Kleftis, but they would be in self-imposed imprisonment. There was Kremasti where they began, but that was impossible. What was let?

"Sally Haggerty," he said aloud.

"How can she help us?"

"She can hide us until we figure out what to do."

"Drive all the way to Sparta?"

"We have no other choice. We can't stay here."

"They can follow us and stop us on a dark road. That would even be worse."

"We have to figure out some way to get out of here without them knowing, like the way we got out of Niata."

"But we don't have Kleftis to help us. We are on our own."

Marcus nodded agreement. He had to figure out a way to leave without detection. He thought to himself, what would Kleftis do? Then he smiled.

"What is on your mind?"

"I have an idea. Clean up the place the way it was, and be ready to leave as soon as I get back."

"What are you going to do?"

"First, see if my room was searched and then talk to the clerk. He is going to help us get out of here."

He walked down the second floor and looked into his room. It was untouched.

He walked downstairs to the lobby and found the clerk dozing in an armchair, a Greek newspaper lying across his lap. This was not the same man who checked them in.

"*Signomi*," Marcus said. Excuse me.

The clerk jumped, embarrassed to be caught napping. He wore a white shirt with sleeves folded up to his elbows, typical of Greek men's attire. He went behind the desk and assumed his professional stance.

"May I help you?"

"Where is the other clerk, the one who checked us in?"

"He went home. I am on the late shift."

Whoever broke into Eleni's room had to bribe the other clerk to get her room number. Well, it looks as if bribery is the only way to go.

"I need a favor. Take my car, the Auto Bianci parked outside, and drive it away from here, pick any street, park it, leave the keys in the car and walk back."

He was apprehensive. "I cannot leave my post," he said.

Marcus held up a 100-drachma note. "You will only be gone a few minutes."

He eyed the money the same way as Panatoulis, then reached for the bill and pocketed it.

Marcus gave him the car keys and ran upstairs to Eleni's room. She was standing in the middle of it, surrounded by perfect order, her packback over her shoulder. "I am ready."

He turned off the lights. "Come with me to the balcony." They stood in the dark, looking down on the garden and the street beyond. "Watch," he said as the clerk came into view.

Eleni became concerned. "He is getting into our car."

"I paid him to. He is going to drive it away. Now let's see if anyone follows."

They waited expectantly and, in a few seconds, a taxi came into view, headlights out, following the Auto Bianci.

Perfect, Marcus thought. "Let's go."

"Where?"

"To the square."

They picked up their gear and left the hotel.

Marcus expected the square empty of people at this hour, after one in the morning, but he was wrong. There were tables along the perimeter corresponding to shops across the street that served food, coffee, ice cream or pastry. Several tables were occupied, attended by waiters running back and forth. This was where families gathered. Marcus even saw a yiayia pushing a stroller with a sleeping child. What a nightlife.

Two yellow cabs were at one corner, their drivers leaning against a fender chatting. Marcus and Eleni approached them carrying their bags.

"Where to?" one of the drivers said, the eternal question from cabbies no matter what the language.

"Sparta."

He shook his head. "I can take you into Athens to the central station where you can hire an overland taxi. I only drive locally."

"I'll make it worth your while."

"The trip will take most of the night and I will return empty."

"I'll pay you a thousand drachmas down and another thousand to get back."

Eleni stared in shock. Marcus was spending money like a drunken fool. She was right—he was not only spending it like a fool but also spending money he didn't have. He was counting on Sally to bail him out.

The two drivers exchanged glances and then one of them nodded. "He has a wife. I don't. Climb in."

17

They arrived in Sparta at dawn, driving down the same divided highway Marcus, his mother and Kostas traveled on only three days earlier, but seemingly much longer—as in eternity. Marcus directed the driver to the Library, the building lacking definition in the long shadows created by the early morning sun. The windows, cornices and decorative balustrades blended with the wall, creating a flat image like a stage set.

The driver parked in front and Marcus got out. "Wait here." He walked to the entrance and rang the bell. Marcus knew that government buildings always were guarded, at least one security person taking the overnight shift. Presently the door swung open a few inches and a uniformed man peered out.

"We are not open yet," he said in Greek.

"I must talk to Sally Haggerty. My name is Marcus Giannou, a friend from America. Please call her and ask her to meet me here. It is an emergency."

The guard, cautious by nature, peered at Marcus suspiciously. "She will be here at nine."

"I cannot wait till nine," he pleaded. "Please call her and let her make the decision."

The guard eyed him a few more seconds and closed the door. A minute passed as slowly as the sun rising, making Marcus more nervous. Finally the door opened, wide this time. "*Ella mesa*," Come in, the guard said and ushered Marcus to a telephone on the receptionist's desk.

"Sally..." Marcus began in English.

"My god!" Sally interrupted, "I was really worried about you. I got a Telex from Art Prager yesterday afternoon that you and the Stathos girl came to see him, and he asked me to check on your mother."

"Have you?"

"I was planning to drive down today. You called just in time. We can go together."

Not likely, Marcus thought. "I have to see you now, Sally. There is a lot to tell you."

"I'll be there in a half hour."

The cab driver was not happy having to wait, even though Marcus gave him the first thousand drachmas he promised, wiping him out. He hoped Sally had that much on her. Otherwise he'd have to find an American Express office to buy more currency.

When Sally arrived behind the wheel of a gray Chevrolet Malibu, Marcus was glad that Eleni had shopped for new clothes so she would not feel like a drab country girl next to Sally, who was dressed in a linen business suit. Sartorially, at least, the two women were now on an equal level of style with looks that would turn heads, especially those of Greek men.

The first thing Marcus said to Sally as she approached him was, "Lend me a thousand drachmas."

She looked over at the taxi. "It's a good thing I got paid yesterday." She reached into her handbag for her wallet, counting out ten 100-drachma notes and handing them to the driver, who was now all smiles.

"*Efharisto! Efharisto!*" he called out as he pulled away from the curb on his drive back to Athens. He had a story to tell his cohorts once he got there.

"Sally, this is Eleni Stathos. She remembers meeting you when you visited Kremasti about the bookmobile."

It was clear Sally did not remember. The two shook hands and eyed one another warily the way women do when both are involved with the same man.

"I am perishing for a cup of coffee and the staff doesn't arrive for another hour. Store your bags inside and let's walk over to Kipris for breakfast."

Marcus remembered it as the restaurant they had stopped at on their way to Kremasti. "I wonder if it will be safe for us to go there."

Sally raised a curious eyebrow. "Why not?"

Marcus then briefed her about the extraordinary series of events that brought them to Sparta: being shot at, the trek from Kremasti to Niata, driving a hotwired car to Athens, their hotel rooms being ransacked… "I had to ditch the rental car. That's why we took a taxi from Athens."

"My god, Marcus! You steal one car and abandon another? You have become a fugitive. You can never leave the country without being arrested. You will go to jail for sure."

All this time Eleni had said nothing but she found her voice. "What can we do?"

"Let me think. This is a lot of information you dumped on me in a few minutes. For one thing I will Telex Prager to retrieve that rental car. You said you left the keys in it?"

"Yes."

"Thank goodness Greeks are not as lawless as you appear to be. No one would steal it. I'm sure the car is still parked where you left it. Tell me where so Prager can have it returned. At least we can erase that off your list of crimes."

"Thanks."

"I feel strongly that you have to face this head-on. You can't keep running and you can't keep hiding."

"What do you think we should do?"

"Go back to Kremasti. Try to get to the bottom of what is going on. Eleni is better off staying with me. Take my car. Do you think you can find your way?"

"One way in and one way out. How can I go wrong?"

"Beware of Greek drivers. They are not timid."

"I haven't met anyone yet who is," Marcus replied.

The trip had plenty of ups and downs because of the rocky road but it was pleasant to have an American car to drive. Marcus reached Kremasti at nine fifteen and parked as close as he could to the square, the oversize Chevy looking as out of place as a spaceship.

He walked the now familiar path to the Stathos house. Everything was quiet, almost too quiet. He climbed the porch and tapped on the closed door.

The door swung open and his mother looked out at him in astonishment. Then she stepped outside and shut the door behind her. She gripped Marcus by his shoulders. "My son! You are safe!" Tears welled in her eyes. She looked beyond him. "Where is Eleni?"

"With Sally Haggerty. Don't worry, she is safe." He went on to explain what had happened since he and Eleni left, dressed in village clothes with their backpacks. He spared her the grossest details, knowing it would be difficult for her to follow and would unnecessarily frighten her. The important news for her to grasp was that her son and Eleni were fine.

"Can't we go inside?" he asked.

She hesitated. "I have to tell you something."

"What is it?"

"Dimitri had a stroke."

"Oh my god," Marcus said. The heavy burden Dimitri had been carrying finally was too much for his frail body to manage.

"Where is he?"

His mother led him inside the house. Caliope was sitting on a stool by the bed. Seeing Marcus through the doorway she jumped to her feet and came out, putting her hands to her mouth to stifle a cry of relief. Taking a fresh intake of breath, Marcus explained that Eleni was safe in Sparta and would fill her in later but right now the important question was, how is Dimitri?

Marcus looked into the bedroom to see his uncle covered up to his chin with a blanket. A small pillow propped up his neck keeping his throat in a straighter line to facilitate breathing. Even so, air rasped in and out of a dry, open mouth. His eyes were closed and the skin stretched over the sharp bridge of his nose was deathly pale.

"Is there a doctor?" Marcus asked.

"He drove up from Niata yesterday. He did what he could. In the meantime, Dimitri must rest."

"Is he conscious?"

Mrs. Giannou shook her head.

Caliope returned to the stool and her vigil. The woven seat creaked in a cadenced rhythm as she crossed herself over and over. Her lips moved in prayer, and every now and then Marcus heard a word audible enough to understand. The look on her face told him all he needed to know about her agony.

Marcus and his mother went outside and sat on the whitewashed steps.

"We need to get him to a hospital," he said.

"This is not America, Marcus. Besides the doctor told me it would be too hard on Dimitri to drive over the rough roads. Imagine what it would be like for him. He would not make it."

"What happened when Eleni and I left? Do you think that had anything to do with his stroke?"

"It was hard on him to see her leave but it was the treatment from Kostas."

"What did he do?"

"He came later on the morning you left. We told him that Eleni and you had left with the icon. I thought Kostas was going to go crazy. He ranted and raved, he shook with rage. I never saw a man act like that before. Poor Dimitri was trembling.

"And then he collapsed?"

"Not immediately. Later that morning, Dimitri began to complain that he did not feel good. His face lost its color. Then his eyes kind of disappeared into his head. It was frightening to see. He sank to the floor—did not cry out, did not sigh, he just sank."

They sat side by side on the steps, looking out at the yard and in the distance the white campanili of the church reaching above the trees.

"Thank god you are back. It has been a terrible ordeal."

"We walked into a mess, didn't we?"

Footsteps along the hard dirt path interrupted their conversation. Marcus looked past his mother's shoulder and saw a man carrying a small bag cautiously making his way along the uneven terrain. He turned into the yard and Marcus and his mother rose to their feet as he approached.

"*O yios mou,*" she said to the doctor. My son.

He stared through steel-rimmed spectacles at Marcus and nodded soberly. He climbed the steps and went inside the house.

He returned after a few minutes.

"There is nothing more I can do," he said in Greek. "Make sure Kyrie Stathos gives him the digitalis I left. She is so distraught she may forget about it."

"You will return?"

"A woman is ready to deliver in Maoli. I will try to stop by before returning to Niata."

Caliope appeared at the doorway and reached for the doctor's arm in heavy silence and pulled him back inside the house. Marcus and his mother followed, squeezing into the bedroom.

Dimitri's eyes were open, staring ceilingward. His hands were clutching the blanket on his chest and he was desperately trying to say something. Caliope dabbed his brow with a wet cloth. Dimitri's desperation grew as his voice became caught on the sharp edges of his rasping breath.

"*Mystras!*" he cried out.

His body settled slowly and the color drained from his face.

Marcus thought he had died. The doctor quickly drew his stethoscope from his bag and probed Dimitri's chest for a heartbeat. Presently he straightened. "His heart is stable. He will rest now."

The doctor left a small vial of sleeping pills for Caliope who was near exhaustion, but she refused to take one offered by Mrs. Giannou.

"Please, you must sleep a little. I will be here."

Caliope shook her head no and kept her lonely vigil in the bedroom while mother and son went to the kitchen.

Mrs. Giannou sliced bread and kasseri cheese and poured wine for Marcus

"Mom," he asked between bites, "what is Mystras?"

"A monastery near Sparta."

"Did you see the way Dimitri willed himself into consciousness to utter that one word? What is so important about it? Tell me."

"Wait for a better time."

"Mom, there is no better time. What if he dies?"

The question was blunt but had to be asked. She nodded. "Caliope is the person you should talk to, not me. But don't push too hard."

Marcus returned to the bedroom. Caliope was holding Dimitri's bony hand and staring at him fixedly.

"Theia," he said softly in Greek. "May I talk to you?"

"What is it, Marcus?" she whispered.

He got down on his haunches and balanced himself by holding on to the frame of the bed. Dimitri's breathing was raspy, but not as forced as it was before.

"Dimitri seems better." Marcus wanted to sound hopeful. "He will get well."

"I hope you are right."

"Theia," he continued, "Why did Dimitri say Mystras?"

Caliope concentrated on pulling her dress across her lap as though pondering where to begin. "I must start with the war," she said, recalling memories that can never be erased from her mind. "I will always remember Monday, October 28, 1940, the day Italian soldiers invaded our beloved Greece. They were beaten back by our valiant soldiers but the Germans came with their panzers and finally defeated us. The Nazis treated our homeland as though it was their own, raiding our museums and monestaries, helping themselves to anything they wanted. The monks at Mystras were worried about their precious icon, the Virgin of Theophanes…"

"The icon in Eleni's bedroom?" Marcus asked. "Is that where it came from, Mystras?"

Caliope nodded. "They were afraid if they hid it the Nazis would still find it so they gave it to to Anna Koulouris"

"Eleni's mother," Marcus confirmed.

"She was a student staying in the village above Mystras. She was allowed to visit the monestary to research Byzantine art. They could trust her to return the icon when the Germans were finally driven off our land. But she died giving birth to Eleni." Sadness enveloped Caliope like a shroud.

"Why did she come to Kremasti?" Marcus asked gently. "Did she know anyone here?"

"No. She was brought here."

"Who brought her?"

"Kostas."

Marcus stared in shock. "Kostas?" This was so incredible he couldn't believe it was true or, worse yet, Caliope was getting dementia and her mind was wandering. "Anna knew him?"

"They met at Mystras. He was a novice studying for the priesthood. I was a midwife. He was looking for privacy for Anna, away from Sparta to a small village where she was not known."

Marcus found it difficult to reconcile the two images of Kostas: one a disciple of God and the other a disciple of greed. If his goal, even then as a young man, was to steal the icon he could not have found a better place to hide it until he was ready: a girl's bedroom in a remote village. He simply bided his time, knowing the icon would not be discovered. When Eleni grew into womanhood he could claim the icon by claiming her. Eleni had a rich dowry and did not even know it.

But was there more to the relationship between Anna and Kostas than the icon? It was fascinating to speculate about two young persons, an American student and a Greek novice, in a time of war, when there were no guarantees. He imagined them as unformed, uncertain about themselves in an uncertain world. No one knew how the war would end and each day could be their last. As his imagination continued on this course, Marcus conjured up an image of Anna and Kostas possibly becoming young wartime lovers. The image took a moment to settle in to realize the consequences if such a relationship had actually happened. It hit him like an unexpected blow. Could Kostas actually be Eleni's father?

The mere thought made his flesh crawl. Could this be? Kosta fathered Eleni and then, when she is a young woman, become engaged to her? It was a plotline out of Sophocles. Is this why everyone is so fearful of Kostas? Marrying Eleni would be incest of the severest kind. It was not uncommon in Greek villages for cousins to marry, but a father and child? Impossible. No one, not even Kostas, could be so depraved.

Caliope was trying to read the alarmed look on his face. "What is the matter, Marcus?"

"Oh, nothing, Theia, nothing." He kissed Caliope on her wrinkled cheek and returned to the kitchen, drawing the separating curtain to the parlor behind him. His mother was sitting at the table. "Did you find out about about Mystras?"

"Yes, Mom, maybe more than I want to know." He was about to elaborate when there was a tiny tapping at the front door. Marcus's mother got up to see who it was. A girl of six or seven came in carrying a wood pail covered with a wet cloth. She was wearing a homespun dress and a shawl over her head. When she saw Marcus she acted surprised and a bit confused. She apparently wasn't expecting to find him there.

"This is Ourania," his mother said, "Athena's daughter."

At last Marcus met the mystery child who was either asleep or absent whenever he was in Athena's house. She was pretty in an anemic sort of way. Wrists so thin you could almost circle them with a wedding band and legs showing disproportionately large knee joints. He felt sorry for her. Like her widowed mother, Ourania also faced a future of limited opportunity.

"Ei mietera mou efiaxai yaourti," Ourania said in a tiny, tinkling voice.

Mrs. Giannou lifted the wood pail of fresh yogurt onto the counter. "Thank your mother. We will have it later with dinner."

"Ohi," the little girl said, reaching for Mrs. Giannou's arm. "Please have some now."

"Later, my dear. I will put it by the north wall where it will stay cool."

The girl shook her head and her eyes darted between Mrs. Giannou and Marcus. Then she spun on her heels and ran out of the house.

Mrs. Giannou shook her head. "Silly child, yogurt will not spoil."

"Just a minute." Marcus picked up the pail by its metal handle and set it on the table. "There was something suspicious about the way Ourania insisted that we eat it now."

His mother was slightly exasperated. "All right if you want some, I will get plates."

"No, I just want to look under the cloth. He lifted it and the pungent odor of fresh yogurt filled the air. The smooth yellowish top had a slit in it as though someone had stabbed it with a knife. "Mom hand me a spoon."

Mrs Giannou gave him a spoon from the cutlery tray assuming Marcus was going to taste it but instead he poked into the slit and separated it.

"What are you doing? You are spoiling the yogurt."

As she admonished him, he pulled out a slip of paper that had been hidden in the yogurt and wiped it clean on a napkin.

"What is that?"
"A note."
He read the Greek words:

Kyrie Giannou:
You must know where Eleni is. It is essential that I see her. Tell her she must come alone.
I have her documents. Number 45 Zografu,
Apartment 16, Sparta. I will be waiting.
Kostas

"When did he write this?" Mrs. Giannou asked.

Marcus thought a moment. "How long does it take to make yogurt?"

"At home I boil the milk and it sets overnight but here it is made with milk fresh from the goat, warm but not hot, so it takes longer. Two days."

"That means Kostas wrote this the same day Eleni and I left, and gave it to Athena to put in the yogurt after it set."

"But why write a note and then hide it? Why didn't he just talk to me?"

"Kostas could not say anything with Drovich around. What he did not expect was that I would be here when Ourania delivered the note. Remember the look on her face when she saw me?" He stood. "Mom, I have to get back to Sparta and find out what Kostas is up to."

"Please be careful, my son. Remember, Kostas wants to see Eleni alone."

18

Number 45, a three-story apartment building jammed into a narrow lot, was typically Greek modern, a far cry from the classicism that made Greece great: cement block construction coated with rough masonry and painted a pale pink. The main entrance was landscaped with flowerbeds and low-growing shrubs.

In this neighborhood, Eleni appeared out of place wearing the fashionable dress she got in Athens. She turned at the doorway and waved to him, not knowing what to expect but feeling safe with Marcus waiting nearby.

He drove to the end of the block, turned left, and made a U-turn before parking in the shade of boulevard palms where he could watch the building in relative obscurity.

Sitting in the shade with the windows down, his elbow hanging out, the radio turned to a music station, he reflected on his quick trip to Kremasti. Caliope had shed tears of fear and uncertainty as she bade him goodby even though he assured her that he will take good care of Eleni and everything will be all right. Marcus made good time driving back to Sparta. He drove like a native Greek.

Sally was surprised to see him back so soon until he showed her the note scented with yogurt. She let him use the Chevrolet again to drive Eleni to Zografu Street as long as he promised to keep US government property out of sight.

He had made the decision not to tell Eleni about Dimitri's stroke, at least for the time being. No need to worry her if she was helpless to see her father. Now that the icon was "in protective custody," as Sally referred to her office safe, and they couldn't do anything until they heard back from the American Embassy, there was nothing to do but wait. Not only that, Eleni was seeing Kostas to get her documents. That's what his note said. Everything was coming together. So why not return to Kremasti? Think how Dimitri will react when he hears Eleni say, "I'm home." Marcus smiled with satisfaction. Things are working out after all. He will cash in some traveler's checks, hire an overland taxi and head back to Kremasti where they belong.

Marcus relaxed, feeling much better, but time passed grudgingly and the longer he sat in the car the less confident he became. He began glancing at his watch. After twenty-five minutes he decided to give Eleni five more and if she did not appear he would go fetch her. Now that he was counting seconds, time seemed to stand still. To hell with it, he said aloud, and got out of the car. He crossed the intersection against traffic inviting a honk or two, his mind clouded with worry, and headed for the apartment building, simmering in the afternoon sun.

As he approached the entrance he became aware of the distant sound of a siren—the two-note signal used by European cop cars and ambulances. The persistent *da-da, da-da, da-da* got louder and louder. Marcus stopped walking and waited for the siren to commit itself or fade away.

It did not fade away. In another moment, the *da-da*s reached a crescendo punctuated by screeching tires as a black and white police car burst into view, careening around the corner at high speed. It slammed to a stop in front of the apartment building. The doors burst open and four policemen jumped out, drawing their pistols and shouting in such rapid Greek that Marcus could not understand them.

They ran past him into the building, and it was quiet again—eerily quiet, the siren choked off, the police car sitting in the street more abandoned than parked, the two doors on the curbside hanging open.

In spite of the hot sun, Marcus felt a cold shudder run down his back. He ran to the entrance, pulled the glass door open and entered a foyer with mailboxes and a bench. He heard the impact of heavy feet running along the terrazzo hallway on the secnd floor. Marcus reached the stairway as an officer was coming down.

He asked what was happening in Greek but the officer gave no indication of having heard him and ran outside to the police car. Marcus saw him through the front window making a call on his two-way radio.

Marcus climbed the stairs and looked down the hall. At the far end several residents were standing in a tight knot looking into the apartment whose door had been broken through, barely hanging by its hinges. A brass plate attached to the frame gave the number: 16.

His body trembling, Marcus walked toward them, and using the advantage he had over most Greeks, being several inches taller, he looked above the sea of heads and into the apartment. What he saw made his heart clutch. Eleni was sitting on a sofa—her eyes, wide with fright, were darting back and forth between two officers who were firing questions at her. He separated the knot of bystanders using his shoulder as a wedge and stepped into the room. What he saw next was even more frightening: on the floor as though forgotten lay a body covered by a bed quilt hastily thrown over it. One thin hand was visible and the scalp of a bony head. Blood was oozing out, staining the threadbare carpet. Even without seeing the rest of him, Marcus knew who it was. Kostas was lying dead under the quilt.

When Eleni saw Marcus she jumped from the sofa, separating her inquisitors and rushing to him. She clutched his shoulders in desperation. Her skin was as cold as a frosted windowpane. Her face swam in tears as she tried to tell him something, her hysteria and rapid Greek too much for him to comprehend.

Marcus looked past her at the inscrutable faces of the Greek officers who were staring back at him, wondering no doubt who was this man who suddenly appeared out of nowhere.

One of the officers, wearing white stripes on his black collar, tried to separate them. The more he tried to insert his arm between their bodies the harder Eleni gripped Marcus.

"*Ella, deh,*" he said, his voice rising with impatience.

"Do you speak English?" Marcus asked trying to keep his voice from quavering.

The officer looked at him in surprise. "Americanos?"

Marcus nodded. "Can you just let her be for awhile? Give her a chance to pull herself together?"

The officer smiled, a half-twist of his mouth. His beard was so heavy it seemed to grow before Marcus's eyes. The officer's own eyes were hard and calculating, mean and unrelenting.

"Impossible," he said in excellent English, "there has been a crime here." He pointed at the body.

Eleni pulled her head from Marcus's shoulder and looked down at Kosta. She cried out. There was no comforting her. Marcus held her to him, a couple in the eye of a hurricane of policemen.

Eleni and Marcus were locked together in a kind of impasse until the fourth officer returned with a man carrying a medical bag, apparently the coroner.

The officer in charge told the onlookers to return to their rooms and pushed the door against its battered frame. He turned and barked an order to the coroner who busily opened his satchel and brought out a plastic bag containing a syringe and a small bottle with a cork. It happened so fast Marcus had no time to protest or to protect Eleni. The doctor filled the hypo and poked the needle into her trembling arm.

She shrieked, a continuous sound that slowly lost its power as the drug took effect. She began to sag in Marcus's arms and gently he guided her rubbery feet around the body and to the sofa. She was fighting the hypo but her motions were getting cottony and formless. Presently she lay still, her breathing labored but regular.

"What did you do to her?" Marcus demanded.

"A mild tranquilizer. She will be fine in a few minutes. Only to calm her down... hysterical women...." He let his words hang, which was enough to irk Marcus, insinuating how Greek men, especially those in authority, dismiss women.

"Now that she is quiet, may I have your name?"

"Marcus Giannou."

"Passport?"

In his confused state Marcus had to think a moment "Oh, yes" he withdrew his passport from his shirt pocket and handed it over.

The officer leafed through the pages. Marcus expected him to return the passport but he held onto it.

"My passport..."

"In due time. Who is the girl?"

"Eleni Stathos. She lives in Kremasti."

"Why were you in Sparta?"

"We came to visit..." Marcus glanced down at the body. "...him."

"We?"

"Well, Eleni did. I dropped her off and parked."

"I saw no car."

"Around the corner."

"The victim? You know him?"

Marcus nodded. "Kostas Kanellos."

"Is there a relationship?"

"She was engaged to him." Marcus looked down at the body.

The officer leaned over and lifted the blanket to expose what was left of Kostas' head.

"He was shot at close range."

Marcus winced, wondering if the officer was trying to intimidate him, even frighten him, to make him say something careless, incriminating. He had to be careful what he said.

He tried to distract himself by looking around at the apartment, seeing it finally for the first time: cheaply made furniture one would see in a cut-rate motel, like the sofa Eleni was lying on. Above it on the wall was a seascape print of the Mediterranean. Draw curtains shaded the windows and a kitchenette off a short hall ended at a bedroom so narrow only a twin bed would fit in it.

"Kyrio Giannou…is that correct?"

"Yes."

"May I introduce myself? I am Captain Tsatsos of the Sparta Police. Now then, what was the purpose of her visit?"

"Business."

"Monkey business?"

One of the officers chortled. He apparently also understood English. The Medical Examiner had pulled the blanket off Kostas' body and Marcus tried to keep from looking but he could not. It was Kostas all right even though much of his face was missing and what was left was covered with blood.

"Mr. Giannou, let me emphasize that the young woman…"

"She is my cousin."

"Then you should be even more concerned. She is in serious trouble unless you explain to me why she happened to be found in an apartment with a dead man."

"He left a note." Marcus pulled it out of his trouser pocket and handed it to the officer.

Tsatsos wrinkled his nose. "Where was this?"

"In a pail of yogurt."

He waved the slip of paper as if airing it out. "You certainly are lending an air of mystery to this case," Tsatsos said in Greek over the laughter of his fellow officers. "Now, if you please," he said, returning to English, "tell me why the note was delivered in such a manner?"

"Kostas did not want anyone else to see the note."

"Even though it states that she was to come alone, you were with her."

"I waited in the car."

"How long was she in the apartment?"

"About a half hour."

"Half hour?" Tsatsos repeated. "What went on during that half hour?"

"I don't know."

"You don't know?" Tsatsos repeated. He was getting under Marcus's skin.

"That's why I was heading for the apartment when you showed up."

"You wanted to find out was going on, is that it?"

"I was worried about her."

"You were worried about her?"

"Yes!"

"Maybe you were coming into the building because you knew the job was finished."

"Job? What job?"

"The murder. You knew the victim was dead by that time and since the girl had not come out, you decided to go in and get her."

"What are you suggesting? That I...that Eleni had anything to do with this?"

Tsatsos shrugged noncommittally

"This is crazy. Where is your proof?"

"Proof?" Tsatsos said as though this was so obvious even Marcus could understand.

"If you want proof, how about a gun? If she shot Kostas there has to be a gun and I don't see one anywhere."

Tstatsos glanced at the open window, the curtains billowing slightly in the breeze.

"After she shot the victim, she threw the gun out the window where you conveniently picked it up."

Such an extravagant lie could not go unchallenged. "And what would I have done with it?"

Tsatsos shrugged as though this was not a problem. "We have a corpus delecti, we have a pretty young woman standing over the body, we have a handsome young man waiting outside. Are you with me so far?"

Marcus stared mutely.

"You said that the girl and the deceased were engaged. He appears to be fifty or sixty…"

"Fifty-five."

"…As I said, a man of fifty or sixty. Quite an age difference, even for Greeks. So why would a stylishly dressed young woman want to marry an ordinary old man, especially if she is in the company of an American with whom she is obviously in love?"

"Captain, this is crazy!"

He gave Marcus a contemptuous smile. "We all witnessed a very loving reunion when you entered the room, Kyrio Giannou. The young lady gripped you as a leather glove would grip a hand."

"She was hysterical. She saw a man get killed. I am the only one she knows here. That is all there is to it."

"Perhaps so, perhaps not. It is for the Court to decide."

"What Court?"

"The Court of Penal Justice where I will present my case and where Miss Stathos will present hers."

The blood drained from Marcus's head with such speed he felt faint and had to lean against the wall. Tsatsos held out his arm but Marcus shook it off. This was all a dream, no a nightmare, and it would disappear when he woke up in his apartment on Columbia Pike in Alexandria, Virginia. Surely he would wake up, wake up, wake up…

"Kyrio Giannou, are you all right? Should I have the doctor give you some ammonia?"

Marcus shook his head. "No," he said, "I'm ok, just not used to bad jokes."

"If it is a joke, Kyrio Giannou, we all would be laughing, including the corpse. This is a serious matter and you will have to come with us."

Marcus stared at the inscrutable face of the Captain trying to read what was behind it. Nothing—a sheet of blank paper. "Am I under arrest?"

"Yes. You and the young woman."

"She did not come here to kill Kostas. That is absurd. Does she look like someone who could use a gun, let alone have one with her?"

"There is ample circumstantial evidence," Tsatsos said cryptically.

"What about motive?"

"As I said, a handsome young man, an attractive young woman, an older man…"

"Are you suggesting a love triangle?"

"Love triangles as you call them happen all the time. Our prisons are full of hypotenuses." He translated for his fellow officers who roared with fawning laughter.

"What about the documents?"

"What documents?"

"Eleni's birth certificate and the passport of her mother, who was an American citizen. These are the documents Kostas mentioned in his note."

"This smelly little note?" More laughter but it stopped as soon as Tsatsos asked his men in rapid-fire Greek if they found any documents.

They shook their heads. "We searched the apartment."

Marcus straightened, towering over the men. He looked at Eleni breathing heavily, her body flattened out on the sofa and, on the carpet worn nearly bare lay Kostas, not breathing at all. "The documents are in a manila envelope, legal size, worn around the edges."

"I will give you the benefit of the doubt," Tsatsos said almost sypathetically. "If you care to search the premises, be my guest." He held out his hand like a maître de showing the way to the best table.

Marcus randomly began to open cupboards and drawers, lift carpet corners and look behind the seascape on the wall. The whole thing was a charade, a joke, to make Marcus look bad, but he had been backed into it and now had to play the game. Doggedly he walked into the bedroom with Tsatsos following him. Marcus opened the dresser drawers, all empty, and poked around the sheets of the unmade bed, forcing back a lifting bile as an unpleasant body smell was released into the air. The closet was bare.

"Doesn't look as if he actually lived here," Marcus said.

The offhand comment played into Tsatsos' hands. "The apartment was used as a trysting place, perhaps."

Frustrated, Marcus pulled the sheet off the mattress and shook it, holding his head out of the way. Then he pushed on the pillows and looked under the mattress. Tsatsos was losing interest and returned to the living room to talk to the Medical Examiner who appeared to be wrapping up his investigation.

As Marcus lifted the mattress to expose the springs, he noticed a wood frame with hinges on the floor. He dropped to his knees and pulled the frame out from under the bed. It was a folded-up easel. He looked under the bed again and found a long narrow metal box used by artists to store tubes of paint and brushes, and a palette with dried circles of paint. He opened the cover. Inside were paint tubes, some partly rolled up, some new, spotted with blotches of pure color. Their names printed in English were as rich as the colors themselves: burnt umber and yellow ochre, cadmium red and raw sienna, terra verte and titanium white, cobalt blue and manganese violet. There were also brushes of various sizes.

He swept his hand under the bed for one last check and his fingers bumped a piece of cardboard. He pulled out a square of illustration board with four pushpins securing a page cut from what looked like an art catalog. Marcus stared. The illustration was of an icon, a familiar one. My god, he thought, Theophanes' Virgin!

Just then Tsatsos yelled from the front room, "Almost done, Kyrie Giannou?"

"Almost." Quickly Marcus unpinned the image from the illustration board, folded the page and slipped it into his pocket, trying to make sense of what he found. Art supplies and a quality reproduction can only mean one thing: making a forgery. Is this why Kostas was killed?

Tsatsos returned wondering, no doubt, what was keeping Marcus, and saw the easel and the paint box on the floor.

"What is this?" he shouted. "What are you handling?"

Tsatsos grabbed Marcus by his shirt collar and roughly pulled him away from the bed. Still on his knees, Marcus went sprawling on the floor, his head glancing off the edge of the dresser, stunning him.

Tsatsos, now in a fury, shouted an officer's name. The officer rushed in, his face caked with fright. Tsatsos angrily held up the paint box and dropped it on the bed. Some of the tubes of paint fell out.

"Did you search in here?" he shouted in Greek.

"*Nai, nai!*" an officer cried out in panic.

"Then why didn't you find these instead of leaving it to the idiot American? *Boufos!*"

"I am sorry, my Captain," he quaked. "The room appeared empty…"

"Your head is empty!" Tsatsos thundered. He looked down at Marcus who was rubbing his bruised head.

"Put him in handcuffs!"

He stormed out of the bedroom.

19

Marcus was marched outside between two of the officers, held by his upper arms, his wrists handcuffed, stumbling to keep up and desperately trying to clear his mind, still in a jumble not only from the harsh treatment but also a headache from hitting the dresser. He was shoved into the back seat of the squad car, now heated up from sitting in the sun. Perspiration ran down his forehead. He looked through the windshield and saw Eleni being carried out in the arms of another officer and placed on one of two stretchers in the rear of the Medical Examiner's van. Shortly after, two other officers brought out Kostas's body covered in a gray zippered bag and placed him alongside Eleni.

My God, Marcus thought, they are making her ride with the body! What if she wakes up and sees him lying next to her! He squirmed in the back seat, pulling on the handcuffs wanting to help her. He cried out in dismay at his helplessness.

Tsatsos, still fuming with anger over the ineptness of his officers, came outside and looked at Marcus through the window. "Where is your car?"

"Around the corner. A gray Chevy."

"As in Chevrolet?" he said snidely. "Expensive rental."

"It belongs to the US government."

Tsatsos grinned, his anger shifting from high to low now that he had Marcus to toy with. "Stolen?"

"No, borrowed!"

"Get the keys," Tsatsos ordered the officer standing next to him.

The officer reached through the window. Marcus lifted his hip and said, "back pocket," to make sure the officer would not begin searching his pockets and discover the page with the icon.

As the officer walked off with the keys, Marcus said to Tsatsos, "The car is the property of the American Library. Will you return it?"

"Return it?" Statsos replied. "I am confiscating it as evidence." He was grinning now, his anger replaced by satisfaction that he had Marcus where he wanted him.

They drove in silence, the windows down, hot air blowing on them to a police station on the outskirts of Sparta, in a neighborhood of dried-out buildings and dusty parking lots. There were no trees, no shrubs—an area shorn of beauty. They parked in front of a cinderblock building whose whitewash glowed in the sun. There were narrow slits of windows and an entrance with a sign above it reading *Sparti Astynomia*, informing Marcus that he was entering the Headquarters of the Sparta Police.

The van with Eleni and the deceased, which had been following them, went around the back and disappeared,

Marcus was led to a chair in the anteroom and his handcuffs were removed. Across from him on the wall hung a framed color photograph of Pappathopoulos. His smiling face told Marcus what a bad boy he was.

He looked away in disgust. In the corner, hanging from a stand like a limp dishcloth was the flag of Greece. It needed dry cleaning. Official business was being conducted at a raised desk, but he did not pay any attention to the Greek being spoken. For one thing his head still hurt and for another he was worried about Eleni. More than worried, he was really troubled. If he was being treated like this what could now be happening to her?

Finally Tsatsos came over. "As an American citizen, Kyrio Giannou, you will be treated fairly."

"If you are treating me fairly because I am an American citizen, then you have to give Eleni the same consideration."

Tsatsos raised an eyebrow, but not too far.

"Her mother was born in America. Her documents prove that."

"Ah, the so-called documents."

"Her birth certificate and her mother's passport. They were stolen by Kostas Kanellos."

"Where?"

"A hotel in Athens."

"A hotel?" Tsatsos repeated, getting more and more interested.

Marcus did not answer, realizing he saying too much. "I want to talk to someone in the American Embassy."

"Do you have a particular person in mind?"

"Arthur Prager, Consular Section."

Tsatsos nodded. "I will, as you say, use PR and try to reach him for you."

Fortunately for Marcus, Prager was at his desk. He yelled into his phone, "Giannou, what in hell have you gotten yourself into?"

Marcus told him. Prager listened patiently, interrupting occasionally for clarification, as Marcus recounted how he got to where he was, the Sparta Police Station. Tsatsos was taking this all in but Marcus did not care nor did he think it would make any difference since all of this would have to come out in his defense, so Tsatsos might as well hear it now as later.

"You said Kanellos was murdered?" Prager asked.

"In his apartment here in Sparta. He had left a note for Eleni to meet him there."

"Big trouble, you are both in big trouble. Where is the girl?"

"Somewhere in this prison where I'm at. She is not in good shape, and I know she did not kill Kostas."

"You don't have to convince me, it's Tsatsos you have to convince. And he's tough. I've heard of him. You would have the rotten luck of being in his jurisdiction."

"What can you do?"

"I'll fire off a cable to your Senator. In this case, Tolson is a plus. We may be able to work something out between our ambassadors."

"VIP status?"

"Something like that."

"What about Eleni?"

"She doesn't have any status, VIP or otherwise."

"We have to help her."

"You better leave well enough alone. She's their property not ours."

"Wait a minute, Prager, the reason I'm here is for her."

"Not for her, Giannou, because of her."

"Prager..."

"I have work to do if I'm going to spring you out of there. Sit tight and forget about the girl. You're in enough trouble as it is and if you try to meddle in her problems you will only make things worse for yourself."

Prager hung up. Just like that he left Marcus dangling like the cord on the phone.

Tsatsos had a smile broad enough to lock his jaw.

"Ha, ha, ha!" Marcus said but he wasn't laughing. "I have to call Sally Haggerty about her car."

"Car?"

"The Chevrolet. It's US government property, remember?"

"In due time."

Marcus festered. "You keep saying that. She needs to know her car is safe."

"You should be more concerned about your own safety."

Marcus returned to his chair and sat for an hour until a guard brought him something to eat, a piece of lamb wrapped in pita bread with garlic sauce and a glass of water. The lamb tasted stale, even the sauce didn't help, but he had no other alternative. No one would take him to lunch at Kipris Estiatorio. He spent the afternoon waiting, trying to doze off in the stiff-backed chair but every time he nodded, the sore on his head jerked him awake. At four o'clock Prager called back.

"I have good news."

"I can't imagine any news that's good right now."

"You will. It took a ton of effort and I hope you appreciate it, Giannou. The Greek government will release you on one condition."

"What is that?"

"That you get out of Greece."

"You mean be deported?"

"Right away, as soon as I can spring you from jail. And don't ever show your smiling face in this land again."

"That's insane. I haven't done anything wrong."

"Maybe not, but the courts here can make anything stick. Would you rather stand on principle and go to prison for a year or two? Don't be a martyr."

Marcus asked, "What about my mother…"

"What about her?"

"She is in Kremasti. We flew on a charter and it doesn't leave for ten more days."

"Why didn't you tell me this?"

"How was I to know it was important till now?"

"You just complicated my life, that's all. I'll send a car down to pick you up. Tsatsos will let you go as long as I guarantee you stay in our Embassy. In the meantime we will contact your mother and get her to Athens so you two can fly home together."

"Why can't I go back to Kremasti?"

"Do you think Tsatsos will let you do that? Not a chance. Your only option is to hang out here in the Embassy. I have a nice cot for you in the marine guard quarters."

"But I can't abandon Eleni. What will happen to her?"

"She'll be tried for murder."

"And convicted?"

"No doubt."

"Oh my god. Then what?"

"A life sentence. There is no capital punishment in Greece. She will end up at Korydallos prison in Pireaus."

Marcus groaned.

"The Greek justice system likes neat packages. Eleni makes a neat package."

"Can you get Tsatsos to let me see her?"

"Take my advice, Giannou. Forget the girl. Her life is ruled by a society far different from ours."

"But can't I even see her to say goodbye?"

"That's up to Tsatsos. But be careful because you are not off the hook."

"What do you mean?"

"Once you are out of here you will be tried, too, in absentia."

"For what?"

"Ironically, for fleeing prosecution."

Marcus could not believe what he was hearing. "They are forcing me to leave the country so they can charge me with fleeing prosecuton? A Catch 22 if I ever heard one."

"I never said it was a perfect world, especially Greece. Put Tsatsos on. I'll ask if he will let you see the girl."

Tsatsos agreed to give Marcus five minutes with Eleni, a big concession but it probably was worth it to get Marcus out of his hair.

He told Marcus, "follow me," and led him down the corridor to the women's detention unit at the rear of the building. They came to a cellblock.

"I want you to see how well we accommodate our women prisoners so you Americans will not think of us as barbarians." He pointed to a corner cell. "Your lady friend has a window to let in the light." He laughed. "The window has bars of course. After all this is not the Conrad Hilton."

Marcus thought if he heard that phrase one more time he would throw up.

A uniformed matron unlocked the metal door to the cell and Eleni emerged as if sleep-walking.

"As you can see, she has recovered from the tranquilizer."

If standing erect was a sign of recovery then Tsatsos was right but it was heartbreaking to see Eleni now wearing a gray prison dress reaching her ankles and an ID wristband as wide as a dog's collar. Her shoulders sagged from the weight of the world, in her case, a world gone mad. She looked up when she neared Marcus, her face tear-streaked, her eyes filled with terror, her lips locked in a thin straight line.

Marcus sensed that she wanted to rush into his arms, but the matron had other thoughts. It was an awkward moment until they were escorted to an interrogation room and the door clicked behind them, obviously locking them in. Then Eleni hugged Marcus as though her life depended on it, and in a large way it did. The compact room contained a table and two chairs. The walls were lined with gray insulating material that had small indentations. Overhead was a light hanging by a cord. The space was bleak and forbidding and Marcus wondered what methods were used in here to make an inmate talk. Eleni shuddered because she no doubt was sharing those same thoughts.

Marcus pulled the chairs over so they could sit across from one another. Eleni lowered her head into her hands and wept.

He leaned over and put his lips close to her ear. "Speak English but softly in case they have hidden microphones."

She lifted her head wiping away tears and nodded in understanding.

"Can you tell me what happened in the apartment?"

Seconds passed before Eleni began whispering, obviously the memory still too close and too terrifying to make sense. She spoke randomly, recalling things as they came to mind. "The door was open a little...I peeked in...Kostas was standing in the middle of the room...nervous...I asked him what do you want...I have your papers...how did you get them...never mind...you stole them...I did not...I made a deal...what deal...the icon for your papers...tell me what deal...he got angry...shouting...there was a fight...I screamed...noise like someone hitting a pillow with a fist...Kostas falling...blood all over...police coming..."

She covered her face with trembling fingers. He realized he should not push further. Whatever was still locked in her mind was too awful to contemplate, too deeply imbedded in her subconscious to surface.

"It's all right, Eleni, it's all right." Even though he said this he knew it was not all right.

There was a moment of silence while they stared into each other's eyes, their faces physically inches apart but spiritually a chasm separated them—Marcus free to return to America, Eleni trapped in a merciless prison.

"It is hopeless," she moaned. "My life is over."

"No!" Marcus said defiantly, hoping his voice stunned the ear of anyone listening in on them. Then he whispered to Eleni: "It is *not* hopeless, it is *not* over."

"I wish I could believe you."

"I will get you out of here."

She leaned back to look at him fully. "How will you do that?"

"I don't know but I will. I promise."

"You will be caught and then you will suffer my fate."

He closed the physical difference between them and pressed his lips on hers.

"I could not live with myself," he whispered against her mouth, "if I left you in prison without trying to save you."

20

Watching Eleni escorted back to her cell, Marcus knew he had to act fast before she was emotionally destroyed, burdened forever by the hideous memories of prison brutality and degradation. Tsatsos had Eleni in his control, and Marcus had nothing but nightmarish images of what this sadistic jailer might do to her. In his unbridled frustration and impotence he wanted to charge the jail right now, like Don Quixote attacking a windmill, but his rational self calmed him down and he took his time surveying the exterior of the building while he was escorteded to the parking lot for a ride to the American Library.

He made a mental picture of what he saw. Police cars cooking in the sun were lined up along an eight-foot chain-link fence that met at the corners of the cinder-block jail. The windows were secured with vertical bars and the back door was guarded by an overweight and dozing security guard sitting on a folding chair shaded with what looked like a beach umbrella. It all had a casual and vulnerable appearance, and Marcus immediately thought of Kleftis. With his cleverness he ought to have something in his bag of tricks to break into an unsuspecting Sparta Police Department.

Sally was at her desk when he returned. She jumped up and embraced him, her fresh American smell seeming almost foreign to Marcus. "Thank god, you are safe. I heard from Prager. He is sending a car to pick you up tomorrow."

"What about your car?" He was asking about the impounded Chevy.

Sally laughed, a happy sound out of synch with how he felt. "Tsatsos likes to play the big shot. A call from our Charge d'Affairs in Athens put him straight. The car is parked in back where it belongs."

"At least something has gone right." Marcus drew from his pocket the page he found, unfolded it and gave it to Sally.

"What is this?" she asked.

"You tell me. Looks like it was cut from an art catalog."

Sally studied it carefully. "This is a high quality reproduction of Theophanes' Virgin. Where did you find it?"

"Hidden under the bed in Kostas' apartment, along with paint supplies and an easel. The page was pinned to a piece of illustration board. What do you make of it?"

"Well, if you ask me, I'd say Kostas was in the forgery business."

"What?"

"Looks like he got this reproduction to make a forgery. Why else would he have paint supplies and this reproduction together?"

"My god, maybe that is why he was killed."

Sally studied the page again. "This is a plate, no identification except a number, see there? Number 17 referring the reader to another section of the catalog. This must have come from a library, perhaps the National Library in Athens. It could be a catalogue raisonne."

"What is that?"

"A comprehensive listing of all the known works of a particular artist, in this case Theophanes."

"How could Kostas have gotten it?"

"With his connection to the government he could easily have borrowed the catalog. I'll see what I can find out. There would be a record of who checked it out and when. It may take a few days. Mind if I keep this?"

"No. I appreciate your help. But it is the least of my problems."

"You should be relieved, Marcus. Tsatsos let you go."

"I worry about Eleni."

Sally became somber. "I'm sorry. I know how you feel about her. I wish I could do something."

"You can. Let me borrow your car."

"Again?" she asked suspiciously. "Are you up to something?"

"I want to drive to Niata. There is a resistance cell there that Eleni is a part of and they have to know she is in the Sparta jail. Maybe they can do something to break her out of there."

Sally stared, her mind sorting through the implications of what he said.

"I just can't walk away and do nothing. I'll have your car back by morning."

"Marcus," Sally said emphatically, "if you get involved with those resistance people, there is nothing I or Prager can do to help."

"I am not expecting any. In fact, I don't want you to know about it. What time will Prager's driver pick me up?"

"Noon."

"I will have your car back before then."

"Maybe I should go with you."

"No, I have to do this alone."

Kleftis and Haralambos gave Marcus huge bear hugs when he showed up in the middle of the afternoon, even though he woke them from their naps in the dayroom of the Taverna.

After the greeting, all was serious. Occasionally corrected by Haralambos, Marcus used his improving Greek to bring the two compatriots up to date on what happened after leaving Niata in the dead of night: the unresolved meetings at the American Embassy and the Greek Consulate, abandoning the Simca, losing Eleni's papers in the robbery, making it to Sparta, Kostas murdered and, worst of all, Eleni locked in the Sparta jail.

The two men listened intently, their deep emotions revealed only through their eyes.

"Captain Tsatsos has an evil reputation," Haralambos said. "Ever since the junta took control, he has become the chief interrogator in this region. Eleni will be treated harshly. He will force her to tell him about our cell in Niata. Not only is she under threat, so are all of us. I do not see how she can withstand his techniques. We must get to her before he does."

Kleftis smiled grimly. "I know that jail. I have been in it."

"You have?"

Haralambos returned the smile. "He has been in many jails, but not for long."

"But not a woman's ward," Kleftis replied ruefully. "And that is where Eleni is imprisoned."

"I've seen it," Marcus said. "Tsatsos was showing off, bragging about how nice the the women prisoners are treated. Eleni's cell is in the corner and it has a window."

Kleftis became attentive. "It is an old building, badly built."

"What are you thinking?"

"We can rip out the window."

Marcus stared in disbelief. "How?"

"The car you drove here, what kind is it?"

"Chevrolet. I borrowed if from the American Library."

Kleftis grinned. "I have seen it on a visit by the attractive librarian. It has a solid bumper and an eight-cylinder engine. We will tie a cable from the bumper to the bars and hit the gas!"

Haralambos shook his head. "Kleftis, you have seen too many gangster movies. We will have the entire ESA after us. How many Chevrolets are there in Greece? Half a dozen, maybe, all belonging to the US government. How long before we are arrested, including Marcus and that librarian?"

Kleftis shrugged. "You have a better idea?"

Haralambos thought a moment. "No."

They fell into a troubled silence until Haralambos said, "We have to bribe a guard."

"That takes time and money, and we have neither."

"How about starting a fire?"

They laughed at the absurd direction of their conversation, struggling to find a way to free Eleni.

They fell into another silence.

Suddenly Marcus said, "The plant."

Kleftis stared questioningly. "Plant?"

"The dieffenbachia you told me about, the plant that makes you sick when you chew on it."

Kleftis's steely eyes glistened. "The dumb cane that sent my *compatrioti* to the hospital in Nafplion? If it worked there it will work in Sparta."

Their outlook went from madly impossible to wildly possible.

"We need someone to eat the dieffenbachia and create a diversion."

"Who will do that?"

"You said there is a guard who sits by the door in back."

"But how will we get the guard to eat the plant? Sprinkle it with sugar?"

"Then I will eat it," said Haralambos.

"You?"

"I will bite the plant and then run into the jail, creating a diversion. In the meantime, you overpower the guard in back, and rush in."

Kleftis shook his head. "Too risky. Besides we don't have enough manpower."

Again they fell into a protracted silence. Finally Kleftis said, "Eleni has to bite the plant."

Marcus could not add another layer of pain on top of what she already was suffering. "No, I can't do that to her."

"There is no other way."

Marcus reflected a moment and then said, "What would happen?"

"Painful burning as if her mouth was on fire. Then her face would get numb and she would start drooling. Her tongue would swell. All very unpleasant but not fatal."

Marcus thought about Eleni going through this. "I don't know…"

"What is the alternative? Torture by Tsatsos? It is the only way. Eleni has to bite the plant. She will scream. She will writhe in pain. She cannot help herself. The guards will come running. Guards are not only stupid, they are afraid for their jobs. If they lose a prisoner, Tstatos will torture them instead. So, they rush Eleni to the hospital and that is when we make our move."

"How do we get a plant into the jail and have Eleni chew on it?"

"We pass a leaf through her window with a note explaining that she has to bite the stem where the white juice is. The dieffenbachia will do the rest."

"What about the guard at the back door?"

"Knowing Greek guards, he will be fast asleep. If not I will make sure he gets that way," Haralambos replied, making a fist of his hand and smacking it into the palm of the other one.

Before getting serious again, they took a moment to relish the image of the guard taking a knockout punch.

"But where will we hide Eleni after the breakout? She has to go someplace where Tsatsos would never think of looking."

Devoid of ideas, Haralambos and Kleftis looked at Marcus.

He thought a moment and then broke into a wide grin.

"What are you thinking, my friend?"

"You said someplace Tsatsos would never think of looking?"

"Yes, of course."

"I've got it."

"Where?"

"Mystras."

21

Haralambos wrote a note on the outside of a plastic bag with a crayon using big letters so that Eleni could read without much light:

Eleni
Follow these instructions. Inside the bag is a stem. Bite it at the thickest part, then flush everything down the toilet. You will taste bitter juice that will make you sick but it will not harm you. You will scream from pain. The guards will take you to the hospital. We will be there to rescue you.

Kleftis had a closet filled with enough clothing to outfit the three men in black, like bank robbers or jewel thieves. They sat in the back room till two in the morning blending in the dark, exactly the way they wanted to appear, or disappear, while on their rescue mission. Nervous energy kept them from dozing. Haralambos constantly shifted his worry beads from finger to finger, reaching the end and starting over again. In the corner sat the freshly watered dieffenbachia plant, Kleftis's floral pride as well as his secret weapon. Just before they were ready to depart, he cut a fully grown leaf at the main trunk of the plant, the stem dripping white sap which he plugged with a damp bar cloth.

They followed the path behind the church where Marcus had parked the Chevrolet, climbed in and began their tense drive to Sparta, without lights till they reached the main road.

"You have enough petrol?" Haralambos asked, his face aglow from the dash lights.

"Yes," Marcus said, checking the fuel gauge. "The tank was full when I left the Library."

Sitting in back with a cloth sack containing a rope ladder and the dieffenbachia stem, Kleftis marveled at the interior of the car. "I haven't seen such luxury before," he said, rubbing his hand along the fabric.

"Our getaway car," Haralambos said, recalling Chicago's gangster era in an attempt at lightheartedness despite the heavy atmosphere. Even the air coming through the open windows, as cool and comfortable as it was on their bodies, nevertheless had an undercurrent of oppression.

They left the Chevy on a residential street two blocks from the jail and headed in the general direction of the Sparta Jail, giving it a wide berth and approaching it from the rear. The only streetlamps were at intersections, which they avoided, crossing instead in the middle of the block. They followed a narrow alley, passing garages and trash barrels, until they reached the chain link fence guarding the jail's parking lot. They crouched behind the line of squad cars and surveyed the scene, the security lights illuminating circles on the asphalt, the darkened cell windows, and interior cellblock lights visible through the slotted window of the back door. On the stoop was the folding chair and the large umbrella lowered for the night—but no guard. What a stroke of luck, they nodded in agreement.

Marcus pointed to the corner window. Kleftis nodded and opened the sack. With cool efficiency that truly impressed Marcus, Kleftis pulled out the rope ladder and the plastic bag containing the dieffenbachia leaf. He tossed the rope ladder over the fence and hooked it on the other side to the chain links. He clamped the handles of the plastic bag in his teeth and clambered up and over faster than a monkey peeling a banana. He ran to the wall, dodging the circles of light, leaped for a vertical bar in the window and pulled himself up till he could see into Eleni's cell.

Harsh whispers reached Marcus's ears, "Eleni Eleni! Read the note. We will save you!" Kleftis dropped the bag through the bars, fell to the ground and ran back to the fence. He clambered over and yanked the rope ladder behind him just as the rear door swung open and the guard came out stretching, apparently returning from a bathroom break, unaware that three men were crouched on the other side of the fence not twenty yards away.

Holding their breaths in an effort to contain racing hearts, they waited for a sign from Eleni, anything to let them know she had read the message, a wave from the window at least. If after a few minutes nothing happened they would return to the car and get out of town. If this was a hair-brained scheme none of them was willing to admit it.

Then, just as they felt they could wait no longer, a sudden shriek filled the air, so piercing and so alarming that even the trio who expected it were startled.

They waited long enough to hear the clatter of the big metal door being unlocked and see the light come on in Eleni's cell.

"Quickly, back to the car," Kleftis whispered. As they ran up the alley in the direction of the parked Chevy, all hell broke loose behind them. Guards were hollering, a squad car started up its engine and the big gate swung open. The police car sped down the alley, it's siren in a full-throated *da-da da-da.*

Kleftis directed Marcus to the hospital, *Geniko Nosokomeio*, a four-story stucco building with two wings separated by a courtyard. The emergency entrance was in back, where the police car, brakes suddenly locked, skidded to a stop. Two guards jumped out and carried a limp Eleni inside. Marcus, seeing her in obvious pain, parked the Chevy across the street. It was nearly three. They had to move fast and get her out of there before sunup.

Marcus stayed with the car while Kleftis and Haralambos walked around to the front entrance so as not to arouse suspicion. Marcus wondered what a Greek hospital other than those in the huge metropolitan area of Athens looked like. He imagined dimly lit hallways, mop-stained floors, blood-spotted sheets, but he would never know nor did he care. He just wanted Eleni out of there safe and sound.

The waiting was interminable. He nervously checked his watch every few seconds, resisting an impulse to run inside and see if he could help. Ten minutes passed before he spotted Klefits and Haralambos holding Eleni upright between them running around the back of the hospital. Marcus got out and opened the doors so they could climb in quickly. They lay Eleni across the back seat, and then Haralambos and Kleftis jumped in front with Marcus.

Marcus pushed back a desire to floor the gas pedal. Instead he drove slowly to the outskirts until it felt safe to speed up.

Eleni was starting to recover from her painful encounter with dumb cane even though she was having trouble speaking with a swollen tongue. Haralambos was humming a song to keep her calm. The fact that she had escaped Tsatsos's dungeon had yet to reach her consciousness. She trembled frequently, her eyes blinking, her nerves in shambles.

Marcus spoke up only to ask directions to Mystras while the two men tried to calm down from their daring rescue. Finally he could wait no longer. "How did you do it?" he asked.

Kleftis smiled. "A hospital in the middle of the night is no place for security. Small staff, the emergency room doctor and nurses on night duty."

"What about the guards who brought Eleni to the hospital?"

"You mean the two men locked in a utility closet, their mouths shut tight with hospital tape and their hands tied with rolls of bandages? Whatever we needed was right there in the hospital."

"But they saw you, they can identify you!"

Kleftis reached in his pocket and pulled out a surgical mask. "Not with these covering our faces."

The drive to Mystras was far from forgiving as Marcus punished the Chevrolet, its struts and shocks making odd noises over the rough roadbed. The government's motor pool mechanic will have to overhaul the suspension after this trip, he thought, as the rising sun revealed ahead of them the monastery that commanded the view of the valley they were now leaving behind.

Originally a medieval fortress dating back to the thirteenth century, Mystras clung to the side of a steep hill, sharing nature rather than interfering with it, blending into the environment unlike architecture that imposes itself like an invasive species. Not so Mystras.

Marcus parked at the foot of the hill where the road dead-ended. No vehicular traffic beyond this point.

They got out and stretched their taut muscles, the exhausting ordeal over for the time being, but what lay ahead was equally uncertain. Marcus was convinced this was the only safe haven available for Eleni even though she was a woman. Could the monastery, traditionally male, turn a fugitive away because of her gender?

What lay ahead for Eleni beyond the sanctuary of the monastery Marcus could only guess at or hope for. The State Department had to find a way to get her safely out of the country. Until then she would have to remain here. There was no other place to hide without threat of recapture and certain death.

Eleni was slowly recovering. Her tongue was no longer swollen from the effects of the plant poison, and her eyes once filled with fear were now filled with gratitude.

"How can I ever thank you?" she asked.

"Seeing you safe is thanks enough."

She looked down at her prison gown self-consciously. "I wish I had my nice clothes."

"I promise we will go shopping again," Marcus said, wishing he could do it right now—anything to lift her spirits.

The quartet climbed a stone stairway to a locked gate. Kleftis, being the monkey that he was, easily climbed over it, fell to the ground on the other side and unlocked the gate, ushering the others in like the doorman at a four-star hotel. In his own way, he too, was trying to make Eleni feel better.

They followed the path to a spacious square of ornately decorated buildings connected by arched porticos. Everything was old, very old. Dominating the square was the church, Agios Dimitrios, designed in the traditional drum shape, impressive yet humbling. The dome, encircled by arched clerestory windows, was tiled in a parched dull-red color. Extending from the church like arms on a body were interconnected brick-clad buildings with arched porticos. These, Marcus assumed, were the living quarters for the monks.

They saw no one this early in the morning as they walked across the baked earth to the church. It was eerily quiet—they felt as though they had entered a place of make-believe, a stage set. Nearing the entrance they heard a psalti chanting and an occasional chorus of *Kirie Eleison* coming from within.

There were no doors, only a wide, arched opening. Marcus signaled for the others to remain outside. He passed through the narthex, and took a metaphysical step backward to the time of Byzantium. In the shadowy nave, kneeling on the hard stone floor, were perhaps twenty-five monks in brown cassocks, their covered heads bowed, their prayerful bodies moving to the cadence of their prayers.

On the walls around them and from the dome above, covering every square foot of plaster, were frescoes of saints and holy figures glaring at the bowed backs with disdainful scowls as if warning them that no matter how hard they prayed they were still not yet good enough to enter God's glorious kingdom. By comparison, what chance would Marcus have? None.

Beyond the worshipers was the *ieron*, the chancel, where the solemn liturgy was being performed. He knew every word intoned by the priest and every response from the psalti. And why shouldn't he? He was not only raised Orthodox he was indoctrinated in it. The holy screen separating the chancel and the nave, the spiritual and the temporal, was called the *iconostasis* because it served as an exhibition wall for large iconic depictions of the life of Christ.

The priest stood before the altar, his robed arms lifted up in praise of God. The pungent smell of incense was overpowering to Marcus even though he stood in the rear of the nave. He stared overwhelmed by the scene and the powerful memories it evoked. Every Greek Orthodox Church in America was a direct copy of Byzantine architecture and iconography. Marcus was not only raised but also smothered in the Greek church, as an altar boy holding the cross and the candlesticks by the Bible stand for the priest, as a choir member, first as a tenor until his voice changed, singing the hymns and responses, as well as the weekly recitation of the Apostles' Creed. He had memorized words without a clear understanding of their meaning, Greek words permanently imbedded in his brain like nursery rhymes.

Up till this trip to Greece, he regarded his upbringing as an intrusion on his freedom, his Americanism. He grew to resent having the hollow rituals forced upon him. Born into this dichotomy, he was torn between two worlds, two cultures: urban America and rural Greece. He then flaunted and made fun of the autocratic customs and the mumbo jumbo superstitions of the church.

But now, in this moment, immersed in a medieval treasury of sound and sight, he felt ashamed of his attitude. The priest's untrained yet controlled baritone spilled out of the *ieron*, and sprinkled like a welcome shower upon the lowered heads of the brothers. The nave was an echo chamber of sound. Without engineering degrees or computers, stonecutters and masons knew how to create perfect acoustics. And the artists, following ancient practices, painted the saints and the holy figures in accusing attitudes so that mortal man knew precisely where he stood in the order of things.

Marcus suddenly felt devastated. For the first time in his life he had the sense of what his mother was trying to drill into him. For the first time he understood the full impact of what she, an immigrant, had left behind and always missed. But she couldn't transplant it to another garden, she could not hand down to her son the awesomeness, the everlasting beauty, the quiet force of her religion. Who was to blame? Marcus? His mother? He could not fault her for trying. And he could not be blamed for missing the point. Timing was off, distance was too great.

If he had been raised in Greece, he would have accepted and understood, he would have complied with her every wish and given in to her unreasonable demands. Marry a Greek girl, stay in the church, speak the language. He would have had no other choice.

He wanted to drop to his knees as the brothers before him, but too many years of resistance had locked them into an arthritic-like stubbornness and all he could do was show humility by bowing his head.

His deep thoughts were broken by the sound of tiny bells tinkling. The priest was now blessing the monks with the censer on whose chain the bells, symbolizing the preaching of the apostles, were ringing in cadenced rhythm. With practiced grace, the priest swung the censer back and forth, sparks of burning incense sent smoke aloft. His eyes met Marcus's for a split second as his gaze swept the congregants, and then he disappeared behind the screen. For the first time Marcus had an unobstructed view of the altar. It was solid marble and gleamed with pink and gray streaks. A gold chalice and paten were placed upon it, as was a row of gold candlesticks. Slim candles burned in perfect arrows of light. In the center of the altar, in the place usually reserved for the cross, in a position of honor rested a gold embossed frame meant to hold an icon.

But the icon was missing.

22

Following the dismissal prayer, the monks rose to their feet, crossed themselves and filed out, their sandals scraping the worn tiled floor. They did not acknowledge Marcus's presence, their heads were still bowed and their hands clasped in a beatific embrace of God.

Marcus remained in back waiting for the priest to emerge from the *ieron*. It was some time before he appeared, dressed now as his brothers were dressed: a simple habit with the cowl over his head and a sash tied around his waist. The habit was made of wool dyed a tan color. It seemed heavy for the weather but he showed neither discomfort nor perspiration.

He smiled cautiously as he approached Marcus. "Welcome," he said in Greek, "but may I ask how you got in? We have a locked gate."

"But easy to climb over."

"You have to be very determined," he said, "or you would not be here."

He was exceptionally large and taller than Marcus but how much taller he could not tell because the priest was bent at the waist. Maybe this was an affectation given the vows the priest had chosen, but then maybe he really was stoop shouldered, no doubt having to bend over when addressing his fellow monks because Greek men were generally shorter. Regardless, this made him seem particularly holy and spiritual. He straightened to his full height and pulled his head erect, revealing a face of ruddy complexion which surprised Marcus assuming that men whose dress code included hoods would have complexions resembling those of troglodytes. It was as if the monk were reading his mind.

"We spend much time in the sun tending to our garden and olive trees." He extended his hand. "I am called Yianni."

"Pater Yianni," Marcus said, addressing him as Holy Father. "May I speak with you?"

"Of course. But if you refer to me as Pater you must also use the same term with my fellow brothers. We are all equal here at Mystras."

"But you celebrated the *Litourgia*."

"We take turns. Today it was my turn to celebrate the Mass."

"And my name is Marcus Giannou."

"You are American?"

"My bad Greek gives me away."

"Not that bad. Even so, I knew before I heard you speak. I could see from the *ieron* that you are American."

"We have a special look?"

He smiled and nodded. "There is a bearing in the manner you carry yourselves, a sense of energy and self-confidence that are not as apparent in people of other nationalities."

"Have you met many Americans?"

"I studied Theology at Holy Cross School in Brookline, Massachusetts."

"You're kidding," Marcus said in English

"You find that unusual?" he answered, also in English.

"Maybe more lucky than unusual."

"I am pleased you feel lucky, but why should it make any difference if I spoke only Greek?"

"It is much easier to express myself to you."

"Shall we continue in English then?"

"Yes, please." Marcus stared at the monk named Yianni. "I have a favor to ask."

"How can I be of service?"

"I have a friend outside who needs help."

"What kind of help?"

"A place to hide."

Yanni straightened slightly "This is someone wanted by the authorities?"

"Yes, but she is innocent."

When Marcus said "she" the monk straightened fully. "Are you speaking about a woman?"

"I'm afraid so."

"Mr. Giannou, this is a monastery not a bed and breakfast."

"She has nowhere else to go."

"Mystras is next to a village. She can find a place to hide there."

"She will not be safe. My friends and I just broke her out of the Sparta Jail…"

Yianni extended his arm as if warding off a blow. "Wait a minute. You broke her out of a jail?"

"Yes, an hour ago."

"I cannot believe this."

"She is in grave danger. If she is caught she will be tortured."

"You exaggerate."

"Really? Have you heard of ESA?"

Yianni reacted as if he had been insulted. "We may live in isolation but we are not isolated from the world."

"Then you know what I say is no exaggeration."

"You are asking my order to become involved in a jail break? All we can do is pray for her."

"Pray, yes, but you must also put your prayers into action."

"My brothers and I live as one. We cannot share our devotion, our faith, our quarters with a woman. Such a departure from tradition cannot be re-ordained with a snap of the fingers."

"You are signing her death warrant."

"It cannot be helped."

"Are you speaking for yourself or for your God?"

Underneath his cassock, Yianni's shoulders sagged from the weight of his dilemma and Marcus wedged himself into that opening of vulnerability. "Eleni's mother was an American citizen. I will work as quickly as I can with the help of my government to get Eleni safely out of Greece. In the meantime she has nowhere else to go but here."

"You are driving an impossible bargain."

When Yianni mentioned bargain, Marcus thought of Dimitri uttering the word: Mystras. What Dimitri implied and what Caliope confirmed was that they could make it possible for Theophanes' Virgin to come home.

"Brother Yianni," Marcus said, sensing he was shifting the argument in his favor, giving him an opportunity to strike a bargain. "On the altar I saw an empty frame. What is the significance of that?"

Yianni was happy to change the subject. "Ah, yes, it once held an icon of the most precious symbol of our or any order, the Virgin Mary."

"Is the missing icon valuable?"

"Do you mean in terms of monetary worth or as a holy relic of the Orthodox Church?"

"Both, but what personally is it worth to you?"

"Ah, everything that I value including my life to have it back. It is one of the world's great art treasures yet few have ever heard of it."

"I don't know much about Byzantine art," Marcus said, intentionally leading him on.

"In that case, I will give you a lesson in art history." Yianni led Marcus to a long bench with a hinged seat that could be raised out of the way. "Now then," he began as they settled themselves. "The missing icon was painted in the Middle Ages. We do not know precisely when since these religious works were never dated and never signed, but it was painted by one of the masters of that age, Theophanes, who lived from 1350 to 1415. He was Greek but lived most of his life in Russia and this is probably why he is not popularly known in the Western World.

"He developed into one of Europe's greatest religious painters. There are very few icons ascribed to him, and so they are very rare. You may well ask, what made Theophanes a great artist? What made Leonardo a great artist? Both had skill certainly, but something more than that. It was their ability to transform, to change what went before. That is what Theophanes did. He forever altered the way of Byzantine art. He endowed his paintings with emotion and compassion.

"An icon has special characteristics that separates it from other portraiture. After Theophanes, iconographic convention required that the subject, whether a religious figure, a holy person or a saint, have human qualities. This is an important point. See the frescoes on the walls of the dome in this church? They were painted before Theophanes. See how removed the saints are from human qualities? Note how grave and accusing the faces are? Worshippers in the Middle Ages were left desiring something more accessible and compassionate, more human."

It was clear that Yianni was passionate about his subject and was more than happy to have someone's ear.

"Painting a religious figure with human qualities is not as easy as it seems. It was necessary to invest the contours of ordinary human beings with the celestial presence of God. In other words, icon figures had to appear human but they were never to be mistaken for an ordinary human being."

"A tall order," Marcus ventured.

The monk nodded soberly. "Very tall. And there is something else. Each icon figure also had to be endowed with the distinctive features that render the subject recognizable at a glance. For example, a worshiper had to be able to tell St. John from St. Jude. This restriction created a good deal of mediocre art, as you would expect. Few icon painters mastered these demands as well as Theophanes. He was the first to succeed." Yianni, speaking in reverent tones, cast his eyes in the direction of the altar and the empty frame sitting on it.

After an interval of silent reflection on what was lost, Marcus asked, "What happened to the icon?"

"It was removed from the monastery during the war to keep the Germans from finding it."

Just then another monk entered through a side door with a bucket and a mop, no doubt doing his daily chores of cleaning the church.

"Brother Christos, come here please," Yianni said in Greek.

The monk set down his cleaning equipment and came over, walking with a stoop and a shuffle.

"Christos will remember. He was here during the war. He is in his nineties and hard of hearing, but his mind is as sharp as yours or mine."

Yianni addressed Christos in a loud voice speaking Greek. "This young man is from America and is asking about the Virgin of Theophanes."

The old monk wore an untrimmed beard of pure white. He smiled and revealed a few craggy teeth that were like pieces of yellow corn candy stuck to his gums. He sat next to Marcus on the bench.

"When did you last see the icon?" Yianni asked the old man.

He scratched his beard, thick and wiry and matted with dried food. "During the war. When the Germans invaded we were afraid she would be stolen by the soldiers."

It impressed Marcus that the old monk thought of the icon as a "she," endowed with humanistic qualities of tenderness and vulnerability.

"The brothers decided it was necessary to send her away. We placed her in the care of a young student."

Marcus's scalp prickled. "What was her name?"

"The student?" Light poked through his rheumy eyes as he opened them wider, trying to remember. "Anna, yes, it was Anna."

Marcus leaned against the back of the bench filled with awe at hearing the old monk mentioning Anna's name. It was as if fate had taken him by the hand and guided him here, returning Eleni to her roots.

"Anna was from America," Christos continued, "and came to Greece to research Byzantine art. She stayed in the village of Anavriti, a few kilometers away. She was here every day, asking permission to visit our library, and we allowed her because of her persistence. She rode on the back of a donkey, wearing a large hat of American fashion to ward off the sun. She was a familiar sight kicking the stubborn beast up the hill."

Marcus smiled to himself imagining Eleni's mother beating her heels against the donkey's flanks with the same determination as Eleni. Like mother like daughter.

Christos continued: "The war came and Anna received official notice from her Embassy, warning that Americans were in danger if they did not leave Greece. But she wanted to stay. 'Greece is my home,' I remember her saying. She was very attached to Mystras. We were now her family and she worried about us more than she worried about herself.

"We knew it was only a matter of time before the Germans would overrun the whole country. We convinced her that she must leave. We asked her to take the icon with her, to keep the Virgin Mary safe until, we prayed, the Germans would be defeated. I remember the day she left with the icon in a brown envelope along with her other important possession, her passport."

The same brown envelope, Marcus realized with amazement, that he and Eleni carried to Athens.

"Was Anna alone?"

Mist covered his eyes. "No, she was in the company of a young novice whose name I cannot recall. I do remember that he had a talent with a brush and learned the art of icon painting. We never saw them or the Virgin again."

Marcus looked up at the saints scowling at him from the dome. If they could smile, he thought, they would do so right now.

"I have seen the icon," he said. "I know where it is."

The brothers stared at Marcus, shocked into silence. Finally Yianni said, "If what you say is true, then God delivered you to Mystras."

"He delivered more than me, Brother Yianni. He also delivered Anna's daughter."

23

"The young woman you have asked to provide sanctuary is Anna's daughter?" Yianni asked, his voice rising in pitch to match his excitement.

Marcus nodded.

"Where is she?"

"Waiting outside."

Yianni jumped up from the bench. "Take me to her."

"May I join you?" Christos asked, wanting to connect his memory of Anna with her daughter in real time.

They walked out to the sunny courtyard. Eleni was sitting on a bench under the portico, hands folded in her lap, all alone. She stood when she saw Marcus and the monks coming out of the church.

"Where are Haralambos and Kleftis?" Marcus called as they approached.

"They left. They said it was better to keep moving."

"But where did they go?"

"They will hide in the hills and then make their way to Niata. There are *compatrioti* along the way who will help them. They will be fine."

Christos could not hide his excitement. "I knew your mother, Anna!" he said, as he embraced Eleni. "And now I have met her daughter. I can die happy now."

Theophanes' Virgin

Eleni was flustered by the unexpected attention.

"You resemble her, and from what I have heard, you inherited her indomitable spirit."

She blushed. "You are very kind to say that."

Yianni was observing Eleni carefully, analytically. "Young lady," he said to her, "your friend has asked me to give you sanctuary. I explained to him that it is against the rules of the monestary." He smiled benevolently. "But I think he has in mind an interesting proposition, your protection in exchange for Theophanes' Virgin." He looked at Marcus for confirmation. "Am I right?"

Marcus nodded.

"We would have to foresake a thousand years of tradition, but I also cannot ignore God's will that brought you here."

"Then you can appreciate the perfect symmetry, can't you, brother Yianni." Marcus said. "The icon given to Anna returned by her daughter."

"I will have to get unanimous approval from the brothers. We are all equal here." He looked at Eleni uncomfortable in her prison uniform. "At least you would not have to wear that any longer. But you cannot wear a dress. You must appear as a monk so no one from the outside world will suspect you are in hiding. You will impersonate one of us not to mock God's will but for your protection."

"As you say," she replied shyly.

Yianni crossed himself. "What I have learned on this morning of prayers is that God answers you even if His words come from a mere mortal."

"So the answer is yes?"

"Only with the approval of my fellow monks, but I do not foresee a problem if Eleni accepts the conditions of living with us—sleep in a cell, work in the garden, help prepare meals, wash dishes. She may take her prayers in the privacy of her cell. She is not allowed in the church. Most important, she must always cover her head in a cowl to hide her identity."

Eleni nodded, accepting the conditions of becoming the first woman in the histroy of Greece to live in a monestary.

Brother Yianni looked at Marcus. "Now, then, can we discuss your end of the bargain? Where is the icon and under what conditions will you return it?"

"The icon is under lock and key at the American Library in Sparta. I will ask the librarian, Sally Haggerty, to return it to you. I wish I could be the one to bring it back but I have to leave Greece."

"Why? Are you in danger?"

He was in danger, all right, big danger, unless he got to the library in time to catch that ride to the Embassy. In a way, the American government was providing him sanctuary, too. He said this as much to comfort Eleni as to inform Yianni.

"Eleni needs to rest, but I'd like to have a few minutes alone with her before I leave."

"Of course, my son," Yianni said.

The two monks bowed and went into the church leaving Eleni and Marcus together. Marcus was having difficulty finding words to express his feelings. He didn't even know where to start. But it did not matter. Rare moments can't be enhanced by mere words. There was nothing either of them could say to describe the wonder and relief of sitting alone in a quiet place where serenity, not fear, was the norm.

"What will happen now?" she asked, breaking the mood they had fallen into. She was so tired she could barely keep her eyes open.

"You will be well taken care of," Marcus said. "The monks may even want to adopt you." He laughed hoping to ease the concern she felt.

"When will I see you again?"

"Art Prager is sending a car to take me to Athens. I will have to return to Washington and I will work from there to get you out of Greece. The entire force of the American government is on your side." He used hyperbole to comfort her, but he was still not sure how he would carry out what seemed like an insurmountable feat.

He stared at her, wanting to take her in his arms while wondering how this would be perceived in a monastery, and so he held back. But she could read what was on his mind, what was expressed in his eyes.

She pulled the prison dress she was wearing away from her body as though it was contaminating her skin. Spiritually it was.

"You are beautiful," he said to reassure her.

"Not as beautiful as the day in Athens when you took me shopping and you bought me new clothes." She sighed with regret. "They took them away from me."

"They can have them as long as I have you."

Tears formed in her eyes. "Marcus, I never expected to see you again. It is so confusing. I cannot think clearly...Captain Tsatsos told me you were arrested, too."

"He told you that?" Marcus asked angrily. "He was lying. My Embassy made a deal with him. I will not be arrested if I leave Greece immediately."

"I thought you were somewhere in that jail, locked in a cell where they torture prisoners." She shook her head. "You should not have taken this risk for me." She shivered involuntarily.

"I could not enjoy freedom knowing you were without it."

Eleni began to unravel. She needed to let it all out and Marcus knew he must be quiet and let her talk.

"Tsatsos told me you were locked up and he would not let you out until I confessed to killing Kostas. He told me that his men were torturing you and he brought a machine that records sounds. He turned it on and made me listen to screams. Your screams."

"That is what he wanted you to believe." The bastard, Marcus thought.

"He played the tape over and over until I could not stand it. Only I could stop my boyfriend's screams, he said, and he gave me a sheet of paper with a statement that

I killed Kostas." Eleni looked pleadingly at Marcus. "I signed it. What else could I do?"

Then, as if she were reliving the nightmare of the screams, she began shivering despite the warm air. She folded her arms and gripped her shoulders. He pulled her toward him and wrapped her firmly with his own arms. She buried her face against his neck and he felt her hot tears running down his collar.

To hell with religious taboo, he thought, and kissed her. Her mouth was warm, grateful.

On his drive back to Sparta, Marcus missed the companionship of Haralambos and Kleftis, his co-conspirators as he joyfully thought of them. What a pair. He hoped they were all right and he wondered when he would see them again.

He was in a good mood when he parked the Chevrolet behind the library. Just as he promised Sally, he was back before noon after an adventure to remember. Eleni was safe, mission accomplished. He followed the sidewalk to the front entrance and walked in. The receptionist was at her desk and when she looked up her eyes widened with alarm.

"Anything the matter?" he asked, still in an uncommonly good mood, and dropped the car keys on her desk. "Tell Sally her Chevy is back. Is the Embassy driver here yet? I'm ready to leave but I'd like to have something to eat first. I'll walk over to Kipris Estiatorio for a bite."

She just stared at Marcus, her lips parted as if she were ready to say something but changed her mind.

"Are you ok?" he asked. He turned and saw that the door to Sally's office was closed. That was odd since he always remembered her preferring to have her door open so she could keep an eye on things. As he thought about this the door did open. Fully expecting to see Sally, the breath was knocked out of him when the person staring at him was Captain Tsatsos of the Sparta Police.

225

"Ah, there you are," the officer said in well-crafted English, an I've-got-you-now grin splitting his face. "The entire constabulary has been looking for you and you walked right into my arms. How convenient."

Sally was standing behind her desk, which was flanked by two police officers. She was anxiously rubbing her hands. "My god, Marcus, what have you been up to?"

"I will tell you what he has been up to, Miss Haggerty," Tsatsos answered for Marcus, smiling smugly. "He was involved in a foolhardy attempt to help a prisoner escape. An American car, a Chevrolet as it turned out, was seen leaving the city following the jailbreak. It was simply adding two and two to trace the car to this library, and Miss Haggerty was quite helpful in letting us know that you had borrowed it. How convenient, using an American car to commit a Greek crime."

The glaring stare Marcus got from Sally told him what she was thinking: How could you be so stupid?

"I have to take you in for questioning, Kyrio Giannou."

Fingers of fear clawed up his back.

"I released you on condition that you leave Greece. But you did not take my advice."

"Yes, I did. A car is coming to pick me up and take me to the Embassy."

"But in the meantime, in a very short time I might add, you managed somehow to free the murder suspect."

Sally was clearly concerned. "I must remind you, Captain, that Marcus Giannou is an American citizen and cannot be detained without legal representation."

"Do not worry that pretty head of yours, Miss Haggerty. I will simply ask him a few questions."

"How long will that take?" Marcus asked.

"An hour or two?" Tsatsos answered, as though he was not at all sure how long.

Marcus tried to sound confident. "I have to be back by noon. That's when the driver picks me up."

Tsatsos smiled that smug smile again and his two officers were grinning like a pair of Cheshire cats. "I will do my best."

Marcus was escorted out of the library and down the block to a police car. "My apologies for making you walk in the hot sun but I did not want to park too closely to the library and have you spot my car and try another escape. Good police work, don't you think?"

Marcus was led into Tsatsos' office. On his desk was a prism-shaped sign that read in Greek: Aristidis V. Tsatsos Captain. Behind the desk were the obligatory photo of Pappathopoulos and the limp Greek flag.

"Sit there," Tsatsos motioned to a wood chair with a straight back next to the desk. A gooseneck lamp was twisted so that the bare bulb shone in Marcus's face.

"Now, then, a few questions if you don't mind. First, how did your girl friend get sick so suddenly? The toilet in the cell was plugged with a plastic bag and a leaf from a plant. A note on the bag instructed her to bite into the leaf. What was in it, some kind of poison?"

"Not deadly. The effect is only temporary. The plant is called a dieffenbachia."

"I am not familiar with it."

"I wasn't either till I was told about it."

"By whom?"

Marcus suddenly realized he was tricked. He had to be careful how he answered. "Oh, my mother. She knows all about plants."

"A very clever escape. Eleni Stathos, where is she?"

"She is safe. You cannot touch her."

Tsatsos scowled. He did not like being talked back to. "If she is safe as you say then you can tell me where she is."

Marcus thought it was ok to tell him. Besides it gave him satisfaction to know he could needle the Captain. "The Monestary of Mystras."

"You are lying. Women are not allowed in the monastery."

"I am not lying. That is where we took her after getting her out of the hospital."

"We?"

Marcus looked down, upset that he was so easily trapped.

"Are you talking about two men wearing hospital masks who overpowered the guards?"

"I don't know who you are talking about."

"Kyrio Giannou, do not take me for a fool. You have committed a serious crime and I want to know about your accomplices. Tell me who they are and where I can find them and I will release you in time to catch that ride to Athens. As for the girl I will wait to see if the monks get bored with her and kick her out or, if not, they will easily fold under a bit of pressure from ESA. They will turn her over to us when we charge them with harboring a murderer. They will suffer legal as well as moral consequences. Their Christian belief is in conflict with the rule of law."

"She is innocent," Marcus said.

"Ha!" Tsatsos shot back. "You are blinded by love. Look at this." He opened the narrow middle drawer and pulled out a sheet of paper and laid it in front of Marcus. It was titled: The confession of Eleni Stathos for the murder of Kostas Kanellos.

Marcus looked at it but did not pick it up.

"Perhaps your Greek isn't good enough, so I shall I read it to you."

He used a monotone as though he was reciting directions for mixing cement.

"On the morning of Saturday, August 28, 1972, I was driven to the apartment building of my fiancé, Kostas Kanellos, 45 Zografu Street, Sparta, District of Laconias, by my cousin, Marcus Giannou, who waited outside. I went to apartment number 16 and knocked on the door.

Kostas answered. He was drinking and abusive, and accused me of having sexual relations with my cousin.

He made nasty comments of my infidelity, saying he was unwilling to marry a woman whose virginal body was already dirtied."

My god, Marcus thought, recalling the night he and Eleni spent together in the shepherd's hut. Did Tsatsos force her to tell him about this or was he just making it up?

Tsatsos was watching Marcus's reaction. "Is this having some affect on you, Kyrio Giannou? Perhaps it is too close to the bone, as we say in Greece?"

Marcus looked away. "I don't want to hear any more."

"But you must and you will. Pay attention." Tstatos was having the time of his life. He continued reading:

"Kostas said that if I was available to my cousin, then I should be available to him. He forced me against the wall and touched me in extremely unpleasant ways. I tried to make him stop but he forced himself on me even more, pulling up my skirt and touching my private parts. I was able to push him away and ran to the door but it was locked. I was so frightened I could not find my voice to scream. He grabbed me by the waist and threw me to the sofa, lifting my dress and running his hands along my legs. I fought with my fists, trying to stop his advances.

"I held my legs together as tightly as possible and beat him as hard as I could. Finally he fell off my body and rolled to the floor where he lay stunned by my blows. I was hysterical and thought only that he would rape me as soon as he cleared his head. I ran around the apartment looking for the key to unlock the door. I went into the bedroom and searched the nightstand where I found a pistol. I returned to the parlor with the gun in my hand. Kostas was on his feet and he came toward me. I was so afraid he would rape me I pulled the trigger and the gun went off, striking Kostas in the head. He fell to the floor. When I realized what I had done I went to the window.

Marcus Giannou was waiting for me on the sidewalk. He told me to drop the gun to him and he would hide it. That is why no murder weapon was found.

"I openly and willingly confess to this crime and ask for leniency by the court. May God have mercy on my soul.

(Signed)
Eleni Stathos"

Marcus snorted with disgust. "You forced her to sign this piece of crap using screams she believed were mine. Is that what you want to do to me? Force me to scream enough so that I will sign another made-up confession?"

"Do not toy with me, Kyrio Giannou. You have one option and one option only to walk out of here a free man—the names and location of the two men who entered the hospital and took your girlfriend away. Otherwise I will keep you here, as you say in America, where you can cool your heels. But you may not like that because here we heat your heels." He laughed derisively. "We will see how long it will take you to trade cool for hot, as in hot answer. It is up to you."

Tsatsos got up and spoke to one of his lieutenants in rapid-fire Greek that Marcus could not understand.

The officer took him by the arm, roughly pulled him to his feet and led him down the same dank corridor that Eleni disappeared in. They turned into a narrow hallway that made an L with the corridor. At the end was a guard standing by a door of heavy steel with rivets and huge hinges to hold its weight. The door was painted a dull gray and in the center was a small slot covered by a piece of metal set in a track. Under it was a shelf. The guard pulled the huge door open. The hinges made a grinding noise.

"Welcome to the luxury suite in our four-star hotel," he said in vulgar English, his face greasy from sweat.

"Are you the doorman?" Marcus asked, looking in. The confining space had a bench with a thin mattress, a sink with a towel bar, a drain in the floor, and a bare bulb that hung from the ceiling by its cord. There was no window, only blank walls. He realized with a shudder that the room was used for torture.

As an answer, the "doorman" pushed him into the cell. "On the bench is a bag. Open it."

As much from curiosity as following orders, Marcus opened the bag. Folded neatly were a gray sweatshirt and gray pants with an elastic band.

"Your prison uniform. Remove your clothing and place them in the bag. You can keep your shoes because they have no laces. Leave everything else including your passport and wallet."

Marcus stared in shock.

"Do as you are told."

He undressed, embarrassed at being stared at, the beginning stage of humiliation that he did not yet understand, a calculated process of turning him into a non-person. He quickly put on the prison clothing to cover his nakedness.

"Your watch."

"What?"

"Your wristwatch. Put that in the bag and hand it to me."

"How do I keep time?"

"You don't."

The guard took the bag and banged the door shut, locking it with a resounding clank.

Somewhere in the ensuing silence Marcus thought he heard a scream. In his fragile and confused state he wondered it if was coming from him.

24

Time lost its dimension and Marcus lost his sense of place. He could not separate hours, he could not tell night from day. The gray-painted concrete walls wanted to close in on him like the terrifying story by Poe. The lone light bulb hanging by its cord was so bright that he cast no shadow, as though he did not exist. He sat on the bench, the only place to sit other than the floor, which was stained permanently with what he did not know or want to find out. What kind of hellhole is this? he asked himself.

All he had to do was tell Tsatsos that the men he wanted were named Haralambos and Klèftis—no he did not know their last names, only that they were from Niata—and he would be let go in time to catch that ride to Athens, find safety in the American Embassy and eventually passage back home to Washington where he belonged, not here in this filthy dungeon.

There was a sudden banging on the metal door, which made him jump and his heart almost seized. My god what was that?

Silence followed, an eerie lapse of time, how long? Five minutes? Ten minutes? An hour? And then there was another banging on his door, jarring and ominous, as though a guard walking by hit the metal with a truncheon.

The only break was mealtime, when the metal cover was slid open and a guard pushed a tray of food through the slot. Not food as one would define it but a knot of mush that resembled wet lint and tasted even worse. But he ate it. He had no other choice. Either that or starve. Water he got from the tap, warm and metallic-flavored, and the drain in the floor was used for everything else. He cleaned himself with a roll of coarse paper and rinsed himself with a rag folded over the towel rod. The guard was wrong about one thing, this hotel was not four stars.

Even though it was stained from god knew what, throw-up, urine, semen, he lay down on the mattress, exhausted and deflated, hoping at least to nap, but the bright overhead light pierced his eyelids and then, without warning, another bang on the metal door, harder this time, hard enough to vibrate the metal. He realized now that they were forcing him to stay awake and wear down his resistance, a prelude to being grilled.

Tsatsos meant business all right—tell me what I want to know and you can leave. God, but he yearned to see Haralambos and Kleftis. But this line of thought was futile. They were somewhere en route to Niata, safely he hoped, and they had no idea where he was, certainly not in the same wing that they broke Eleni out of. The irony was inescapable and added to his sense of defeat and desperation, just what Tsatsos wanted. Kleftis and Haralambos could not try using dumb cane. No jailer was dumb enough to fall for that trick again. Marcus should not even entertain the notion that these two intrepid men could do anything to free him. He would have to do it himself.

And then the screams began. Where they came from he did not know. Were they real or a recording meant to break down the last vestige of resistance, he had no way of knowing.

Tsatsos was playing mind games and the only way to fight back was to play a mind game of his own. Pretend he was broken, ready to spill the beans, anything to get out of this horrible cell.

Marcus rubbed the gristle of his beard to gauge the passage of time. He had been in this place for several days, maybe a week. He laughed wryly. He missed that ride to Athens. He began to wonder if time really existed. Like a tree falling in the forest not making a sound if no one hears it, does time pass if you have no way of measuring it? The riddle kept rolling around in his head like a loose ball bearing, driving him almost as crazy as the incessant banging on his metal door. He had to think of something else do drive out the repetitious thought, like the drip-drip-drip of Chinese water torture. And then he thought of Eleni. He conjured up her face, listened to her voice and her laugh, and felt her god-given sense of composure. She was his lifeline. She survived and so can he!

With determination he did not know he had, he worked the towel rod loose from the wall, the screws finally coming out imbedded with concrete dust from the holes. He wielded it like a batter and stood by the door, waiting not in trepidation but in anticipation. He did not have to wait long. Inexorably, the intimidating bang came from the other side. Using all his strength Marcus swung the towel rod and struck the door so hard the rod vibrated his arms and left a dent in the metal. The noise echoed and reechoed in his tight quarters almost to the level of pain in his ears. It had to make just as much noise outside his cell.

He held his breath, wondering what the guard was doing, reacting with surprise he hoped. A few seconds passed and then the guard hit the door as though testing a trial run, not as hard this time.

Marcus responded with another bang on the door. The metal cover to the slot slid open. "What is going on in there?" the guard shouted through it.

Marcus hit the door right at the slot and then bent over to look through it. He saw the guard hurl back against the opposite wall, his eyes stricken with fear and uncertainty, his truncheon hanging at his side.

"I want to see Tsatsos right now!" Marcus shouted through the slot.

The guard, totally confused, as it was clear he had never experienced disorder like this before, shouted back, "It is late! He is at home asleep!"

Aha, Marcus thought, nighttime. He banged the metal door and waited. Silence. He banged again and kept at it this time, the reverberating noise like explosions ripping through his skull—bang after bang till his shoulders ached so much he had to stop. Through the ringing in his ears he heard the key turn the lock and watched the door swing open. He could not believe his extraordinarily good luck. Curiosity finally getting the better of him, the guard stuck his head into the cell.

Without a moment's hesitation, Marcus swung the towel bar down on the guard's shoulder, splitting his collarbone in two with a loud crack. The man yowled in pain and went down like a chimney collapsing. Marcus threw away the towel bar, jumped over the writhing figure and ran down the hall, turning where it made the L, and following the corridor to the front entrance. Somewhere in the sheer madness of the moment he heard shouting from other places in the jail, inmates who were joining the mayhem with yelling and pandemonium of their own, just what Marcus needed.

At the end of the corridor a second guard had taken a wide stance to head Marcus off. Nothing like this had ever happened before in the Sparta Jail and guards were not trained to handle an angry American in the middle of the night. Marcus ran pell-mell into him, sending him sprawling across the floor on his back.

In another moment Marcus was outside, breathing fresh Spartan air and wondering what in hell to do now. As he looked around, the soft night air was suddenly shattered by a confusion of headlight beams splitting the darkness, tires squealing to a stop, car doors opening, shoes scraping on asphalt and shouts of Greek epithets. The scene unfolded like a Keystone Kops two-reeler. Men clambered out of the car with such haste they bumped into each other. One stumbled to his knees, cursing another who tripped over him. They were brandishing guns and waving at Marcus who took off on foot and ran faster than he had ever run before, down dark streets, past dark warehouses and shuttered stores.

All he knew was he had to make it to the library, a mile or more, running almost helter-skelter, calling on his memory of the city. He came out of a side street and suddenly found himself on the boulevarded main drag. He ran past the restaurant, Kipris Estratorio, and then he knew where he was. In two more minutes he reached the Library out of breath and his legs burning with pain. He circled the building and lay down on the ground, now cool to his body. Chest heaving and heart thumping, he stared up at the sweep of a black heaven.

An hour must have passed, he didn't know for certain, before he could sit up and take stock of what had just happened. He had escaped Tsatsos's prison. That might be one for the record books if such mad capers are kept track of. His eyes accustomed to the dark took in his surroundings. He was in the back lot of the Library and not ten feet away sat the Chevrolet. My getaway car, he thought wryly, but it was just a big pile of metal within reach but yet beyond reach. Shit, he thought, what now, walk to Mystras to join Eleni or hitchhike to Niata and the safety of Kleftis' Taverna? But how long would he last in the open, dressed in prison garb with several days' growth of beard and a wild look in his eyes. By dawn, Tstatos would find him. He was doomed. He stared at the Chevrolet and the more he stared the more he saw in his mind Kleftis taking apart the steering column of the Simca, finding the wires and connecting them. Hell, Marcus thought, it doesn't take Mr. Good Wrench to figure that out. Maybe he could do it. Worth a try, and if he failed, so what? He was doomed one way or the other.

Might as well go down fighting instead of sitting like a helpless and cowering animal. He got up and went to the Chevrolet. The driver's door was not locked. This was typical. Greeks are honest and trusting and leave their cars unlocked even with valuables sitting in the back seat. No one steals anything unless you happen to be an American fugitive desperate for a car.

He went to work, a kind of hit or miss effort, first cracking the plastic housing with a blow of his fist. He didn't have any tools and resorted to filing the exposed wire harness against a sharp edge of the broken plastic until it split. He used his teeth to eat away the plastic covering to reveal the raw wire. Sweat broke out on his forehead and dropped down on his nose as he worked feverishly, touching several wires, experimenting, hoping a combination would finally work and eventually his effort paid off. The starter suddenly cranked, the engine turned and the spark plugs ignited. The car was running!

He got behind the wheel and drove out of the lot and headed south toward Niata, a road he knew well enough so that he could negotiate it even at night.

When Marcus reached Niata it was nearing dawn. He went off the road at the outskirts and followed the walking path he and Eleni used to enter the town from behind the church. The big car filled the path and scraped bushes and branches as he maneuvered into a thicket where the car would remain out of sight. Only a wandering shepherd would find it.

He came out from behind the church to the back door of the Taverna and gently tapped on it several times before a voice inside said, "*Pios?*" Who?

"Marcus."

The door flung open and Haralambos, in his skivvies, stared at Marcus with a combination of disbelief and relief. He grabbed him by the shoulders, yanked him inside and shut the door behind them.

He showered wet kisses on Marcus's forehead, cheeks, nose, neck. "You are safe," he kept saying in Greek, "you are safe."

Kleftis came in from the bar, getting ready to open. When Haralambos released Marcus, Kleftis left his wet imprints all over him as well.

Kleftis went off to bring cheese and bread, and coffee while Marcus and Haralambos sat at the card table.

"We were very concerned about you," Haralambos said. "We knew you were in that ugly jail of Tsatsos the Torturer."

"How did you know?" Marcus said, eating his first decent meal in a week and enjoying every morsel.

"We have a network, my friend, numerous compatriots in Sparta. Your every move was followed. We were planning to break you out of there but you beat us to it."

"You were?" Marcus asked, dumbfounded.

"We had lookouts posted around the jail since the day you were brought there. And last night when you came running out you surprised them. *Compatrioti* tried to rescue you but you ran away."

"Those men who jumped out of the car?" Marcus asked in surprise.

Haralambos nodded.

Marcus laughed in relief. "I thought they were police trying to arrest me!"

"But where did you go? How did you get here?"

Marcus went on to explain that he ran to the American Library, found the Chevy in the parking lot and hotwired it.

"That is how you got here?" Kleftis said, enthralled. "Where is the car?"

"Hidden behind the church."

Kleftis smiled proudly. "With me as your teacher, Marcus, my *compatrioti,* I can turn you into a thief just like me."

"I hope you are kidding. By the way, what day is it?"

"Friday."

"I need to contact Sally Haggerty and let her know where her car is. And I have to let my mother know I am ok."

"We informed your mother that Eleni is in Mystras, but we did not tell her what happened to you."

"You didn't?"

"We lied, just a little, what you call a white lie. We told them that you are also in Mystras. But now we can tell everyone the truth, that you are with us again." Haralambos looked at Marcus, his eyes filled with compassion. "But first we have to take care of you, get rid of those prison clothes and burn them for what they are."

Marcus sniffed under his arm. "I could use a bath."

He cleaned himself standing in a washtub filled with water and scrubbed his smelly skin with a coarse bar of soap that felt as good as a rubdown in a spa. As primitive as his bath was, he never felt so refreshed and clean. Haralambos had scrounged a reasonably well-fitting wardrobe from a neighbor close to Marcus's waistline but not his height, and when he finished dressing he looked a bit like Li'l Abner.

"Do you think you can find out where Drovich is?" Marcus asked, pulling down on his new pants, doing his best to cover his ankles.

"The owner of the Simca?" Kleftis laughed. "He was angrier than a wasp when he saw that his car was stolen."

"I want to talk to him."

"I will send word out. Where do you want to meet?"

"Here in Niata."

"What makes you think he will come?"

"The icon."

That afternoon, when it was siesta time and the Taverna was closed, Haralambos placed a telephone call to the American Library. A harried Sally came on the line. Kleftis passed the phone over to the freshly scrubbed and clothed Marcus.

"Good afternoon," he said trying to sound casual when he knew she would explode as soon as she heard his voice, and he was right.

"My god, Marcus, where are you? This town is swarming with police. I have no idea how you got out of that jail and the less I know the better because they think I was complicit. They are not only looking for you, they are also looking for some men who apparently tried to rescue you. They even think I hired them. This has gotten completely out of control. I have been working night and day to get you released from that jail using every diplomatic channel I can think of. Our Ambassador has been on the phone with your Senator. The entire State Department is involved. Can you imagine the heat we're getting because of you, an aide to Senator Tolson of all people? The Greek government is apoplectic because they pride themselves in their penal system. There is a crisis brewing between our two governments because of you. And another thing, my car is gone. They think I let you use it."

"In a way you did."

"How did you start it? I have the keys."

Kleftis was grinning from ear to ear when Marcus said, "I learned how to hot-wire a car."

She sighed in deep frustration. "I don't want to know anything about that crowd you pal around with. It was bad enough that you were persona non grata and now you are a felon. And if I don't get my car back, include car theft on top of everything else."

Marcus looked at Kleftis. "You'll get it back. I promise. And it will be in running condition. All you have to do is pick it up. It's hidden in some brush behind the church."

"Am I supposed to thank you for that? I'll call Prager and tell him you've turned up. If the Greek government wanted you out of its country before they sure as hell want you out now."

"I don't think Tsatsos is through with me."

"Oh yes he is. He was demoted."

"Demoted?"

"Back to walking a beat."

Marcus called out to Haralambos, "Tsatsos was busted! Tell Kleftis!"

Haralambos translated. The two men hooted and slapped their knees.

"The best news I've had in days," Marcus said, going back to Sally.

"Who are you talking to?" she asked.

"Friends."

Her voice tensed. "Are they resistance fighters?"

He did not answer.

"Oh God..." she trailed off. "Listen to me, Marcus. This is serious business. The Greek government has mud on its face. You are bad PR for them. They will give you and your mother safe passage home. They will even pay your flight out of here, first class, anything to get you out of their hair."

"I need a few more days."

"You don't have a few more days."

"I am not leaving Greece without Eleni. Tell Prager that the only deal I will agree to is an American passport for her. And also tell him that guy at the Greek Consulate should either give Eleni her exit visa or give me back my three hundred bucks."

Sally was quiet for a spell as everything sank in. Finally she said, "You really are serious about her, aren't you?"

"She is my cousin."

"Is that the only reason?"

Again he did not answer.

"Ok, Marcus," she said with an air of finality. "If that is what you want, I will pass on the message. By the way I heard from the Library in Athens."

So much had happened to Marcus that he had to think for a moment about what Sally was telling him.

"The page you gave me from the art catalog of Theophanes' Virgin, remember?"

"Oh, yes. What did you find out?"

"I was right. Kostas Kanellos signed for the catalogue raisonne of Theophanes last month. He was not allowed to take it out of the library, only look at in a reading room. He returned it after only fifteen minutes, according to the time on the checkout card."

"So he didn't steal it."

"No."

"Then how did he get that page?"

"He cut it out with a razor and slid a plain sheet of paper in its place so the gap wouldn't be noticed. That's how the librarian found it. He was furious."

"I can imagine. So there is a forgery out there somewhere, unless he didn't have time to paint one."

"At least the real one is still in my safe."

"I'd like to get it back, Sally. Would you have it delivered to me here in Niata?"

"What are you going to do with it?"

"It's time to return it the monks at Mystras."

What he did not tell her was that before he did, he was going to use Theophanes' Virgin to bait a trap.

25

The next afternoon a white Toyota pickup truck pulled into the square and parked. A young farmer climbed out and came into the Taverna. He was carrying a cloth sack of pistachio nuts and set the sack on the bar counter. Kleftis paid him with drachmas from the cash register. The farmer counted the drachmas before putting the bills into his pocket. He walked out of the Taverna, climbed into his pickup and was gone. To the casual observer he was a farmer delivering the weekly load of pistachios that Kleftis kept in bowls on the bar. To Marcus, he was a diplomatic courier delivering the icon hidden in the sack.

Marcus was still recouping from his ordeal, sleeping long hours, getting up only to relieve himself or have something to eat. His appetite was still fragile, the only thing that appealed to him was bread and *ovgolemono soupa*. He needed to get his strength back if he was going to deal with Drovich. The word had gone out that Marcus wanted to see him alone in Niata. They would meet on the bench below the entrance to the church. Drovich had to be alone.

The Simca turned up three days after Haralambos sent word through his network. Kleftis rushed into the back of the Taverna to alert Marcus. "He is here."

Marcus walked to the front and looked out the window. He caught sight of Drovich heading in the direction of the church, smartly dressed as always, unperturbed by the hot sun. Marcus picked up the manila envelope and went out the Taverna's back door, reaching the rendezvous bench at the same time as Drovich. The two eyed each other like combatants before the match got underway. Drovich was cool, Marcus hot, a disadvantage right off the bat as they sat on the bench in the shade of the church's imposing bell tower. Drovich shifted his body so that he faced Marcus more directly, perhaps a sign of compromise, friendliness.

"Kyrio Giannou," he said, "we meet again."

"Is your car running all right?" Marcus asked, testing the waters.

"The Athens police notified me they found it in a garage near the American Embassy. It cost me five thousand drachmas to repair the damaged wiring. Still, in the end, your little plan has not worked has it?"

"You are here," Marcus said.

"What does that prove?"

"I have the icon."

"What do you want for it?"

"Eleni's good name."

"Is that why you brought me here—to convince yourself that your inamorata is innocent? You should have contacted me earlier and saved yourself a lot of trouble. I would have advised you to plant a story."

"Plant a story?"

"It still may not be too late. The more lurid the better, Greeks love lurid stories."

"What are you talking about?"

Drovich shrugged as though there was nothing more to explain. "Justifiable homicide, so justifiable that a Greek court would exonerate her. Instead you and your compatriots willfully helped her escape, sealing forever the opportunity for a pardon. Am I making myself clear?"

If Drovich expected Marcus to become speechless he was correct. Marcus's rattled mind whiplashed back in time when he speculated about Eleni's relationship to Kostas. If this is what Drovich was implying—that Kostas forced Eleni into a relationship so grotesque that killing him was forgivable in a Greek court.

Marcus dropped his gaze and stared at the flagstones under his feet, their haphazard arrangement a metaphor for his state of mind. "By claiming Kostas was her father," he asked matter-of-factly, "Eleni would have had justifiable reason for killing him?"

"Exactly. You are a man with more imagination than I gave you credit for."

Marcus spoke as if to himself: "Eleni was his ticket out of Greece. He was so desperate to live in America he was willing to force his own daughter to marry him?"

Drovich waited a few seconds before answering. "A very believable scenario, especially for Greeks. An argument in the apartment, an emotional confrontation in which the truth comes out, she finds a gun and kills him. "

"You know she did not kill Kostas."

"You have to accept the reality of the situation, Kyrio Giannou. Proving innocence is far more difficult than appealing for mercy."

Marcus shook his head. "So Eleni could have walked out a free woman."

"If you had just let the Greek system of justice run its course, yes, she would have walked out a free woman. Instead you flew in with all your American self-righteous attitude about fairness and justice."

Marcus sighed heavily, feeling discouraged and defeated. "This is a crazy country." He passed the worn envelope to Drovich. "Here it is."

"What?"

"Theophanes' Virgin. What you dreamed of having."

Drovich examined the envelope as he would a package lost on a tram. With slow methodical moves, he opened it and pulled out the icon. He held it close to his eyes and studied the brush strokes in fine detail.

"Not bad," he said and handed it back.

"What do you mean?"

"Not bad for a forgery."

"*A what?*"

"A forgery. Well-done but still a fake."

Marcus picked it up and stared at it. So Kostas had painted a forgery after all and passed it off as the real one. Even this came back to haunt him. Everything he had hoped to accomplish on his short, tortured visit to Greece lay in ruin, from not being able to help Eleni to being taken for a sucker.

Drovich stared accusingly. "Were you planning to pass off this forgery for the real icon? Did you really expect me to be that naïve?"

Marcus was completely dumbfounded. "I had nothing to do with this. I thought it was genuine."

"You would not ask to meet me with this forgery unless you knew where the real one was. Everyone has his price. You must have an idea what the genuine icon is worth. Hold it for ransom, no questions asked for its return. We are talking a hundred thousand dollars, maybe more."

"I swear to you I did not know it was a fake. Eleni and I have been carrying this all over Greece assuming it was the real Virgin. Kostas painted this. I found paint supplies and a reproduction of Theophanes' Virgin torn out of a catalog hidden under the bed in his apartment."

Drovich settled himself against the back of the bench as though he were going to be there awhile. "In case you missed something let me bring you up to date. I made an arrangement with Kostas, perhaps a better word for it is a deal. He was to deliver the icon to me the night before your arrival in Greece."

"Is that what the phone conversation was about at the restaurant? I heard him talking to you, at the time I did not know who. He was very agitated."

"Yes, but instead of completing his end of the bargain, he chose instead to drive to Athens to meet your plane, using my car which I had entrusted to him. He was playing the big man, as you say. And so when he called me from the restaurant he still did not have the icon. I was quite upset. I smelled a rat because after you and your mother arrived, he thought he was in a stronger position to bargain, perhaps thinking he could get more money than what we had agreed upon. And that is why Weber and I chose to ride with you to Kremasti. I see now that Kostas thought he could pass off his forgery as the real one, pocket the money and still have the original in his possession. A true double cross, wouldn't you say?" Drovich rubbed his chin. "I have to give him credit, though, this is not a bad forgery. He had a talent I did not know he possessed."

"He learned the art of icon painting at the monestary when he was a novice," Marcus said recalling what the old monk, Brother Christos, had told him. He looked at the icon with disdain. What he thought was a precious work of art was nothing more than a curiosity, not even worth the paint brushed on it. Wait till he tells his mother she had sent him off with a fake. He was unbelievably disappointed. "We both got taken."

Drovich turned his frown into a smile. "The real one is still out there. Don't you want to find it? Suppose we join forces, you and I…" he let his sentence hang in midair waiting for a reaction from Marcus.

"What are you suggesting?"

"By working together we might have a better chance of finding the icon."

Marcus wondered if this was another trick.

"We can also keep an eye on one another. Doesn't that make sense?"

Marcus understood that it did make sense, at least for the present. Better to have your target in the crosshairs than have him disappear into the trees.

"If we find the original icon, what's in it for me?"
"The same deal I made with Kostas."
"Ten thousand dollars?"
"Yes."

"What would I do with it?"

"You said you wanted Eleni's good name back. Hire a lawyer. For ten thousand dollars, thirty-three thousand drachmas, you can get the best lawyer in all of Greece."

"Not a bad idea, but why do you want the icon? So you can hang it in your home in Zagreb and admire it every day?"

"On the contrary, I would want everyone to see it. I would contribute it to a great museum."

"And get a plaque bearing your name?"

"At least, Kyrio Giannou, but you have to agree that the icon is much better off in a museum than hanging in the bedroom of your relatives. Theophanes is more widely known in Russia than in Greece. It would be an artistic coup to give the icon for presentation and preservation to the world's oldest museum that happens to be in the Soviet Union..." he hesitated for effect, "...the Hermitage." Drovich's thin face seemed to light up as he talked. "Imagine, the prestige it would bring. I come from a satellite country of limited means and renown, but if I were to bring the icon to the Hermitage where it truly would be a star, it would bestow upon me honor and position, perhaps in time a curatorship as the Russians finally see my talent and dedication, even a Directorship."

Marcus marveled at this man's incredible flight of fancy, his audacious, unbridled ambition. He understood now how vital it was to keep Drovich from getting the icon. Let him assume Marcus did not want the icon itself, only for the money it would bring.

Drovich leaned back already basking in future glory. "Agreed?"

"Agreed," Marcus said, hoping he was making the right decision.

"Where shall we start?"

"At the scene of the crime."

Drovich looked at him questioningly.

"Kremasti."

26

The two men arrived in Kremasti an hour later, the whitewashed church and the original landmark campanili greeting them as Drovich dropped off Marcus in the square. A boy ran ahead to announce his arrival and so, when he approached the house, Marcus's mother and Caliope were on the front porch waiting with open arms, wet cheeks and pounding hearts.

Mrs. Giannou gripped her son tightly and then crossed herself several times. "Thank god, you are safe."

Then it was Caliope's turn and Marcus pulled away with his cheek moist not only with her kisses but her warm tears as well.

"How did you get here?" his mother asked.

"Drovich drove me."

She looked around with alarm.

"He went to the house he rents with Weber."

"I hope he stays there. I don't like him."

"It's ok, Mom. How is Dimitri?"

"He has come out of his coma."

"Great news. Is it too much if we go into his bedroom so I can bring you all up to date?"

"Of course."

Dimitri was sitting up in his bed. His pale face brightened considerably when he saw Marcus.

Marcus leaned over the old man and kissed the top of his head, then touched his hand, his bony knuckles.

By now he felt confident enough to launch himself into Greek. If he faltered he had plenty of help to correct his grammar and syntax. "The last time I saw you," he said to Dimitri, "the word Mystras came from your lips. Do you remember that?"

"Only as in a dream."

"It is no longer a dream, Theio. I found Mystras."

His eyes glistened.

"And Eleni is there."

He appeared a bit befuddled. "She is in Mystras?"

"In the care of the monks."

Dimitri grunted as he shifted against his pillow. "Sit next to me. I lost many days. Tell me everything I have missed."

Marcus sat on the edge of the bed. "It is a long story but it has a happy ending."

Caliope and his mother stood in the doorway and listened as Marcus reprised the events that brought Eleni to Mystras, careful to leave out harrowing details that could traumatize them. There would be ample opportunity in the future when they could manage the full story with the benefit of elapsed time and mellowing.

"An adventure no less than Homer's Odyssey," Dimitri said.

Marcus smiled at his uncle's hyperbole. Except for the fact that it lasted ten days, not ten years, it *was* packed with adventure and, to be honest, with a cast of characters that could fill a novel.

"I long for the strength and confidence you possess, Marcus, but those qualities are beyond my reach. What is left for an old man like me?" He laughed sardonically "Memories..." Dimitri fell into deep thought as though reliving the distant past. He was so remote that

Marcus wondered if his uncle might be suffering another stroke.

"Are you all right, Theio?" he asked, concerned.

Dimitri refocused and nodded. He looked at Caliope and Mrs. Giannou. "Please close the door and leave me alone with Marcus."

Marcus glanced at his mother and aunt and back again at Dimitri, puzzled. "What is it, Theio?"

After they where alone, he said, "It is now my turn to tell a story, Marcus. Not one with a happy ending like yours but one that must be told. I had hoped to bury it in the grave with me because I do not want to hurt Eleni any more than she already has been hurt but it is no longer possible. She, the most innocent among us, has suffered the most, forced to bear an evil that has haunted this family since the war."

Dimitri stared into Marcus's eyes as though building up emotional strength to unburden his soul.

"Does Monodendri have meaning for you?" he asked.

"I remember seeing a monument on the road to Kremasti, but I do not know anything about it."

"That is not surprising. Your history books do not have the story of Monodrendi. In the long tale of man's inhumanity to man, this name will only be remembered by those who survived. The monument marks the graves of 117 young men, shot to death by the Germans in reprisal for the killing of one of their soldiers. They all were young, some of them not yet twenty."

"My god," Marcus said. "When did this happen?"

"November 17th, 1943. There is hardly a person in Sparta who does not have a relative buried in Monodendri."

"Why so many?"

"The officer responsible was a Nazi general who ordered that one man should die for each house in Sparta, 117 houses, 117 men."

"For the death of a single German? That was barbarous! Didn't anyone try to stop him?"

"How could they? If they tried, more would be killed. There were pleas for mercy, to reduce the number at least. One mother lost all four of her sons. An older man begged that he be taken instead of his son. He was refused. The mothers claimed the bodies and buried them at Monodendri. When the war was over a monument was raised, a white obelisk with a bronze plaque and the names of all those who died there." Tears began to flow down the crevasses of the old man's cheeks.

"Their blood will always stain the memories of mothers, sisters, fathers. Their stain is also my stain…"

"Why do you say that, Theio?" Marcus stared into Dimitri's eyes, trying to discover how badly his soul was bruised, but saw stoicism instead, determination to face the issue head-on.

"Because the executioner, the Nazi general who ordered all those men to die…" he hesitated. "…*that* evil man was Eleni's father."

The words were carried on a whisper that was in shocking contrast to their impact. This crushing revelation was the very opposite of what Marcus had initially believed, that Kostas was Eleni's father. Instead, he was a Nazi officer who condemned more than a hundred young Greek men to death. How could anyone have possibly imagined this? Anna Koulouris—so favored by the monks at Mystras that they entrusted their most valuable possession to her, the Virgin of Theophanes—carries the child fathered by this Nazi beast. Was she forced to submit to him? Passion and counter-passion run high in this land, but Marcus could not believe that Anna willingly gave herself to him. It was inconceivable. Unless the executions happened after she became pregnant. If she were only alive to explain it all…

So *this* is what had been haunting Dimitri—not that Kostas was Eleni's father, an irrational suspicion fueled by Drovich's insinuations, but rather a Nazi general who gave the order to kill more than a hundred innocent Greek men.

Another disturbing thought came to him. Eleni is ignorant of this brutal, stark chapter of her life. The terrible secret has been kept from her. It was shameful enough to be a bastard child, but imagine the scorn she would face if the identity of her father became public. Poor Eleni. How could she confront the smoldering hostility and the brooding resentment of her neighbors? Greek women have been stoned for less.

His mother called from the parlor. "Marcus, come here, *amesos!*" Right now!

He rose from the edge of Dimitri's bed and touched his uncle's forearm in a show of compassion, and entered the parlor, his mind so preoccupied with what he had just heard that he was totally unprepared for what was awaiting him. His mother, white-faced, lips trembling, was sitting at the table with Caliope. Their hands were clasped as if in prayer. Curious more than alarmed, Marcus saw Drovich at the front door as though waiting to be invited in. But behind him, standing out on the porch and looking over Drovich's shoulder, was Weber.

"You have company," Drovich said with feigned politeness.

Weber stepped up and stood alongside Drovich so he could be seen in full view, and fear like electricity suddenly enveloped the parlor. In Weber's right hand was a small rifle, more like a pistol with a detachable stock, the long muzzle covered by a canister with tiny holes. There was a telescopic sight clamped over the barrel. Was this the gun used to shoot at Marcus but missed and later used to shoot at Kostas but did not miss?

Following Marcus's stare, Weber affected a strange grin on his pasty face. There was a pathological, sinister and altogether frightening quality about it. He held the weapon as though giving a lesson in gun safety. He checked the clip for bullets, hefted the weight, rubbed the muzzle with the palm of his hand, and held the gun close to his face to read the maker's name stamped on the bluish metal.

"A gun I happen to know," Drovich volunteered. "Mauser C96. A popular weapon used by the German army during the War, now widely coveted."

Weber nodded as though seconding a motion.

"So you and Weber are still a team?"

"Not by choice." Drovich motioned with his thumb. "As you can see he is pointing the gun at me as well as you."

"A falling out?" Marcus asked, keeping his eye on the sinister man whom he had not seen since dinner on his first night in Kremasti.

"That would imply a falling in, which never happened," Drovich replied. "Let me just say that Herr Weber and I are victims of circumstance that brought us to this unlikely position, one which I find distasteful but unfortunately necessary." He looked at Mrs. Giannou "I apologize for this intrusion but I would like to have a word with your son."

"Go ahead, talk to him. I don't feel like it." She rose from her chair and motioned to her sister to join her in Dimitri's bedroom.

"In fact, I prefer that you remain, Mrs. Giannou, as this conversation involves you as well, which we will conduct in English."

Curious now, she sat back down while Caliope joined her husband, softly closing the door behind her.

"Would you mind telling us what this is all about?" Mrs. Giannou asked.

Drovich stepped forward, his courtly manner befitting that of a diplomat on his way to the negotiating table while Weber, with gun in hand, acting like an officer waiting for the command to open fire.

"I would like to propose a financial arrangement that you might find more interesting than did your son."

"Financial arrangement?" she asked suspiciously. "What kind of financial arrangement?"

"I would like to make a cash offer for the icon of Theophanes."

Marcus burst out laughing. "Will the real Janos Drovich please stand up?" he said

"I beg your pardon?"

"I am referring to a game show on American television. The panel has to figure out which of the guests is telling the truth."

Drovich was not amused. He turned his attention to Mrs. Giannou. "I am simply offering you a business proposition. I want to know where the icon is. I was hoping to learn this from your son but he has refused. Perhaps you will be more reasonable. I will pay handsomely."

Marcus was surprised when his mother asked, "How handsomely?" He knew she couldn't seriously be considering his offer. She had to be leading him on.

"Twenty thousand dollars," Drovich replied.

His mother predictably crossed herself, not once but three times. The Father, Son and Holy Spirit all had to be in on this one.

"Is that what you were willing to pay Kostas?" she asked.

Drovich smiled demurely. "Between us, Kyrie Giannou, Kostas was much easier to buy off."

"How much easier?"

Drovich pursed his lips, debating whether or not he should answer. "Half."

"What happened to ruin the deal?"

"Simple greed, Kyrie Giannou. He tried to substitute the real icon for a forgery."

Mrs. Giannou looked sharply at Drovich. "Forgery? What are you talking about?"

"Kostas painted a forgery which he hoped to sell to me. But he could not fool an expert. He could fool only those who cannot appreciate the rarity and beauty of such an exquisite work of art." He shook his head wistfully. "If Kostas wasn't so greedy, I would have had the real icon,

257

he would have been richer by ten thousand dollars and no one would have been hurt."

"Unless you don't count murder," Marcus said.

Drovich lowered his head, his pate showing beads of nervous sweat. "If Kostas had cooperated, he would not have died. It was an unfortunate accident."

"Accident? You expect me to swallow that?"

Drovich reacted as he would from a glove slapping his cheek, more concerned with his honor as a gentleman than his guilt as a murderer.

"I had nothing to do with that unpleasantness."

Weber, standing next to Drovich, suddenly brought his spread legs together. Somewhere hidden by layers of fat his body grew rigid. What was going on inside his head? Marcus wished he could talk, say something, anything, rather than just stare with seething anger.

"I beg to differ with you, Drovich," Marcus said. "Kostas hid the real icon to keep it from you."

"Quite illogical, Kyrio Giannou. Why would I kill the man who had the very thing I wanted?"

"Let me guess. You only meant to threaten him but in your fury the gun went off, the same one Weber is holding. That fits your reference to an 'unfortunate accident' doesn't it?"

Drovich and Weber exchanged nervous glances.

"There is also the possibility," Marcus continued, "and I favor this version, that Kostas told you he had taken my uncle into his confidence, and that he was going to the police to turn you in. I imagine ESA would not be very happy to learn a Yugoslav was trying to steal a Greek treasure. Fearing for your life, you had no alternative but to kill Kostas and hurry back to Kremasti and threaten Dimitri by saying you would kill Eleni, or Caliope, or my mother if he did not tell you where the icon was hidden."

Mrs. Giannou jumped up. "You horrible man!" she cried out.

Weber glared at her, his gun seemingly an extention of his arm as he waved it at her.

Mrs. Giannou was always cautioning her son but now it was Marcus's turn to caution her. "Mom, for god's sake, sit down."

"Kyrie Giannou," Drovich said in a conciliatory voice, "your son is merely theorizing. There is no truth in what he is saying. Please let us put aside our rancor and reconsider my offer, twenty thousand dollars for the icon. A substantial sum of money even in America and here, in Greece, it is a king's ransom that would provide care for your brother-in-law. Look around you." He swept his hand before him, a Shakespearean actor in the middle of a soliloquy. "Eking out a living selling general merchandize from those dusty shelves, three or four hundred drachmas a month income, nothing more. Think of it, twenty-thousand dollars, three million drachmas!"

"It won't wash, Drovich," Marcus said. "You will never get your hands on that icon."

Weber stepped forward, the anger in him finally boiling over, having traveled a long way to reach the surface.

"You are finished talking, Janos," he said in a voice so dry it needed watering. "Now it is my turn."

27

The room suddenly went still. Everyone except Drovich was staring wide-eyed at Weber. He can talk!

"You fool," Drovich snapped, finally breaking the silence. "See what you have done?"

The expression on Weber's face was a strange mix of pleasure and hatred, pleasure from the shock he created and hatred from admitting his private secret.

Marcus tried to untangle the raging mind of this deranged man by separating himself from the reality of the moment, as if he were in a theater watching a melodrama, witnessing an intense, still-developing scene when the villain is found out.

"So you can speak after all," he said. "Why did you pretend not to?"

"A ploy, Giannou. By pretending to be incapable of speech, people assume I am simple-minded and they will be more likely to let their guard down and say things that might otherwise remain private. You learn a good deal that way."

He wiggled the gun to emphasize his point.

"Why don't you put that thing down, Weber. Can't you see you are in no danger from any of us?"

"I have no intention of granting your wish, Giannou. It is the other way around. You are to grant mine." Weber spoke with a heavy German accent, the esses coming out of his mouth as if he were spitting.

Drovich was watching, his face drawn and etched with concern. "Weber, for god's sake. Stop this insanity."

"Listen to your partner, Weber," Marcus said. "If you want the icon you have to get it from me."

Weber stared at Marcus. Can I trust him? he seemed to be thinking. He addressed Mrs. Giannou. "Join your sister in the bedroom and stay with her. Do not try anything foolish."

"Like what?" Marcus taunted. "Climb out the window and run for help?"

"Shut up," he warned mostly for Mrs. Giannou's benefit, "unless you would like to see a bullet enter your head, or your chest, or your stomach." With each mention of Marcus's anatomy he pointed to it with the gun muzzle.

His mother was horror-struck. Marcus tried to calm her fears. "Mom, he won't try anything. He needs me. I know where the icon is."

Mrs. Giannou stared at her son trying to read his mind. He was up to something and she couldn't figure it out. She shook her head from doubt and fear. "Caliope needs me, anyway," she said in Greek. "I need to tell her that everything will be all right." She said this as much to assure herself as her son.

When the door closed behind her, Marcus spoke to Drovich in Greek. "You overplayed your hand. You should have kept him out of sight."

"I have nothing to do with this, you must believe me."

"Really? Where were you when Kostas was shot?"

"I was not in the apartment."

Weber eyed the two warily as they talked, wondering what they were discussing.

"It doesn't matter if you were there or not. You are an accessory. Your obsession for the icon was the motivating factor that led to Kostas' murder."

"I will not be made a partner to murder. None of this was my idea. I was hired."

"Hired?"

"By whom?"

"Weber."

At the mention of his name in the middle of a Greek conversation, Weber looked at Drovich, a sneer building around his mouth. "What are you saying about me?"

Drovich sneered in return. "You told me it would be a simple matter of finding the icon. In and out of Greece in ten days…"

Suddenly Weber brought the muzzle of his gun up and sliced a cut across Drovich's cheek with the gun sight. Drovich shouted in pain and the look on his face was one of sheer horror as he ran his fingers along the line of crimson. Blood began to ooze out of the wound.

The door opened and Mrs. Giannou peeked out.

"Mom, stay in there," Marcus warned.

"What about you?"

"I'll be safe. I know what I'm doing," he said to her in Greek.

She closed the door, her forehead furrowed with worry.

Marcus had to hide his own nervousness. He had to be the man in charge. "You picked yourself a winner," he said to Drovich in Greek.

Weber waved the gun. "Speak English only, damn you!"

"All right," Marcus said, "calm down."

Marcus needed Drovich as an ally. Divide the odds in half and be careful not to antagonize Weber, obviously a genuine psychopath.

Marcus wondered how much life insurance could he buy right now. The premiums would be too high given the image of a crackpot pointing a gun at his heart. Marcus had one advantage, though, of pretending to know where the icon was. He would not be shot if he could keep Weber believing that. Marcus had to get him away from the house, away from his mother, Caliope and Dimitri. Their safety in exchange for the icon—is that the bargain he will have to strike with Weber? Can you even bargain with a killer? Maybe that is what Kostas tried to do, and lost.

"So it *was* you who killed Kostas," Marcus said to Weber in English.

Weber made a bow as stiff as his fat body would allow. "I did so in the performance of a necessary evil."

"No matter how you try to justify it, Kostas is dead."

"Quite so, Giannou. But there were extenuating circumstances."

"So extenuating you had to kill him? Was it over the icon? Did he change his mind?"

"Change his mind? Yes, in a way. He kidnapped the icon, literally. He said I had no right to it."

"Those were his words?" Marcus asked.

"Not precisely but taken in context, yes. I dislike idealism quickly achieved and wrongly placed."

Here was an Aryan looking down on Mediterraneans as weak and indecisive, a clue to his character. Good. Keep him talking—what Marcus needed to do. The more he was able to get inside this man's skull, the better his chances of defeating him.

"What about you, Drovich," Marcus asked. "How did you feel about Kostas' change of heart?"

"I was not in the apartment to hear the conversation," Drovich said.

"Is he telling the truth, Weber?"

Weber laughed. "Janos is an esthete with no stomach for the harder realities of life. I knew he would be in my way. So I sent him out to..." he hesitated looking for the appropriate metaphor "...smell the flowers."

Drovich made a face of displeasure.

"So you were alone in the apartment with Kostas?"

Weber eyed Marcus suspiciously, his mood mercurial, unstable. "You ask too many questions."

"Not nearly enough. I'd like to know what happened."

"What difference would that make to you?"

"A great deal. My cousin was arrested for what you did."

Weber's face went soft for a split second as though Marcus's comment made him remember something. And then he hardened, becoming even more belligerent. "A pity but in any conflict there are innocent bystanders who pay the price."

Marcus felt anger rise in his chest. He was almost shaking and he fought to conceal his feelings. Keep cool he told himself, don't give Weber any psychological advantage. "The real pity, Weber," he said, "is that after all this effort, you still don't have the icon."

He studied Marcus's face for a moment and then said, "Touche."

"What if I were to tell you I know where it is hidden and I would be willing to make a deal with you?"

"I would listen to your offer."

"Good. As long as we understand each other, what harm is there in answering a few questions first, just to clear the air?"

Weber shrugged, giving a little. It was evident he liked being onstage even for an audience of one.

"Let's go back to that day in the apartment," Marcus said. "A young girl brought a note from Kostas hidden in a pail of fresh yogurt asking that Eleni see him in his apartment as soon as possible. Were you in on that?"

Weber hesitated before answering, no doubt debating how much he should reveal to Marcus, but then realizing that if he did not answer there was no hope of getting the icon. "Yes, I told him to write the note. Hiding it in the yogurt was his idea. He is more dramatic than I am."

"But the note did not say why he wanted to see her."

"Because with Kostas, idealism has its limits."

"What does that mean?"

"He wanted to throw out the deal he made with me and make a new one."

"You mean he wanted more money?"

"Oh, nothing as mundane as money. I told you he had become idealistic. He wanted the documents."

"Eleni's documents?" Marcus asked.

He nodded.

"*You* had them?" So Kostas had not stolen them after all. As Marcus took in this revelation he could imagine Kostas going through a primary revision. He must have been suffering sheer agony. What he had thought was a simple deceit, exchanging the real icon for a copy and a hefty reward had turned into a nightmare of problems, not the least of which was losing Eleni's birth documents, thus shattering his lifelong dream of coming to America.

"I found them in her hotel room looking for the icon," Weber confirmed. "And it was a stroke of luck that I did. They were the only bargaining chip I had after Kostas went through his moral crisis and switched the icons. You assumed you had the genuine article, didn't you, but all you had was the forgery. When I searched the room I found the icon and for a brief moment I was ecstatic. But under closer scrutiny I realized it was the fake."

Of course! That is why the icon was left behind. Marcus's mind was traveling at warp speed. The night before he and Eleni sneaked out of Kremasti, Kostas must have switched the icons, knowing they could not tell the difference, and hid the real one so that Drovich and Weber could not get their hands on it. He must have hidden it right here in Kremasti, but where?

"So you broke into our hotel room in Athens," Marcus said, buying time as he tried to think. "And I assumed it was Kostas."

Weber nodded, now proudly taking credit, his initial reluctance to talk replaced by boasting, exactly what Marcus was hoping for. "Kostas did not have the tenacity to do what I did."

"I will give you that," Marcus said, "but why did you steal Eleni's documents? What possible use could they be to you?"

"Simply as leverage. I really wanted the icon. When I did not find it, how could I justify a hasty trip to Athens without something to show for it? As it turned out, I made a wise decision."

"How did you know where we were?"

"Greece is a small country," Drovich interjected. "Only one road connects Athens from Niata and a telephone call to an ESA contact in Corinth spotted my stolen Simca as it traveled through town. He followed you, reported back to us where you were staying and we took the overland taxi into Athens, convinced we would find the icon by searching your room."

Weber stared angrily at Drovich. "You and your stupid ideas."

"Why are you blaming me? You were as responsible as I, believing the icon was in that envelope."

"Envelope?" Marcus said, and began to laugh.

"You find that amusing?" Drovich said, irritated.

"I find it more ironic than amusing."

"What are you talking about?"

"Anna Koulouris carried the icon to Kremasti in that very same envelope. You had the right envelope but you were twenty-five years too late."

Weber gritted his teeth but Drovich merely smiled. "After what happened the preceding night it is no wonder we jumped to conclusions."

"Preceding night..." Marcus said, trying to remember. His life had been swept up in such a tornado of jarring events his head was constantly spinning.

"The night of your arrival," Drovich said, "you went to bed tired from your long trip, but we were not sleeping. Weber and I were having a rather pointed discussion with Kostas who was beginning to have second thoughts about our agreement. I tried to impress upon him the danger of second thoughts. He began talking about principles. Can you imagine a man like Kostas Kanellos getting a conscience so late in the game? I can guess that his change of heart had something to do with your arrival. I do not know and he did not explain. He just said that he had to think about our agreement a little longer."

Weber interrupted. "He could not be trusted, I told you that all along. He was weak, undisciplined."

"Not at all like you, my Aryan friend?" Drovich replied with more than a hint of sarcasm and then picked up the thread of his narrative. "He left the house we were sharing at the edge of town. Weber and I presumed he was just letting off steam and would return. We were offering him a sum of money he could not refuse, or so we thought, but as the minutes went by we became worried that he might go to you or Dimitri, Eleni even, and expose us. You grew restive and concerned, right Weber?"

Weber nodded.

"Would you like to take up the narrative again since hearing if from me would be secondhand. It would be better to hear it from an eye witness."

"If you are trying to incriminate me, Drovich, it will not work. No one was hurt that night, only frightened."

"Then be my guest."

"All right, I will finish the story if it will make you shut up for a while."

No lost love here, Marcus noted to himself.

"Drovich is right about one thing," Weber said in his thick German accent. "I was worried, so I went outside to look for Kostas, following the path to Dimitri's house. I saw him at the front door talking to Dimitri. I was worried that he was spilling the beans."

"You were more than worried, you were furious," Drovich said. "I know, because you came back for your gun."

Weber looked down at it admiringly. "This is a very sophisticated weapon," he said, "useful for both short and long-range targets. It has a silencer and an infrared sight," he pointed to a device with an eyepiece locked over the barrel. "Ideal for night shooting, a true precision instrument."

"Not unlike you, Weber," Marcus said, "a true precision instrument?"

Weber smiled appreciatively.

"But if the gun is so accurate why did you miss your target?"

"I did not miss my target. I only intended to warn Kostas that he could not get away with doublecrossing us."

"What about details?"

"Details?"

"Features that can identify one person from another when you take aim."

"I can tell a man from a goat." He laughed at his joke and patted the gun for extra emphasis. "The infrared provides a clear outline."

"But can you tell one man from another?"

Weber looked at Marcus with renewed wariness. "What are you driving at?"

"I just happened to be your target for the night." Watching Weber's reaction Marcus felt as though he had taken Weber's queen with his pawn. "You weren't firing your so-called warning shots at Kostas, you were firing them at me."

"*You?*" Weber asked, his voice faltering. "No, I shot at Kostas, I know I did."

"You backfired more than you fired, Weber. You missed him by at least a minute. I was in the outhouse when I heard footsteps. I was curious so I went to Dimitri's house and hid around the corner. Kostas was talking to Dimitri and after he left I climbed the porch. Suddenly a bullet exploded in the wall by my head."

Weber managed a wry smile. "So, the figure in the dark was you. At least my aim was accurate because, as I said, I did not shoot to kill."

"How would I know that? I took off and ran back to Athena's house."

"It appears we were both mistaken," Weber said gamely.

"But you made a much larger mistake. By frightening Kostas you ended up completely alienating him, an unintended consequence of your actions."

"I did not frighten Kostas, I frightened you."

"You frightened both of us, Weber. Kostas witnessed the shooting on his way back to the house. Even in the dark he could see enough to come to the inescapable conclusion that he was the intended target, not me. He had no reason to believe you missed on purpose. He believed you intended to kill him. so he decided to hide the icon. It was his life insurance policy."

Weber looked at his gun, not admiringly as before but as if it were now a liability. "Anyone can make a bad decision, especially under duress."

"You made a string of bad decisions, Weber. That one, following Eleni and me to Athens on a wild goose chase and, in the end, killing Kostas."

Weber was clearly unsettled, the way Marcus wanted him to be, but not so unsettled that he would lose control and do something rash. Not right now.

"Let me explain the circumstances of that fateful day in the apartment, Giannou." He waved the gun at the table. "I have to sit down. My feet are tired."

Marcus was glad to get off his feet, too, but he wasn't going to admit it. The three drew back chairs and sat down. Weber rested the gun on the tabletop next to his elbow. He let out a sigh of relief. "One of these days I must lose a few pounds, eh, Janos?"

Drovich gave him a steely look. "A few?"

Weber's cherubic cheeks took on a pinkish glow of resentment.

Keep needling him, Marcus thought. "Ok," he said, "start explaining."

"Let me begin with the night we borrowed the documents belonging to your cousin."

"Borrowed? You stole them," Marcus said testily.

"Oh, but we were very willing to give them back. We returned to Kremasti and asked your uncle if he would act as intermediary in a deal to trade Eleni's documents for the icon. He was the perfect host. He invited us in. His wife made coffee. Even your mother was cordial to us."

Marcus was surprised they were friendly when in the past they were fearful of this pair. What was going on?

"Drovich did the talking. I stood humbly by and listened. They assumed of course that I could not speak."

"What did you say to Dimitri?" Marcus asked Drovich.

"Once we had the icon we would leave Greece never to return."

Marcus eyed Drovich with suspicion. "Did you threaten him?"

Drovich looked at the door of the bedroom where Dimitri lay. "Are you implying we caused his stroke?"

"I am not ruling anything out."

"He was fine when we left," Weber said dismissively.

Nevertheless, Marcus thought, poor Dimitri must have been under extreme pressure dealing with Weber, pretending to be cordial when in his heart he was hating every minute with him. A stroke could easily have been a delayed reaction to this invasion of his home.

"You left empty-handed, right?" Marcus said, dealing a small modicum of revenge on behalf of his uncle.

Drovich nodded. "Your uncle said he did not know where Kostas was. We drove to his apartment in Sparta rather depressed. To our complete surprise who do you think was waiting for us?"

"None other than Kostas Kanellos?"

"None other, and we finally learned the fate of Theophanes' Virgin."

"What did he tell you?"

"He told us he kidnapped her!" Drovich spoke so dramatically Marcus wondered if he wasn't having a love affair with the icon.

"Kanellos was so smug," he continued, "telling us that we were unfit to possess the Virgin and that we would never lay eyes on her again."

"Now you really were depressed," Marcus said goading him a little.

Weber smiled but his teeth were clenched. "Ah, but the last laugh was ours, Giannou. We went to dine at the Kipris Estiatorio, a gesture to show there were no hard feelings. With our stomachs full of good food and wine, he grew conciliatory and we were able to discuss areas of mutual concern."

"I didn't think there were any at this point."

"Indeed there were. One was of special interest to Kostas: the documents belonging to Eleni. I told him they were in my possession and I would return them for the genuine icon. I knew his greatest wish was to go to America, and by marrying a woman who could claim American citizenship by birth, his dream would come true. He valued the documents more than money, actually. No amount of money would get him to America. Only marrying Eleni would provide that."

"Maybe he wanted the documents for Eleni's sake more than his own."

"Really, Giannou, do not invest Kostas with undeserved nobility. He wanted to be a big man but he had a small mind. He thought only of himself."

"Is that why you don't feel any guilt killing him?"

Weber snorted. "Guilt is an indulgence of the weak. Besides, why should I suffer guilt over what had to be done?"

Marcus wanted to object on moral grounds, if nothing else, but Weber held up his hand. "Before you jump to any unfair conclusions, let me tell you what happened."

Marcus settled back. "All right."

"Following dinner, we struck a new bargain with Kostas—a simple trade, the icon for the documents."

"Why did Kostas drag Eleni into this, sending her a note to come to the apartment?"

"Lack of trust, I presume. He insisted that he give the papers to her personally and to let her leave before he would take us to the icon." Weber made a face. "The ridiculous idea of smuggling a note in yogurt was his idea."

Marcus smiled. "A flair for the dramatic. But how did you know he would complete his end of the bargain once Eleni got the papers and left the apartment?"

"I am not as stupid as you may think." Weber laughed at his self-deprecating comment. "I told Kostas that Eleni must come alone, a condition that was violated by your presence."

"You saw me?" Marcus asked, surprised.

"Drovich did. In addition to looking at flowers, he was also watching the building. He saw you drop Eleni off and park around the corner under a tree. You were easy to spot."

So much for covert operations, Marcus thought wryly.

"I was to detain Eleni when she came out of the apartment," Drovich said. "Only when Weber had the icon safely in hand was she to be released."

"If not," Weber drew his index finger across the wattles of his throat, "kaput."

Marcus understood the gesture was meant to intimidate him, but he fought down the reaction Weber was looking for and pretended indifference.

"So what happened when Eleni showed up?" he asked casually.

"I hid in the bedroom. I thought the meeting would be over quickly. Kostas gives her the papers and she leaves." Weber brushed his palms together in a gesture of mission accomplished. "How much time does that require? A minute. Two minutes? But Eleni was in no hurry to leave. She was quite upset. She believed, as you did, that he stole her documents. Even though they were speaking only Greek, I had no trouble interpreting the anger in her words. Poor Kostas was having his hair trimmed. I'm sure he was doubly embarrassed knowing I could hear what was going on. Greek men are extremely vain about their masculinity. I shall not bother you with the vehemence of her attack on him, but suffice it to say she not only trimmed his hair, she cut off his testicles." There was a lecherous look in his eyes. "I speak figuratively of course."

"You don't have to spare my feelings, Weber, I am not sparing yours."

The cold-blooded look came back. "Then I shall continue with the gruesome details. Stripped of his virility, Kostas launched a counteroffensive—what is the term you Americans use— spilling the beans?"

"Close enough."

"It was a catastrophic moment, believe me. I could understand that he was ready to tell Eleni everything about our arrangement. I had to stop him. I grabbed my gun and opened the door, but my appearance turned a degenerating situation into a chaotic one. Kostas had his back to me and Eleni saw me first and screamed. All I wanted to do was shut him up but he lunged at me, his hands reaching for my throat. I shot him in order to save my own life. It was self-defense."

Weber settled back in his chair, breathing hard from the exertion of telling his story.

Marcus stared with revulsion at this overweight grotesquerie of a man, the killer buried in Eleni's fractured memory. No wonder she could not articulate seeing him kill Kostas. Could she ever recover from witnessing this horror?

But he could not allow Eleni's suffering to shake him. He had to maintain an exterior as cool as Weber's even though the confession confirmed what Marcus already knew—he was dealing with a madman. "Weren't you concerned that Eleni would turn you in?"

"The police believing an ignorant village girl? You can't be serious."

Marcus stiffened, his anger ready to boil over. Stay calm, he told himself, stay calm. "Of course. How silly of me. So, after killing Kostas you saw an opportunity to frame Eleni. You locked her in the apartment and called the police. Is that right?"

Weber slapped the gun against the palm of his hand. "You are so patronizing, you act like you are smarter because I am German and you defeated us in the war. Well, I won't waste any more time talking to you. All I care about is the icon."

"I wish I could be of service, Weber, but I really think the icon belongs here in Greece."

Weber glanced at the closed door. Inside the bedroom Marcus's mother, Caliope and Dimitri no doubt were wondering what in god's name was going on.

He looked back at Marcus. "Your loved ones are behind that door. Would you risk harming them over an icon that means nothing to you?" His grin had nothing to do with humor, only sadism.

"Suppose I lead you to the icon? How do I know you will let them go?"

"You have my word."

"Word?" Marcus laughed.

Drovich leaned toward Marcus. "Please, Kyrio Giannou, do as he says."

Weber patted Drovich on the shoulder. He shrank from the touch. The small cut on his cheek from Weber's gun had crusted over but not the memory of it.

"Janos," Weber said to the fastidious esthete, "you are finally showing some balls. I thought I was the only one who had any."

Marcus smiled, but he knew Weber's comment was directed to him as well. "There is only one thing I want for the icon."

"I'm through trading, Giannou. No money." He patted the gun as he did Drovich's shoulder.

"I don't care about the money, Weber. I want Eleni's documents."

Weber took his eyes off Marcus long enough to direct a smug look at Drovich. "A fair exchange, wouldn't you say, Janos? We don't need them anymore." Weber puffed up his chest. "All right, Giannou, the papers for the icon."

Drovich sighed with relief. "Let us go. The sooner we get out of Greece, the better."

"Very well." Weber was in good spirits. "We will take you to the documents." He pushed his chair from the table, its spindly legs squeaking from the torque. "After I have the icon and you have your lover's proof of citizenship everyone will be happy."

"Except for the late Kostas Kannelos." Marcus got up walked out on the porch, anxious to get Weber away from the house.

"Where are you going in such a hurry?" he said, catching up. "Don't you think you should inform your mother that you are leaving?" Weber spoke as though he was addressing a thoughtless son.

Marcus stopped walking. "All right."

"Call her."

Marcus did. His mother opened the front door and looked out apprehensively.

"Mom, I'm leaving for awhile."

"Where are you going?" Her fingers against the jam were shaking.

"I won't be long. Stay in the house till I get back."

Weber nodded approvingly. "Take your son's advice, Mrs. Giannou. Do not leave the house for any reason. Do not try to contact neighbors. I will have my gun trained on your son at all times and if I discover that you have not followed these simple precautions, I will end his life." He snapped the safety back for added effect.

Mrs. Giannou rushed to her son, her arms outstretched. She framed his face with her hands and tears formed in her eyes. "Be careful, my son, please be careful."

Marcus could not remember the last time she had looked at him so tenderly.

28

They walked up the steep path to the square. The sun was past its apogee, approaching siesta time. Villagers were inside their homes. Shutters were pulled across windows to darken interiors and block off the stifling heat. Marcus was in the lead, Weber in the middle holding his gun close to his body in case anyone paid them attention, and Drovich followed third.

Marcus hoped Weber believed that he was taking him to the icon, his margin of survival. If Weber for a moment suspected that he was being fooled, Marcus was a dead man. He had to outwit this pathological madman, this squat mass of overheated skin trudging and gasping behind him.

And Drovich? He must know what Marcus was up to and yet he was playing the game, so far at least. Maybe he decided to see how this ruse of Marcus's would play out. He was a winner either way.

Marcus looked over his shoulder briefly. What in the world had crossed this greasy character with that of a saintly icon? Beauty and the Beast, but even that analogy was faulty. Cocteau's version of the beast was of a decent, noble creature. There was nothing redemptive in Weber's character. Marcus had never felt such antipathy for another human. How could Drovich have fallen in with him?

He wondered why these two of such opposite dispositions should appear in Greece like Europeans on vacation and hire Kostas to guide them to a rare piece of religious art? And why *now* when, for nearly three decades, the icon was hidden away in an obscure village presumabley lost to the art world?

They crossed the square, hot and empty like the bottom of a pan after the water boiled away. Weber was squinting and wheezing. Sweat poured down his face. His sporty t-shirt was spotted with moisture under the arms and down the front. Even the waistband of his slacks was stained.

He stopped under a eucalyptus. "I have to catch my breath."

Marcus watched him suffering from the heat. Keep pushing, he thought. "Let's go."

"What is your hurry? This is the hottest time of day."

"I want to see those documents. How do I know you haven't destroyed them? I won't show you where I have hidden the icon till I see them."

Weber wiped his brow with the back of his hand. "All right, all right! It will be a pleasure to get you out of my hair."

They came to the house that Drovich and Weber rented. Behind it was a shed, nothing more than a stall open at both ends and covered by a rusting tin roof. Parked under it was the Simca—tired, spent, a fitting metaphor for the out-of-shape Weber.

The air was still. The only sound was the buzz of insects and his heavy breathing.

"Open the trunk," he commanded Drovich.

The lid sprung open. The trunk was packed with luggage, ready for departure. All that was preventing Weber and Drovich from driving away was the icon.

Wedged between the spare and the jack was the manila envelope, now stained with car grease. Drovich handed it to Marcus who checked the contents, all there,

Anna's passport, Eleni's birth certificate and the completed forms needed for her American passport. Satisfied, he folded the envelope and slipped it into his hip pocket.

"All right, I will now take you to the icon."

"It better not be far." Weber pointed his gun threateningly.

Drovich was wearing down, too. "That thing could go off accidentally. Relax, can't you?"

"Relax you say? I'll relax when I have that icon."

They marched single file to the edge of town where Marcus picked up the trail he and Eleni had taken when they were escaping the man who was now his captor. It was fitting symmetry to haul Weber along the same trail that Marcus hoped and prayed would once again deliver him to safety. But there was no Eleni for comfort, no Haralambros or Kleftis for support. He had only himself.

The mountain trail grew steeper. "Where are we going?" Weber panted from behind.

Marcus turned to look at him. His face was oily from sweat and fatty pores. No wonder there are so few overweight Greeks. Grossness cannot long survive in a hot, arid climate. He almost smiled. His idea was so simple he could work it all by himself. He did not need his friends after all. He did not even need Drovich. All he needed was the sun and Weber's greed and there were plenty of both.

Marcus walked faster and in a moment had put several yards between him and Weber.

"*Gott im Himmel*," Weber muttered in German.

"The icon is hidden in a shepherd's hut, just a little further up the trail. Not far now." Ahead lay a terraced slope used for planting wheat and a thicket of scrubby trees. Marcus quickened his step even more.

"Slow down!" Weber shouted. His face was mottled crimson. Even his scalp showed red through his sandy hair. He was streaming sweat. His t-shirt was soggy and clung to his skin. His breasts and nipples were sharply outlined. He looked like a drag queen.

Drovich was also lagging behind not so much because he was out of shape but because he did not have his heart in the march. He stopped to rest, leaning against a rock with his hand to his chest.

"Drovich!" Weber yelled when he saw that his partner had stopped walking. "Hurry up, will you?"

"Go on," Drovich replied, "I'll wait for you here."

"No! You are in this all the way! If you don't come you get nothing, understand?"

"You need me to sell the icon, Weber, a hundred thousand dollars. Don't be a fool."

"I will find my own buyer."

"Where, a second-hand dealer for a tenth that amount?"

As they argued, Marcus put more distance between them and reached the thicket before Weber realized what had happened.

He shrieked. "Giannou! Where are you?"

Marcus yelled back. "Over here!" He did not want to lose Weber, only tire him into submission.

"Where? I can't see you!"

Marcus waited in the thicket until he heard heavy footfalls and extremely labored breathing. Then branches broke as though an elephant were passing through. Marcus emerged from the thicket and walked into a clearing—a wheat field, no rocks, no trees. The wheat had been threshed and clumps of abandoned wheat stalks stood here and there like the grass huts of pygmies. Dried chaff crackled under his shoes. The brief moment of shade in the thicket reminded him that he, too, was being affected by sun on a bare head. His scalp was burning and his breath was getting short.

Suddenly, Weber crashed through the trees and confronted Marcus, only a few yards separating them. His chest was heaving as he inhaled huge quantities of air. His cheeks were deep purple and his eyes were so red they seemed to be bleeding.

Marcus pointed to the trail. "This way," he said as tantalizingly as he knew how. "Follow the trail, just a few more yards."

"If you are lying...if you are leading me to...nothing." "You don't know do you?" Marcus taunted even though Weber was threatening him with the gun.

The trail now was mostly uphill and Marcus huffed with strain as he put each foot in front of the other. His throat was burning raw. He could not swallow because there was no moisture in his mouth. He looked behind him every few seconds. Drovich was not in sight. He apparently gave up when reaching the trees.

Weber was staggering and the muzzle of his gun occasionally dragged along the ground, as if it were getting too heavy to carry. He dropped the gun once but Marcus could not make a move quickly enough, and watched impotently as Weber retrieved it and righted himself. What was keeping him on his feet? How could his heart manage the heat and the strain of pumping blood through clogged arteries?

Marcus was also beginning to feel the strain. His calves were aching and the heat was making him lightheaded. The trail he had hiked with Eleni and the promise it held was now his enemy. He yearned for water, for cool night air, for the shepherd's hut where he could lie down on soft sheepskin with Eleni in his arms and fall asleep.

He thought he would outlast Weber, tire him out before he himself tired, but now he could only stare helplessly as Weber came inexorably toward him, wheezing and waving his arms to keep his giddy balance, the gun moving up and down like a maestro's baton.

"There is no icon..." Weber gasped between breaths, now standing about a dozen feet from Marcus. "You have been taking me on a wild goose chase." His face took on an angelic glow as he lifted the gun and pointed it, wavering as he took aim.

Marcus stood paralyzed, watching the muzzle seek his body. "If you shoot me," he cried, "you will never find he icon."

"There is no icon, you lying bastard."

"I am not lying," Marcus said, making one last desperate attempt to keep Weber guessing. "It is in a shepherd's hut." Marcus's voice took on a whistle. With each inhalation the sound went down his throat like a robin after a worm. "Over there, behind a stone corral, the icon is wrapped in sheepskin, safe and sound, waiting for you…"

Suddenly the gun went off, the noise echoing up and down the hillside. The bullet missed, sinking into the ground at Marcus's feet.

Weber smiled at his miss, but his smile also had a maniacal finality, implying that the next bullet would hit its target. Marcus decided to make a run for it. Just as he turned Weber fired again. This time the bullet whizzed past his head. The only thing saving him was Weber's unsteadiness. As he ran Marcus tripped on stones that riddled the trail, some big some small, all loose. He groped and clawed to regain balance, his fingertips drawing blood. He glanced over his shoulder. Weber was coming for him, one inexorable step after another, like an automaton programmed to seek him out and kill him.

How does Weber keep his balance? How does he keep walking? Marcus's breath was coming in spurts, as much from panic as exhaustion, and his heart was beating so hard it felt like one solid pounding inside his chest. Images were getting wavy in front of his eyes. Even Weber seemed to be dancing, a dance macabre.

The horizon no longer met the sky and he was losing his sense of direction. Was he going toward Weber or away from him? Which end was up? He thought he was on his feet but then his shoulder struck something hard. It was the ground. He had given out. He could go no further. He lay on his side seeking breath, yet agonized each time he found it. He lifted himself on one elbow, watching

Weber walk up and stand over him. His body exuded so much heat he seemed to be on fire. He stood over Marcus holding the gun to his forehead. Marcus stared into the dark hole of the muzzle imagining a bullet speeding out, splintering his skull and splattering his brains. There was nothing he could do to prevent it. Weber had him now, sweet revenge for making a fool of him.

Go ahead, Marcus was thinking, get it over with. What are you waiting for? Pull the trigger. Stop gloating and kill me! He closed his eyes, his lids jammed together. Now he understood why men were blindfolded before execution, a gesture of compassion to cover eyes squinted shut in terror.

The waiting was interminable. He'd rather hear ready- aim-fire than bear this silence. Eventually he opened his eyes. Weber was still standing over him, his own eyes nearly out of their sockets, his heart under his chest visibly fibrillating, the gun, instead of pointing at Marcus's head, was now hanging listlessly, barely in Weber's grasp. Then Weber looked skyward as if he needed to expand his throat passage to take in more air, and slowly settled to his knees where he remained a second or two like a Buddha figure, then fell sideways and rolled on his back, spread-eagled.

Marcus raised himself and looked down at Weber, sweat from his own nose dripping onto him. Weber was trying to speak.

"Giannou…" he rasped.

As Marcus bent closer so he could hear him, Weber brought the gun up to his chest in the final effort of a dying man. Marcus knocked the gun away with his hand. It clattered to the ground and glinted in the sun.

"Where…" Weber said through his swollen tongue, "…Where is the icon?"

Marcus tried to smile. His dried lips cracked. "I was only fooling you. I don't know where the icon is, but if I ever find it I will return it to the Monestary at Mystras."

Weber's face took on a fatalistic expression as though recalling a distant memory. "How appropriate, completing the circle…"

Marcus was fighting dizziness, even unconsciousness but he still was able to reflect on Weber's statement. What did he mean by 'how appropriate, completing the circle'?

Weber's lids fluttered and his eyes grew moist—tears of regret, recrimination, loss? Marcus did not know.

Air began escaping from Weber's lungs. Marcus had always believed that a death rattle was a figure of speech, but now he heard it with his own ears. Weber's body was too soft to rattle but it did shudder before settling into a lifeless, sweat-stained, spongy mass of blubber.

Marcus was still lying on the ground when Drovich appeared and stood over Weber's body.

"I knew what you were doing," he said. "Weber was too greedy, too deluded to see what was happening. He was in full pursuit of the icon, nothing else mattered, even his own life." Drovich saw the gun and began to lean down to pick it up.

"Leave it alone," Marcus replied, slowly rising to his feet. He planted his hands on the ground and straightened his body, every muscle screaming from the effort. He was so exhausted he only wanted to speak in single words. Syllables would have been even better. "Can't you see it's over?"

Drovich sighed. "I was only entertaining a momentary thought, nothing more." He looked at Marcus. "Just where is the icon?"

Marcus told him, speaking slowly, haltingly, his throat raspy, his voice hoarse. "I don't know."

Drovich laughed bitterly. "I should have known better than to be taken in by Weber's hairbrained scheme to steal the icon, sell it for a king's ransom and then live like one. I should have known better after Weber killed Kostas but I deceived myself into believing we could still pull it off, that you or Dimitri, even Eleni, knew where it was."

Drovich lowered himself to his haunches and bent close to Weber's chest to listen for a heartbeat, careful not to let his ear touch the greasy, inert form.

"He's dead," Marcus said.

"I just wanted to make sure." Drovich closed Weber's lids with his fingertips. "I feel he is still staring at me." He stood. "What can we do with him?"

"Nothing."

"We can't leave him."

"What do you want to do, carry him out of here?"

Drovich looked around as if actually considering it. "That would be impractical."

"We've got to notify the police."

"The nearest is the Sparta Astynomia."

"Tsatsos?" That would be rich, seeing Tsatsos again.

Drovich nodded. "We have to send word."

Marcus noticed flies on Weber, already working at his nostrils and ear canals. "At least we should drag him under the trees. He will rot in the sun."

29

On the walk back they stopped at the *vrisi* to refresh themselves with the spring water for which Kremasti is noted. Four spouts set in a stone wall fed an endless stream, cool and refreshing, that drained into a trough and was channeled to terraced gardens carved into the side of the mountain on which the village was built.

Marcus let water flow until his scalp got too cold to stand it any longer. Then he pooled water into his hand to drink.

"Be careful," Drovich warned as he bent over a spout, "your stomach will cramp if you drink too fast." He splashed water on the cut Weber made on his cheek.

"How is your face?" Marcus asked.

"I will survive."

Marcus held back the overwhelming desire to swallow great gulps of the delicious mountain water. Instead he rinsed his mouth repeatedly and then rewarded himself with a few swallows.

"That is the way to do it," Drovich said, pooling water into his hands. "You are wise."

Marcus grinned. "If my mother heard you say that she would burst out laughing."

They let the sun dry off their heads as they walked to the square. The siesta was over and a long bench outside the taverna was occupied with Kremasti elders—men with white hair, faces grizzled with whiskers, several wearing drooping moustaches, a few resting gnarled fingers on their canes, others working their worry beads. They nodded silent greetings as the two men walked up.

"I have to see my mother and tell her I'm ok."

"I will wait for you here."

"Will you send word to Tsatsos?"

"I will give you that honor."

Mrs. Giannou and Caliope were sitting on the porch when Marcus came into view. His mother cried out, the strain of waiting and the fear had been so great that she jumped up like a jack-in-the-box and was all over Marcus showering kisses, hugging and pounding her palms against his back. Meanwhile, Caliope was crossing herself with such vigor Marcus thought she would end up with pitcher's elbow.

"My son! My son!" Mrs. Giannou burbled through tears of immense relief.

A long minute passed before Marcus could extricate himself from his mother's steely grip. She stood back and looked around finally to the scene beyond that of her son. "Where are Drovich and Weber?"

"Let's go into the house and I will explain everything." As they entered the house, Marcus patted the envelope in his hippocket, Eleni's papers safely tucked inside.

The next day, rested and recovered, Marcus sat on the porch with Drovich drinking lemonade, kept cool in a crock stored under the house. It was refreshing, made from lemons the size of baseballs growing plentifully almost anywhere one looked. They sipped and stared into space, once adversaries and now two men sharing a significant memory—the image of Ernst Weber lying dead, his eyes sightless for all eternity, his quest for the icon of Theophanes ending in failure.

"How did you ever get mixed up with Weber?" Marcus asked Drovich, sipping more lemonade.

"Strange bedfellows, is that what you are implying?"

"Something like that."

"Perhaps not so strange after all. We had similar goals."

"The icon…"

"Yes, but my goal was to give it to a Russian museum, as I told you, for credit and honor instead of opprobrium."

"Somewhere along the way you lost your direction."

Drovich bowed his head in acknowledgment and, perhaps, regret. "Weber contacted me via a letter which contained an interesting proposition: securing a rare icon painted by the master Theophanes. Would I be interested in knowing more? Naturally I was more than interested, I was fascinated. Religious iconography is my specialty, my passion."

He had already told Marcus that several times. "How did Weber find you?"

Drovich tried to give the impression of modesty but it got away from him. "I have a considerable reputation, Kyrio Giannou. Weber would have come across my name sooner or later. Apparently I was not the only person he wrote to, but I was the only one interested enough to write back. Eventually, we arranged a meeting. We met in Zagreb and he brought with him his late father's journal. Quite revealing and historically noteworthy, I might add, written more than 25 years ago and discovered only recently."

"Was there any mention of the icon?" Marcus asked.

Drovich nodded, turning his glass on the wet spot it left on the table.

Marcus asked, "How did he know about it?"

"Therein lies a story. Weber's father was Field Marshall Herman Weber of the German occupation forces assigned to Sparta during the war."

"Weber's father was German?" Marcus asked. "You told me he was Swiss."

"He was born in Switzerland of German parents who moved to Dresden before the war. Weber was concerned about the negative reaction to his nationality."

"How generous of him."

"He was merely being discrete given the deep-seated resentment Greeks have toward Germans."

"But how did his father, a German officer, know about the icon?"

"This is where the story becomes interesting, particularly for you, my friend. The icon was in the possession of a young woman with whom he was having an affair, very clandestine mind you. If Greeks had discovered she was consorting with a German she would have been stoned to death. That was the most poignant part of the journal, their secret romance..." Drovich stopped talking, staring at the shocked look on Marcus's face. "Are you beginning to make the connection?"

The back of Marcus's neck began to prickle. "It can't be."

"But it is."

"Anna Koulouris?"

Drovich nodded.

"Oh my god," Marcus said, connecting the dots.

"Difficult to accept, I know, but it is true. Ernst Weber's father is also Eleni's father, one and the same."

"Eleni and Weber are brother and sister?"

"*Half* brother and sister."

"Half or whole, this is too incredible to believe."

"But believe you must. You can imagine how difficult it was for Weber when he met Eleni. No joyous reunion, nothing like that. He had to maintain his anonymity for our plan to succeed. Moreover, there was his troubling attitude toward her. At a young age he joined

Das Hitlerjugend that exalted the master race and learned to despise anyone of mixed blood. And so, even though she was his sister, Weber regarded Eleni as inferior because she was only half-German."

"But how did Weber's father and Anna meet?"

"She was trying to get out of Greece and appealed to the German headquarters in Sparta for a visa to travel to Switzerland, a neutral country where she could wait out the war and return once again to America. Her plight came to the attention of the officer in charge, Field Marshal Herman Weber. There was nothing he could do, of course, but there was a mutual attraction, a handsome officer—the appearance of his son notwithstanding—and a vulnerable woman. Opposites attract, *machts nichts*? The two fell in love. His father wrote passionately of their relationship in his journal."

"She told him about the icon?"

Drovich nodded. "As lovers do, they shared secrets and she showed it to him. He immediately recognized its rarity but said nothing."

"Why didn't he just take it from her?"

"Do you think there is no honor even among Germans?"

"From what I heard about him I'd say no."

Drovich raised his eyebrows in surprise. "What did you hear?"

"Dimitri told me about the massacre at Monodendri. Remember when we drove past the monument on our way to Kremasti? I had the distinct impression you did not want to talk about it. Now I know why, Ernst Weber's father ordered the execution of 117 young men."

Drovich shook his head. "The journal tells a different story. Herman Weber did not give the order to kill those Greeks."

"Wasn't he in charge of the German forces in the District of Laconias?"

"Yes, but the order came from the high command in Athens where there was growing anxiety over the resistance of the Greek underground, and the reprisals became harsher and harsher. When a German soldier was ambushed, Weber was ordered to count the houses..."

"I know, one-hundred-seventeen."

"It was a brutal order and he refused to follow it. He was relieved of command and stripped of rank. Refusing to obey an order is death by firing squad, but by that time the war was going badly. Allied troops had crossed the Rhine and were knocking on Germany's door. There was a need for officers to fight on the Western Front. He volunteered and was killed in the final days of the war, in the battle for Berlin."

Marcus thought of the body lying on the trail, the stomach curved like a burial mound. "Ernst Weber seemed an unlikely son of the man you just described."

"Young Weber bore the scars of the war, too, even if he did not fight on the front lines. You Americans will never understand what it is like to see your cities destroyed by bombs, your culture vanish, your country occupied by foreigners." Drovich hesitated for a moment of reflection. Finally he said, "Where was I? Oh, yes, young Weber discovered the journal among his father's personal effects that were shipped home following the war, a poignant record of two young persons in a futile love affair. The father suffered untold guilt. An added irony is that he never learned that Anna bore him a child. Young Weber, of course, was far from sympathetic. Believing in the purity of a master race, he resented having a half-sister because of his father's weakness. Out of resentment, I suppose, he embraced brutality rather than compassion.

"The icon became his obsession. He considered it his property, fair payment for a cheated life. From the journal he learned that the monks entrusted Anna, Eleni's mother with the icon on her journey to Kremasti. He had to determine if it was still there or returned to the monastery, which would have provided an added problem but not an insurmountable one. He had no compunction about stealing it from the monks. The whole idea of the adventure fascinated him.

"As I told you on our drive to Kremasti—that fateful day we first met—Kostas and I have known each other since the Greek Civil War, fighting side by side as idealistic partisans. Even though our mission failed our commitment did not, and we remained in contact as political allies. After Weber interested me in the icon, I wrote Kostas to inquire if he cared to join us. We needed in inside man to borrow the American vernacular. Kostas used his position as Sparta's regional agent for ESA to visit Kremasti on inspection tours, a perfect cover to meet the Stathos family and discover, to his amazement, that the icon was still there, hanging in Eleni's bedroom!

"I believed luck was with us until I discovered Kostas had kept a secret from me. He knew Anna. After the war he became a novice at Mystras not only to find a greater calling but also to learn the art of icon painting." Drovich said this with a sneer. "That is where he met her."

Marcus nodded. "And he brought her to Kremasti to have her baby. Caliope told me. Even so I still find it hard to believe you already knew Kostas. What an incredible coincidence."

"Maybe yes, maybe no, Kyrio Giannou. Are you familiar with six degrees of separation?"

"I've heard of it," Marcus said, wondering where Drovich was going with this line of thought. "We are no more than six steps apart from each other?"

"Exactly, a chain that connects any two people in a maximum of six steps. The idea was first proposed by the Hungarian writer Frigyes Karinthy in 1929. Within those six steps, Kostas intersected with Herman Weber. The one person who should be loyal, the one you can trust the most, is a fellow partisan, but too much water had flowed since those days of our idealistic youth. Kostas used his prior connection to the Stathos family to ingratiate himself, and before long he was betrothed to Anna's daughter. I will leave it to you to decide if Kostas suggested he was Eleni's father to force Dimitri to cooperate with him. At the time, of course, we did not realize he had an agenda separate from ours which, alas, brought his life to an abrupt end." Drovich drained his glass as if emphasizing the finality of his story. "And the rest you know."

Marcus drained his glass as well and looked at it, reflecting on its empty symbolism. All this effort came to nothing. He stood. Time to deal with the present.

"The Sparta Police better get here before Weber decomposes any further."

Drovich remained seated. "We should part company before they arrive. It is time I return to Zagreb."

"You can't leave...not yet."

"I have no desire to spend any time in a Greek prison."

"You have nothing to worry about. The police want Kostas' murderer, and he is lying under the trees back there. You weren't in the apartment when it happened. You didn't know what Weber was going to do."

"If the police don't want me, then there is no need for my presence."

"Yes there is," Marcus said quickly. "I need your help to clear Eleni of murder."

"You can do that without me. You have your proof lying in the field."

"Don't you see I need your corroboration? What you told me you must tell Tsatsos."

"You tell him."

"He won't believe me."

"Would he believe me any better? Tsatsos will throw me in his jail."

"What can he charge you with?" Marcus asked.

"He will think of something." Drovich lifted his eyebrows. "Seems ironic that Weber and I unwittingly put the limelight on an icon that hung unnoticed for decades in a village bedroom. It has the quality of poetic justice."

"Poetic, maybe, but there is no justice if Eleni has to go back to jail. Can you go on living with yourself knowing you could clear her and didn't?" Marcus looked at him, at his intelligent face, the kindly sag of his eyelids. "I don't think you are that kind of person."

"You are asking me to take a great risk…"

"Not without good reason. Besides, the risk I'm asking you to take is no worse but far more noble than the one you took when you joined up with Weber."

"You make a strong case." He gazed at Marcus for a few seconds. "You truly love this girl, don't you?"

The question caught Marcus off guard. "I suppose I do…Yes, I do, I love her. Will you help me?"

"You are persuasive, Kyrio Giannou. I may be a damned fool, but I will tell Tsatsos what I know."

Marcus gripped Drovich by the shoulders, showing his relief in this impulsive action. But Drovich pulled his head back, perhaps expecting a kiss on the cheek. Those emotional Greeks, even Greek-Americans, his expression said, you never know what they will try next.

"I need another favor."

Drovich took on a new expression, that of someone being taken advantage of. "What is it this time?"

"Weber's journal, can you get your hands on it? Eleni has gone through so much. Just telling her won't be enough. She has to read her father's journal. It will be bad enough to find out that he was also Weber's father."

Drovich nodded. "It is with Weber's suitcase in the trunk of the Simca."

"Let me to show it to Eleni and I will mail it back to you."

Drovich smiled. "I will do better than that. It is of no use to me. I will give it to you. You will be pleased to know that he journal was written in English rather than German. Weber's love affair was, after all, with an American woman, and with a sense of respect for her memory he recorded their relationship in Anna's mother tongue rather than his own. May I also speculate that Weber's father did not want to make his journal available to the prying eyes of other Germans."

Marcus appreciated what a big favor Drovich was granting. "By the way, we've been through so much that we should be on a first name basis, don't you think?"

"Now that we are winding up our relationship?"

"Better than never."

"Marcus…"

"…Janos."

It was nearing nightfall when Marcus heard distant pounding of feet on the path. He came out of the house, trying to see into the gathering dusk. A village boy was pointing in his direction. Right behind him was Tsatsos with four uniformed police. He pushed the boy aside and took over the lead. His shirt was plain, no indication of rank, no doubt he had none now. The demotion reflected in his face, taut with anger.

As the police approached, they drew their guns. Marcus recognized one of them—he had knocked him flat in his pellmell escape from Tsatsos' so-called high-security jail. Marcus smiled to himself at the memory, and raised his arms to show he was not armed. Nevertheless, he was roughed up out of revenge and his arms were pinned behind his back.

His mother came out of the house. "Leave him alone!" she shouted in Greek, the doorway framing her imposing presence. Even Tsatsos felt it. Marcus saw him nod to his officers. Reluctantly, Marcus was released, but not without one last caressing yank to let him know how unpopular he was.

"So," Tsatsos said, "we meet again." His left eye was swollen and purple around the edges. The ridge above it was taped with a bandage.

"What happened to you?" Marcus asked, trying to be friendly.

His fellow officers looked away knowing it was safer to ignore the injury on his head.

"A slight accident when word came that you broke out of jail. In my haste I hit my head on the door of the squad car." He touched the bandage.

Marcus smiled but his mother was watching him like a hawk. "*Prosehe!*" she said sharply. Be careful

"I will recover," Tsatsos snarled, "but will you?"

"Captain," Marcus began and then looked at the policeman's shirt bare of insignia. He thought he detected needle marks where the bars had once been sewn. "Sorry," he said.

"Because of you, Giannou!" Tsatsos was so upset that, for the first time, he did not refer to Marcus by the formal Kyrio.

The policemen could not contain themselves any longer. They laughed openly.

"Where is the body?" Tsatsos snapped, changing the subject.

"On the mountain trail north of the village, less than a kilometer from here. I made a pile of stones to mark the site. It is getting dark. You will have to wait till morning."

"*Ehoumai fokes*," he said, determined to finish the job. We have flashlights.

"That dead man," Marcus said, "is the one who killed Kostas Kanellos."

"Not your girl friend?"

"Eleni is innocent and I can prove it."

"The judge will decide if your cousin is innocent or not. As for you, there is the matter of assaulting a prison guard…"

"Sparta's finest," Marcus interrupted, perhaps a bit too casually.

"Will you never learn?" Mrs. Giannou cried out in exasperation and pinched him hard in his side.

"*Ouch!*"

There was a faint, barely discernible movement of Tsatsos' mouth. Marcus could not be sure, but he thought the former Chief of Sparta Police was actually smiling.

He knew what it was like to have a Greek mother.

30

His last days in Greece were spent staying out of trouble that his mother kept telling him he was getting into. It took considerable effort and the long arm of the US Department of State, as well as the direct assistance of Sally Haggerty and a personal visit by Consul General Prager, not to mention cables whizzing back and forth between Washington and Athens. Tsatsos wanted his old job back. His reputation was at stake and he needed to save face.

Marcus appeared before the magistrate with a lawyer assigned to him from the Embassy. He was charged with breaking Eleni out of jail as well as breaking the collarbone of a prison guard. He pleaded guilty on both counts and was given a two-year suspended sentence and fined ten thousand drachmas. Marcus gave Prager his IOU who paid the fine for him. Prager muttered under his breath that he hoped Marcus would clear out of his territory, the quicker the better.

Prager's wish notwithstanding, Marcus missed the charter flight home. He did not mind. He'd rather fly Olympic, anyway, hang the expense. There were still loose ends to wrap up, all of them personal, especially his relationship with Drovich. Marcus felt responsible for his welfare. After all, Marcus had convinced him to stay when all he had to do was get into his Simca and drive back to Yugoslavia. Unlike Marcus, Drovich did not have a dependable government to back him up. In the end, the Sparta magistrate dismissed the charge to steal Theophanes Virgin inasmuch as no one could find it. But Drovich did have his visa revoked and told he was no longer welcome in Greece.

Drovich was philosophical when he and Marcus parted in front of the courthouse in Sparta. "I am anxious to develop my film and see what I have of my trip to Greece even if does not include the Virgin."

"But it does include me," Marcus said, smiling.

"You?" Drovich replied, clearly confused.

"Giving the finger at the sign hanging over the Isthmus of Corinth. Kostas took it with your camera as insurance, I guess, in case I interfered with his grand plan."

Drovich shook his head like a school principal. "Is that what you call freedom of expression?"

"You can blackmail me or throw it away. Your choice, Janos."

"At least I have it to remember you by, Marcus."

They both laughed facing each other in the hot sun. There was a moment's hesitation deciding whether to shake hands or hug. They shook hands.

Mrs. Giannou sat with Marcus in the square as he waited for Sally to pick him up for the drive to Mystras to bring Eleni home. Eleni was due to report to the magistrate for a hearing in Sparta but was allowed the weekend to see her family first, given the ordeal she had suffered.

Dimitri was pulling all of his strength together for the reunion. Caliope was busy baking spanakopita and tiropites as well as a large mousaka for a homecoming dinner. Earlier in the week, painters hired by his mother whitewashed the exterior walls of the house. Eleni's bedroom also had a going over—freshly painted walls and wood planking laid down on the dirt floor—a present from the Giannous. All of Kremasti was excited with the anticipation of seeing Eleni come home.

As Marcus pondered the wonderful things happening in Kremasti he was nonetheless still bothered by the most mystifying loose end, the missing icon of Theophanes. Almost every day he wondered where Kostas hid it, finally accepting the fact that it might never be found, or found by accident and not recognized for its value, perhaps ending up once again in a village hanging on someone's wall. What irony.

Sunlight dappled through the leaves of the cypress trees shading the square and caressed his forehead. Beyond the treetops he could see the rising campanili of Kremasti's church, The Assumption of Mary, sitting on its elevated site, visible for all to see if you just looked in that direction. His mind was in idle when he remembered looking at another bell tower, this time belonging to the impressive church in Niata, and thinking that a church would be a clever place to hide an icon, in so obvious a location, so plainly apparent, that no one would bother to take notice.

Marcus stood.

"Where are you going?" his mother called after him.

"To the church."

That Marcus seldom set foot in a church prompted her to add, "Be sure to light a candle for me. And what am I supposed to tell Sally if she shows up, that you suddenly found religion?"

"I'll be right back," he shouted over his shoulder. His mind began to pick up speed as he walked toward the church. It had recently been renovated and the smell of fresh plaster was still in the air as he walked inside and looked at the Byzantine ornamentation typical of Greek churches large or small, resplendent with gold glitter, candle chandeliers, frescos of saints and icons on every square inch of plaster.

Marcus felt like an intruder as he entered the empty nave and approached the Royal Door, the *Agias*

Pilas protecting the *Iero*, the Holy Inner Sanctum. He opened it a crack and peeked into the sacred space where only men were allowed, including those who cleaned up following the liturgy. At least his maleness protected him from what would be a sacrilege if a woman tried it.

With the unwarranted idealism of Don Quixote he studied the line-up of icons depicting the Virgin Mary on a shelf behind the altar table. With great expectation he studied each one—Mary holding the Christ Child, standing with St. John of Chrystostom or the Archangel Gabriel, full length, seated, or praying. He felt his cheeks redden at the silliness of his quest. Of course there was nothing special about these icons, certainly none had the quality of Theophanes. Marcus did not need Drovich to tell him that. He left the church resigned to his fate. The Virgin was indeed lost forever. Moreover, he was too chagrined with the foolhardiness of his mission to admit to his mother why he visited the church in the first place. He only went so far as to to tell her he hadn't yet seen the inside of the church and did not want to leave Kremasti without having done so, however lame that excuse sounded.

Marcus told Sally in the car what he had done.

"I know how disappointed you must be," she said, "but it was a flight of fancy expecting to find the icon in the church. Like the purloined letter in plain sight, is that what you were thinking?"

"In my mind I saw Kostas having a change of heart and wanting to return the icon to Mystras, and so I imagined him hiding it until he could do so in the only logical and spiritual place he could think of outside the monestary—the church in Kremasti. Not just any church but that one, knowing that the priest would protect it until he could return it to the monestary. He was killed before he could do that."

"At least you tried to complete the circle," she said from behind the wheel of the Chevrolet.

Amazing, Marcus thought, what Weber said in his dying breath.

"Maybe the icon will turn up someday."

"Maybe," he said without enthusiasm.

He turned his attention to the cardboard box stamped with a Neiman Marcus logo on its top. It was resting on the back seat. "The last name of the department store on that box is also my first name."

Sally smiled. "Of course, why do you think I saved it?"

She did not expect an answer and Marcus obliged her by keeping quiet.

"Eleni sent word that she needed something to wear and so I brought an outfit of mine in the box it originally came in. We are close enough in size although she is thinner. When she sees you again she wants to look, as she put it, as fashionable as she did in Athens."

Marcus stared straight ahead.

"You changed Eleni from a village girl to a sophisticated woman, like Pygmalion." Sally took her eyes off the road for a second and looked at him. "You realize that, don't you?"

"Yes," he said, "I realize it."

They became prey to private thoughts.

After awhile, Sally said, "I thought the monks would not let me inside but Brother Yianni was very helpful. He was impressed with how you convinced him to allow Eleni to stay there and it must have rubbed off on me. He suspended the male-only rule. I am allowed to tour their library. I researched it, and it's an interesting one, containing manuscripts, monodic chant books and doxologies in Byzantine notation, never seen outside of a monestary. This is a lucky break for me, right in my area of interest, and I have you to thank."

"I'm glad there was something I could do to repay you for all you've done." These words seemed so inadequate but he did not know what else to say.

Sally knew what was on his mind, on both of their minds, actually. "I'll be in the library a long time, so don't feel you have to rush. You and Eleni have a lot to talk about and I'm sure you don't want me butting in."

"Thanks."

"Look, my friend, I won't use boyfriend because I am not sure if that fits any longer. After the two of you sort things out, let me know if there is an act two. I'll be waiting in the wings."

Rather dramatic Marcus thought, but he knew Sally was right. And he will find out soon enough it there is an act two, or even an act three.

Marcus waited for Eleni on the bench outside the church where they parted to face an uncertain future. Even though some issues were laid to rest, chiefly her well-being, new ones had taken their places to make the future just as uncertain as it was before. But the future is never certain, only the past.

And Eleni's past included the journal of her father, the German officer relieved of command because he did not follow an order to execute the men of Monodendri. Marcus debated when and where to give the journal to Eleni, in the privacy of her bedroom, in front of her parents, on the mountain trail they followed to Niata, with her *compatrioti* Haralambos and Kleftis. None seemed appropriate and then it came to him: give it to her here, in Mystras where it all started, where Anna came to do her research in the advent of World War II, where events led her to the Nazi officer who become her lover and finally to Kremasti where Eleni was born and where Anna died. Mystras. This is where he will give her the journal of her father, the origin of her life.

She appeared wearing Sally's outfit, more a caftan than a dress, simple but elegantly cut, pale blue turning almost gray as it reflected the sun. On her feet were soft leather flats matching her outfit, on which she glided rather than walked, and around her slim waist she wore a wide leather belt of fine grain to contain the extra folds because she was indeed thinner than Sally. Everything adorning her was high fashion, affirming the Nieman Marcus label.

He stood to greet her and, as she approached, she flared the skirt the way a model might do on a runway, a graceful move of her hands. "Sally is a close fit to me, don't you think?" she said in English. "I wish I could see her wardrobe."

Marcus had seen Sally's wardrobe in the intimacy of her bedroom back in Washington but he wasn't going to say so. "You look great."

He sensed that Eleni was play-acting, pretending to be light-hearted, doing her best to hide the scar tissue on her soul.

In spite of what they had gone through, there was a shared sense of timidity, even awkwardness, perhaps because they were no longer facing the dangers that brought them together, a commonality lost except in memory and not strong enough to reignite. They both understood this although they were not able to put it into words

"How did you spend your days?" he asked, making small talk the way you do when you run into an old friend.

He was relieved they were speaking English because it had the effect of slowing Eleni down, more involved in finding words than expressing inner turmoil. If she were speaking Greek she could fall apart in an emotional fluency of frightening memories.

"Clean floors, wash dishes, weed the garden. I did not see the monks unless I was working. I ate meals alone. I prayed in my cell because I was not allowed in the church. But I never felt lonely." She managed a wry smile. "It was better than Tsatsos' prison."

Her comment reminded Marcus to tell Eleni that Tsatsos had been demoted, his captain stripes stripped from his shirt. Why that happened, Marcus did not explain. That would come later, not now. However, it did break the spell of their tentativeness and they laughed, even chortled over the setback of her nemesis. It also provided an opportunity to shift the direction of their conversation. Marcus took a deep breath to reload.

"Eleni," he began, "is it all right if we talk about that day in Kostas' apartment?"

She shrugged noncommitally. "What is there to talk about? It is over, isn't it?"

"No, not quite." He watched her carefully, uncertain of the territory he was trying to navigate. "The man who shot Kostas…"

Eleni stiffened but did not recoil. A good sign. "Weber?"

"Yes."

"Why do we have to talk about him? He killed Kostas. I saw it. There is nothing further to discuss."

"There is something you have to know about him."

Marcus withdrew the notebook from his pocket connecting Weber's past to Eleni's present. He handed it to her.

She looked at the worn cover and flipped the pages with her thumb. "What is this?"

"A private journal."

"I don't understand…"

"Read it and then you will."

Delicately, as though handling an ancient manuscript, she opened the journal with the precisely neat handwriting and began reading. Marcus watched her eyes move across the lines, turn a page, read more lines, totally engrossed. Minutes passed but they seemed to hang in the air, unmoving. Finally she closed the journal and placed it on her lap.

"Do you understand now?"

She stared at him as if she did not hear the question. "This man…" she hesitated a moment, as though swallowing something tasteless "…he is my real father." She fell into deep thought, almost trance-like. "You always wonder who your father was and when you find out..." she switched to the third person as though referring to someone else "...you should be happy shouldn't you?"

Marcus remained quiet, careful not to break the spell because it would be like breaking rare crystal that cannot be put back together.

She continued, "He was a Nazi officer, an enemy of Greece. How can you be happy to learn that?"

"He redeemed himself, Eleni. He refused to follow the order to kill those young men."

"He was not as bad as Kostas, is that what you mean?"

"I am not taking sides."

"There are no sides. Kostas worked for ESA and he came to Kremasti to snoop on us. You had to be careful because ESA could arrest you even for making a little joke about the government. Kostas or my real father, both Fascists, which do you prefer?" Eleni paused to reflect on what she just said. "I am confused, Marcus. Kostas brought my mother to Kremasti. He took care of her. Why would he do that unless he was her lover? How strange is it that Kostas, the man I thought was my real father, was killed by the son of the man who *was* my real father?"

A question Marcus could not answer nor could Eleni, and so it hung there as permanent as the earth hanging in space.

"Where did you get this?" she asked.

"Drovich gave it to me. He found it in Weber's personal effects." He decided she was capable now of hearing the rest of the story and he told her how he lured Weber onto the same mountain trail Marcus and Eleni used to escape the same person. Another twist in a tale full of them.

"What you did was very dangerous."

"All in day's work," he kidded.

"You do not need to spare me, Marcus, after what we have been through."

She was right. They were still whole, stronger and, if the truth be told, richer for it.

"My mother and father knew, didn't they?'

"That Herman Weber was your real father? Yes."

She sighed in frustration. "Why didn't they tell me?"

"How could they? As far as they knew, your father ordered those horrendous executions at Monodendri. If any good comes from this, at least you can tell them he was not the evil monster everyone thought he was."

She moved her fingers across the journal, as though connecting with it. "It is all in here."

They were so engrossed that neither noticed Brother Yianni approach them. A braided rope held his cossack around his middle and the fold of his his cowl draped across his shoulders. Marcus wondered how he stayed cool.

"You were having such an intense conversation I did not want to interrupt. I would have expected seeing this from people who have lived longer and seen more, but perhaps what you two have experienced has more than made up for the maturity of your elders. May you wisely apply what you have learned, the hardships you have shared and the relief of having survived them. You gained perspective beyond your years. Let that be your guide."

"Thank you, Brother Yianni."

. "I am sure you both have much more to talk about."

"You are welcome to join us."

"I just want to say goodbye," he said, switching to Greek. He held out his hand for Eleni to grasp.

"Our Order discourages contact with the opposite gender unless it is to conduct business but, in this case, I am sure God will forgive me one small touch. You will remain in our hearts, Eleni."

She looked up, her eyes shielded from the sun by Yianni's body. "You gave me my life back," she said in Greek. "I am forever grateful to you."

"And I to you. Your presence made possible the treasure we all dreamed about but never expected to see again."

The complex conversation in Greek was difficult for Marcus to follow but one word stood out: *Theisavros*.

"Treasure?" he asked, "What treasure?"

"This will be news to Eleni as well since I have not told her. I wanted you, Marcus, to be the first from the outside world to see it."

Yianni led Marcus into the church, replacing oppressive heat with welcome coolness. He pointed to the altar table.

"See?"

The frame that was empty the last time Marcus saw it now held an icon. Puzzled, he approached and the closer he got the more confused he became. It looked like the real thing but it couldn't be. He repeated Drovich's comment.

"Pretty good for a forgery."

Yianni's laughter reached the dome of the church. "No, my friend, it is not a forgery. It is the true one, the Virgin of Theophanes is back home."

Marcus stared at Yianni not tracking, completely bewildered. "But how did it get here?" he asked.

"A miracle, my son, a miracle that began when Eleni joined us. Remember how convincing you were and how reluctant I was? I believe that God tested me to see if I was worthy of the rest of the bargain."

"Bargain?"

"Yes, I'm glad I kept it because the Virgin is back where she belongs, delivered late at night at the gate by a kindly, saintly woman…"

"A woman? Who was she?"

"She left without giving her name."

"What did she look like?" Marcus asked suspiciously.

Yianni looked skyward as though the person he was describing had come from heaven itself. "She was elderly, not very tall, well-dressed and wore her hair in a bun. She had a strong, commanding voice. You could tell in an instant that she was someone you did not take lightly…"

"MO-THER!!!" Marcus cried out.

31

With Brother Yianni's look of astonishment forever emblazoned in his memory, Marcus told Sally in the car that the real icon had been returned to Mystras by a kindly, saintly woman with a commanding voice, namely his mother. Sally was amazed by the news and Eleni was laughing with the joy of it all, but Marcus was upset that his own mother acting like a CIA agent would have carried out a clandestine operation without ever once informing her own son. Her own son!

Sally wanted to know how Mrs. Giannou managed this sleight of hand.

Marcus was wondering the very same thing. "Kostas must have had a change of heart and made a secret deal with mother. He painted the fake icon to dupe Drovich but it turns out that I was the dupe." He had to smile, though, seeing a side of his mother he never knew existed.

The square was jammed with so many people welcoming Eleni home that it was worthy of a traffic cop. To bid goodbye to Sally privately was useless and all Marcus was able to do in the happy mayhem was to wave at her. In the midst of all this joy a ground swell of melancholy coursed through him making him wonder whether his farewell to Sally signaled till we meet again or will we meet again.

They ate dinner on the front porch earlier than was Greek custom, chiefly to accommodate Dimitri who wanted to be part of the festivities, and also to make it inviting for neighbors to visit and express their happiness seeing Eleni again, many commenting on how pretty she looked in the fashionable dress with the wide belt. The spanakopita and moussaka washed down with wine lifted Marcus's spirits, especially the wine. He got a little drunk. His mother, ever watchful of her son's demeanor, kept a wary eye on him but refrained from commenting since she assumed he was celebrating Eleni's return. Was there ever a better reason to get a little tipsy?

After dinner, Caliope helped Dimitri get into bed and Eleni, needing to rest, excused herself, giving Marcus the opportunity to be alone with his mother as the sun was beginning to set.

"What is bothering you?" she asked him. "You won't even let me help Caliope with the dishes."

"Eleni can do that."

"On her first night back?"

"This is more important."

She looked at him expectantly. "Ok, so what is more important?"

He waded right in. "Why in hell did you send Eleni and me off with the fake icon?"

If she was surprised by his question she did not show it. "Who told you that?"

"Nobody told me, I figured it out all by myself. Want to know how? The real one is back at Mystras, simple as that. Brother Yianni told me an elderly woman brought it to him. He called it a miracle. That was no miracle, that was my mother."

"I hired a taxi which cost me almost one social security check." Mrs. Giannou looked hurt. "Brother Yianni called me elderly? But it was dark, how could he see?"

"Mom, just answer my question. Why did you give me and Eleni the forgery?"

"Do you think I could trust you with the real one?"

Marcus spread his arms out in a gesture of frustration. "Will you be serious for a minute? Where did you get it?"

"I will explain. Think back to the night you were shot at. Remember what Kostas said to Dimitri on the porch? I heard the same conversation inside the house."

"Yes, Dimitri said he would not help Kostas with his crazy scheme, and Kostas warned Dimitri that he could not guarantee his or anyone else's safety if he did not help him. What was Kostas talking about?"

"He wanted Dimitri to switch icons, hang the forgery in Eleni's room and give him the real one. When Drovich and Weber insisted on riding to Kremasti with us, Kostas knew he was in trouble. They did not trust him and Kostas was afraid Drovich would simply help himself to the icon and the only way he could preserve the real one was switch it with the fake.

"After Weber began shooting at shadows, Kostas was scared out of his wits. There was no way to know how crazy Weber was. He might kill us all, so I had to figure out a way to get him and Drovich away from us. And I had to act fast. No police to call, no superman out there to come to our rescue…"

"Except me."

"If I remember correctly you were busy looking for the outhouse."

"Come on, mom."

"Never mind. The fact is I did not have time to consult you."

"So you ended up creating a diversion."

"Exactly the word I was looking for. It came to me in a flash. I would switch the icons but not in the way Kostas intended. You should have seen the look on Drovich's face when he showed up in the morning and I told him you had left before dawn with Theophanes' Virgin. He assumed of course that it was the real one, and he and Weber drove off looking for you just as I expected."

"So where did you hide the real Virgin of Theophanes?"

"Where no one would ever think to look, certainly not a man. I wrapped it in my corset and stored it in the bottom drawer of the chest."

"I didn't even know you wore a corset."

"I brought my old one along just in case."

Marcus laughed. "You never know when you might need a hiding place, right, mom? But why didn't you tell me I had the forgery and not the real one? Any other mother would have done that."

"And if I told you how would you have reacted? I could see you with a silly look on your face like you wanted to tell everyone: I have a forgery in my possession but I'm supposed to pretend it is the real thing. How about that, folks? I thought long and hard whether to tell you, and I realized it is easier to keep a secret if you don't think there is one. Ignorance is bliss, right? What if you knew the icon we were using to fool Drovich and Weber was a fake? Do you think you could have kept that lie and fool him? He would have killed you."

He almost did, Marcus thought. "Still, you took a big chance using us as bait."

"Not a nice word but you had a head start and Eleni knows the mountains better than anyone. Once you got to Niata her friends would protect you. You were safer running away than staying in Kremasti."

"What about Kostas? He might have given us away."

"No, my son, there was no reason for Kostas to play the game any longer. He intended to sell the fake to Drovich and pocket the money. A nice swindle if it worked, but everything backfired. He was naïve, not tough enough to cheat. He got cold feet and his conscience was also beginning to bother him. He may have been a crook but he was also loyal to his country and to Mystras. He planned to return the icon to its rightful place, but he never made it." Mrs Giannou inhaled proudly. "He needed your mother to finish the job."

Marcus smiled. "I am proud of you, Mom, but leaving me in the dark was a blow to my pride, you have to admit that. At least when you returned the icon to Mystras you could have said something instead of my having to beat it out of you…"

"Beat your own mother?"

"Figure of speech, Mom. You were playing secret agent, showing up at the monestary late at night. I think you let the whole thing go to your head."

A tear formed in the corner of her eye and rolled down her cheek.

Marcus stared. He did not think his mother was even capable of crying. "Mom…" he began and stopped because he wasn't sure what to say. Tender emotion was not woven into their pattern of behavior.

"I just wanted to surprise you, Marcus." She brushed away the tear with the knuckle of her index finger leaving a tiny rivulet in her face powder. "When you went to the Monastery you found both Eleni and Theophanes' Virgin. Isn't that a nice way to end a story?"

When the day came to leave, Eleni decided to stay at the house rather than join the others in the square. It was a decision Marcus respected. How could they part with dozens and dozens of people staring at them? Instead, they met privately in her bedroom, spartan to begin with but even more so now that the wall above her bed was empty of Theophanes Virgin.

"I have something for you," she said.

Eleni opened the hope chest at the foot of her bed. Inside the chest of cedarwood was her dowry, what a young Greek woman collects in anticipation of marriage—neatly folded linens including a quilt, pillow cases, table cloth and towels, handwoven or embroidered. It was bittersweet for Marcus to realize that Eleni expected no more than to marry a villager and live in the home Dimitri and Caliope shared with her until they died and then it would be her home to raise her children until she too died and the house would be handed down to the next generation, and so it went, predictable, boring by American standards, but yet filled with a sense of completeness and continuity that was calming and reassuring, making Marcus wonder how Eleni and he might share a life together. It would depend on how much one was willing to give up for the other.

Tucked in the corner of the chest was something wrapped in tissue paper. She handed it to Marcus.

"What is it?" he said as he unwrapped the paper. He stared in surprise. It was the icon of the Virgin Mary, courtesy of the late Kostas Kanellos, a far cry from the original but still better than most. "The forgery," he said and smiled broadly.

"It brought us together," she said.

But will it keep us together, he wondered. "Are you sure you want to give this to me? Don't you think you should hang it over your bed like the original?"

"I have a memory of the orignal. That is all I need. I want you to have this one to remember me by."

"Don't you think we will see each other again?"

She shrugged noncommittally. All she said was, "Where will you put it?"

"On my desk so I can look at it every day."

Time to bid farewell, and once again a crowd gathered in the square but on a different mission this time: not to greet but to say goodbye to Marcus. Two men carried Dimitri up the path in his chair so he could join the leavetaking. He was becoming more alert, understanding what was going on even though he could not express his thoughts.

Mrs. Giannou decided to stay on and not to fly home with Marcus. Uncle Dimitri's condition, uncertain as it was, was reason enough to remain and help Caliope around the house. Being with her sister was far more desirable than living alone in Minneapolis where she would only fret and worry. Most important, she finally concluded, Marcus was old enough to take care of himself.

There was so much hugging that the taxi driver eventually beeped his horn, alerting Marcus that it was time to leave or risk missing his flight. Reluctantly he climbed into the back seat. As the taxi pulled away, dozens and dozens of handkerchiefs waved goodbye.

Epilogue

Sally entered her final year at the American library in Sparta, still trying to raise funds for a bookmobile in Laconias. But the likelihood that the military junta in Athens would allow the free dissemination of information shelved her idea, to borrow a phrase, until there was a change of government. She telexed Marcus in Washington that her next assignment was in Izmir on Turkey's west coast. She gave him an invitation to visit.

Marcus opened a savings account at his neighborhood bank in Fairfax, depositing twenty dollars a month for an education fund for Ourania, Athena's daughter.

As for Kleftis and Haralambos, Marcus did not contact them—just as well, since doing so might have jeopardized their safety. But he did honor his *compatrioti* by promising to keep his beard until the junta was overthrown. Senator Tolson thought that it looked more at home in Haight-Ashbury than in the Senate but he understood Marcus's dedication and the ordeal he had gone through to suggest that he shave it. In any case, the political winds were beginning to shift and the work of his friends and thousands more in the Resistance, as well as pressure from the United States and other NATO countries, began to weaken the stranglehold of the repressive government.

Marcus shaved his beard on July 24, 1974.

Peter Georgas, author of Dark Blues, The Empty Canoe, The Fifth Slug, and The Curse of the Big Water earned a BA in Journalism from the University of Minnesota. Following a decade in advertising, he joined the staff of the Walker Art Center in Minneapolis as the museum's first full time publicist. Later, along with his family, he moved to Austria, where he was Director of the Salzburg Seminar. He and his wife now live in the Linden Hills neighborhood of Minneapolis.

Made in the USA
Lexington, KY
08 June 2018